THE GODDESS BINDING

UNDERWORLD RISING

BOOK ONE

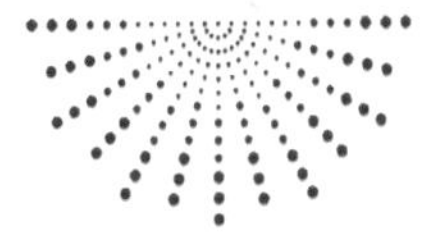

LYDIA RUANNA

To the one who seeks adventure.
May you overcome all fear.

GLOSSARY

LOCATIONS & TERMS

Rhizole - **rye**·zohl
Persephone - pr·**seh**·fuh·nee
Cerberus - **sir**·bur·ris
Hades- **hay**·deez
lyre - **lai**·ur
Neró - **neh**·roh
Sionnan - **shan**·in
Solaris- **soh**·lah·ris
Máni - **mah**·nee

THE HOUSE OF THE EARTH QUEEN

Alira- **ah**·leer·ah
Dhara- **dahr**·rah
Flint- **flint**
Pebble- **peh**·bl
Gemma- **jeh**·muh
Ilesha- ih-**lee**-shuh
Jade- **jayd**
Clay- **klay**
Demeter- duh·**mee**·tr
Arani- uh·**rah**·nee
Berilo- **beh**·ril·oh
Carnelian- **karn**·ee·lee·in

THE HOUSE OF THE RIVER GODDESS

Wade- **wayd**
Lynn- **lin**
Misty- **mis**·tee
Clara- **klair**·uh
Marshall- **maar**·shl
Ripley - **rip**·lee
Delta - **del**·tuh
Bradán- **bray**·dawn

Quill- **kwil**
Kai- **kai**
Torin- **tohr**·ihn
Onora- uh·**nor**-uh
Patience- **pay**·shns
Keane- **keen**
Marilla- **Muh**·ri·luh
Isla- **eye**·luh
Vale- **vayl**
Creek - **kreek**
Serenity - sr·**en**·nuh·tee
Morgan - **mohr**·gn
Muriel - **myoor**·ee·uhl
Marina - **mah**·ree·nuh
Brook - **bruk**

THE HOUSE OF THE ILLUMINATOR

Tayn - **teyn**
Profit - **praa**·fuht

VAGABONDS

Peri - **peh**·ree
Cal - **kal**

TABLE OF CONTENTS

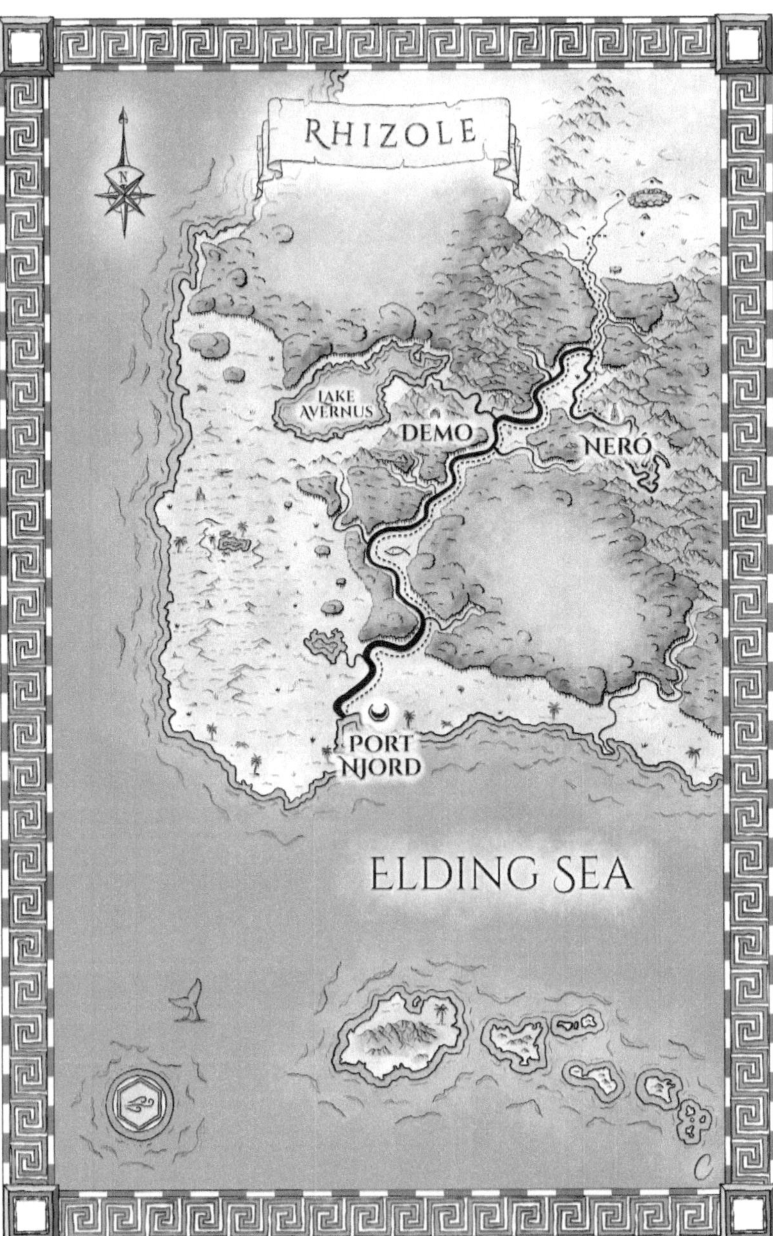

RHIZOLE
N
LAKE AVERNUS
DEMO
NERÓ
PORT NJORD
ELDING SEA

1

ASPHODELS

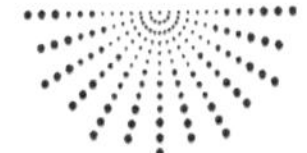

Twelve minutes: that's how long it takes for eggs to boil in the center of Persephone's Spring. It's about the same as the time it takes for the scalding steam to become absolutely unbearable.

My fingers itch to wipe the sweat off my brow, but the rock outcrop is overcrowded with villagers. Any movement could cause a stir, and I'd rather not attract attention to myself. As the discomfort rises, I remind myself it could be worse. Summer is worse.

I sense a shift as someone leaves. My shoulders lower from their hunched position and my elbows expand out from my sides, filling in the space they left behind. As nice as this feels, it won't last long.

As the eggs dangle from one end of the pole into the spring, I steady the other against my hip, using my free hand to wipe the steam off my brow. I take an extra moment to swat away the tawny hair that clings to my cheek. It's a darker color than usual when saturated with steam like this. It almost makes me feel like one of them.

Sweat beads just as fast as I can wipe it off. The eggs are almost done.

"Hey!" A nasally whine jolts me out of focus. I look behind me and see a girl, about thirteen, glaring up at me. Behind her, a long line of villagers wait for their turns, too.

She stands there with her arms crossed, her foot tapping against the rock. Her hair is black, her eyes brown, just like everyone else. She will never change.

"Are you done, mutt?"

The label, condescendingly casual, turns my red face even redder. The steam of the spring hides my embarrassment well, but the urge to flee rises like bile.

"Yes."

I snatch the twine hanging from my pole and pull the net of eggs out of the water, only for them to pendulate into my arm with searing heat. I bite back a yelp and step back from the pain, letting the eggs drop to the ground with a dull *thunk*. I look down and find myself slipping past the ledge. Time stands still.

Then a woman grabs my arm and yanks me away.

"Be careful," she hisses.

She's from the northern village. I can tell. Her voice is full of raw disgust, and she pulls away as though she has just touched fresh manure. All while the girl sneers.

"I'm fine." I say it more to myself than anyone else. I grab the net bag from the ground and rush off the rock outcrop, weaving through the line of villagers until my boots sink into hot-spring sand, perpetually warm and wet.

The ashen sands are far less crowded than the outcrop. Villagers sprawl around the edge of the spring, digging for morrow bread. Each one I pass is too focused on their hole to look up. I smile politely to the few that do, but it doesn't matter: They dismiss me immediately.

Even Mother is unaware of my presence at first. She hovers

over her hole, a pot and a pail of thick mittens beside her. Her braided black hair drapes down over her shoulder. She takes a hand to tuck a loose strand behind her ear and notices me standing in front of her.

"Are you ready, Alira?" Her umber eyes glance at me before refocusing on the task at hand. It doesn't matter whether I'm ready or not. She will assume I am.

I snatch the mittens from the pail beside her and shove them into my armpit. I replace them with the net of eggs, pulling the string to undo the knot and detaching them from the pole in one smooth motion. They slump into the bucket.

Mother wastes no time. Her spade is already deep in the hole as I set the pole aside. I scramble to put the mittens on as Mother hoists the sealed clay pot of morrow bread up and into my hands. Warmth seeps through, as though I'm not already hot enough.

The empty hole is wet. Thick bubbles form at its depths. Each pop releases an eggy smell of sulfur that sits in the air. It's so strong I almost set the morrow bread down to plug my nose, but I know doing so will only inspire harsh criticism. I turn away, looking for anything to distract me from the smell as Mother places a fresh pot in the hole.

I spot the girl at the dock and my cheeks flush. I can't help but play back the events. The villagers stare at me like I'm an albino deer, targeted by hunters and coyotes alike. The hunters see something unmistakably different, a trophy to hang on the wall. The coyotes, hungry for an easy meal, see my light hair and blue eyes as a sort of sickness: a weakness.

That girl is a coyote.

"What happened here?"

My heart flutters. I whip my head around in fear and see Mother studying the pail, running a finger over the hairline cracks that decorate the eggshells.

"It's nothing. Someone asked for my spot. I fumbled and they fell."

"Alira, you're sixteen. You should know by now that you don't have to rush off the rock if you aren't ready to. It's okay to say no."

I bite my tongue to keep myself from talking back. She doesn't get it. She's a different type of outcast, voluntary and content in her solitude. If the girl had tapped her shoulder, she would have ignored her or told her to wait her turn, simple as that.

But even biting my tongue does me no good. Frustration bubbles up and over my lips.

"Why can't there be an easier way to do things?" I ask.

"The Earth Queen provides everything we need."

It's a motto she has repeated for as long as I can remember, as if trying to convince herself of its truth. She turns and walks away with the pail and shovel in hand, leaving the pole to mark our spot in the sand. A sense of purpose drives every step she takes, purpose that I don't have.

The farther we get from the spring, the fainter the smell of sulfur becomes. The smell of asphodel, sweet as honeysuckle, takes its place. Hundreds of them bloom around the edges of the spring, protecting the ashes of the dead.

Suddenly, a cry rings out, a cry so shrill and full of anguish that even the blooms of the asphodel flowers quiver, as though the veil between life and death has been opened. Mother spins around and I do the same, looking back at the rock outcrop, where several villagers are scrambling to pull someone away from the dock and onto the sand. I see her short-cropped black hair and know exactly who it is.

Mother's voice drops in dismay, "That's not good."

Ms. Ilesha, the house professor, whimpers from the pain as the villagers pick her up and carry her away. Her foot, all the way up her calf and creeping up her knee, is a bright, scalded red.

"Come now." Mother turns away from the spectacle, "No use gawking."

Whimpers to fade into the whispering wind as I turn to follow her home.

~

This isn't the first time someone has hurt themself in the spring. An unskilled villager can easily burn their hands if they aren't careful enough. Simple burns only take a few days to heal. Ms. Ilesha, though, scalded her entire lower leg. All I can think about on the way home is how it could have been me.

When I almost slipped, the girl simply smirked. The gravity of the situation didn't set in until now. A burn like that, throughout the body, would be no less dangerous than fire.

Unlike the spring, though, fire is highly restricted; only hunters and potters are permitted to use it. Unpermitted uses are considered heretical, and straying too far from our beliefs has disastrous effects. At least, that's what I've been told.

Soon enough, we reach our allotment and our dwelling comes into view, a small hill in a field of flat, even pastures. The autumnal flowers that paint it are a welcome distraction. Purple phlox creeps down the lush green roof, goldenrod hovers over the windows, and chrysanthemums line the dirt path all the way to the solid slate door.

This house is of the earth.

As Mother shuffles inside, I pause to study the house insignia on the door. A single meandering line is carved along the edges. It weaves in and out of itself without ever touching, as though forming a sort of labyrinth. It surrounds the delicate hands of our Earth Queen, Persephone. She holds the world tenderly in her palms, like an fortune teller reading from a crystal ball.

It won't be long now before Persephone returns to the Underworld, where Hades awaits. Her absence will leave the surface so cold that crops will cease to grow.

But her warmth will keep us safe in our underground dwellings, and she will continue to heat the spring, as well. When she returns, the snow will disappear and the crops that sprout beneath her tender feet will feed us through the year.

In winter it is true that the Earth Queen provides what we need, but I wonder if she would allow us to appreciate more than her naked power.

In lectures at school, Ms. Ilesha often mentioned that our house was once much larger and far less restrictive. There's a reason it is no longer so, a reason that most would rather not rediscover. Whatever caused our house to shrink into itself, Ms. Ilesha made it clear that it was deadly.

Even so, I can't help but wonder if there's a way to make life easier without straying too far. Is it possible to bring more balance without accidentally tipping the scales?

"Alira? What's taking so long?" Mother calls. Her voice is stern and rushed. There are more chores to do. This problem will have to wait until they are done.

I enter the dwelling and set the morrow bread on the countertop for extraction. When I remove the lid, the rich buttery smell wafts upward. It's sweeter than usual; Mother must have added honey or syrup to this batch. When I tip the pot, the dense bread slides out in one beautiful piece.

I grab a slate shard and cut three pieces out, slicing each lengthwise before setting them aside. Then, I grab a vibrant tomato off the windowpane above the wash bin. As I do, I glance at Mother, diligently peeling the shells from the eggs to reveal smooth, creamy whites underneath. I smirk when I find they weren't damaged after all, but I know better than to rub it in. Instead, I return to my spot at the table and begin slicing the tomato.

It's sloppy. Slate doesn't always cut well, but Mother refuses to trade for a proper blade. The sun merchants often have knives to trade, but they've stopped coming to us for anything after Mother drove them all away. She often speaks of them as though they're dirty for offering us what we may not need, but she never seems to have an answer for the fact that the merchants are the ones who send us pomegranates, a necessary part of every ceremony.

"Go fetch Flint for breakfast." She takes the tomato slices out from under my hands and begins constructing our sandwiches. The movement is so abrupt that I lose my train of thought. I pause for a moment, wondering if I should bring up Ms. Ilesha's fall, but Mother is engrossed in her work. Instead, I follow her orders and fetch my older brother.

While mother and I were at the spring, Flint should have been tending to the sheep. It's possible he's still in the barn.

As I get closer, I spot a few of the ewes out in the fields of vetch and clover. They flick their ears as they hear me coming and lift their heads. It only takes a moment for them to catch my scent and recognize me. They should; I lambed each and every one of them.

I leap down the steps that line the stone ramp down to the barn door and burst through it to find it empty, save for a pail of fresh milk that sits on the table against the wall. Remnants of grain still sit in the feed bins and soiled straw litters the floor. He's moved on.

I step outside and scan the rooftop garden, shading my eyes from the morning sun. The squash are harvested, the potatoes mounded, and the weeds pulled. There is only one other place he could be.

A basket of vegetables sits on the ground near the gate to the orchard and next to it, our sheepdog, Pebble. She stands at the sight of me, her tail wagging furiously, but she remains next to her basket, ever diligent. This is the only proof I need. He's in there, hiding behind a wall of bark and leaves. Venturing in, I sense movement near the berry thicket. A slim figure with sleek black hair hovers over a raspberry bush: Flint.

He's wearing his favorite gray cotton flannel, pushed up to his elbows. His brows are furrowed, his blue eyes focused on the berries in his hand. He inspects each one before plopping them into his basket of woven honeysuckle.

Though I am certain he knows I am here, he doesn't show it. He keeps working, diligent and unwavering.

Mother claims that Flint took after her and I took after Father, but that wasn't always true. I don't know anything about the man who left us, but the Flint I grew up with hated chores and loved to explore the woods on the edge of the village. He was nothing like Mother.

Eventually though, Flint realized he was the only man around. Almost overnight, he changed. All his childish quirks are overshadowed by a dark and brooding persona now, convinced he must act like an adult in order to be a man.

I sidle into his thorned shelter, trapping him in his precious space of distraction.

"I'm busy," he says, expecting me to pry out the Flint I used to know. Normally, I would fire back a smart reply, but today I just watch. My silence draws his eyes upward.

"What's that face for?" he asks.

"Ms. Ilesha fell into the spring."

His hands freeze in tense anticipation. "How bad?"

"Up to her knee."

"That's not good."

Of course it's not good. None of this is good. I want to go on a rant about what we can do about it, rather than talk about how bad it all is, but that's not why I'm here.

"Breakfast is ready," I compose each word through gritted teeth as anger ruminates, waiting to escape.

I step aside for Flint to leave and follow him out of the orchard. Pebble is happy to see us, her tail thumping against the gate post. Flint scoops up the basket she's been guarding and we walk in deafening silence back to the house.

My eyes are trained on the ground as I calm myself. I want to say something, but every time I open my mouth, the words die on my tongue.

Mother would say that now is no time for ranting. I should abide by that, but my thoughts are pounding against my skull.

We should do something. We should help Ms. Ilesha, prevent more injuries, and find a way to make life easier. But no one in their right mind will listen to me.

Of course the house mutt would be the first to suggest we ignore house rules. But what no one seems to understand is that, as much as I hate it here, this place is home. I nap in the oak tree near the orchard, bathe in the springs, I tend to the sheep and sleep in an earthen home just like them. But that doesn't matter. If it were me who had fallen in the spring, the only people helping me would be Mother and Flint, and maybe Gemma.

Gemma.

As soon as her name pops into my head, my eyes adjust and I see her at the door. Her hand hovers as if about to knock.

"Gemma!"

I bolt past Flint toward her and she spins around at the sound of my voice. Her creamy white dress twirls with her, cinched at the waist by a burgundy corset. When I pull her aside, she comes easily. Her short black curls are pinned back, revealing eyes of liquid caramel rimmed in red. She's been crying.

"What's wrong?" I ask.

"Did you see it?" Her lip wobbles and she bites to hold it down.

"I got a glimpse."

"I've never seen it worse. They say it could be fatal."

"What?" The word grates against me and I can't believe it's possible. *Fatal.* No one's ever died from a scald.

Flint brushes past us heading inside, but I can see it in his eyes, too. He's scared.

"Who's they?" I ask.

Gemma fiddles with the saffron strings of her corset as she recounts the details, "I saw Tierra and one of the other healers trying to collect water from the creek to cool her off. They were frantic. When I asked what I could do to help, they told me to pray. "

I look away, hiding my distaste. If praying to Persephone did anything, I wouldn't be so cursed and unwelcome here.

"Maybe Persephone wanted this," I mutter to myself a little too loud.

Her doe eyes blink once, then twice.

"You can't really believe that, right?"

"Sorry, I just . . ."

"There's no way. It's utterly backward. And you know what's worse?"

"What could be worse?"

"I have a feeling Berilo will be teaching in her place."

A whimper escapes me as the memories rush back, memories I've worked hard to push away. Berilo, the youngest of the three elders, is from the northern village. He hates me just as much as the rest of them. The last time he covered for Ms. Ilesha, he had everyone stand up in front of the class, one by one, to take an oral exam. When it was my turn, he cornered me with a quiz on biology. He asked me what the probability was that someone with pure earthen heritage could give birth to someone with fair hair and blue eyes. When I told him it was the same as the chances of Arani becoming an elder, he kicked me out of the class and told me not to come back until I had learned my place.

After I left, he gave everyone a project to take home. He had them plot their family trees, going as far back as they could manage. The student who could track their lineage the furthest would have a pot of hot-spring water delivered to their home every day for a month.

My punishment for talking back to an elder was to deliver the water myself.

Gemma's hands grab mine.

"Let's pray right now. It can't hurt."

A fall breeze tugs at my skirts. Praying feels like a lost cause, but I do it for her.

Ms. Ilesha cannot die. It would be a waste of time. So don't take her. Not yet. Instead, show me what to do next. Give me something I can work with. I don't want to pray; I want to take action. I want to fix this.

Gemma pulls away and my hands feel clammy without her.

"Do you think the merchants have anything that can help her?" I ask. It's the only thing I can think of.

"Maybe but"–her gaze falls–"even if they had something, no one's seen them in months."

"Months?" I had no idea.

Gemma nods, "There are rumors that the elders are pulping the remaining pomegranates until their return."

I feel a sense of hopelessness creep in and my chest tightens into a knot. My mind shifts from sadness to anger to grief and back again. We stand there, unable to form the words needed to console the other. I open my mouth to try as a wisp of an idea flutters by, but the door opens. Mother steps out.

"Alira?" When she turns and spots us, her shoulders relax and she smiles in relief.

"Oh, Gemma! Have you eaten? I can make a sandwich for you."

Gemma straightens up, wiping her eyes and smiling politely. I make no such effort.

"Thank you very much, Dhara, but I've already eaten. I should get going anyway; I have a lot of chores left to do before school starts."

She turns away and I feel like a crutch has been removed from my side. I'm forced to look helplessness in the eyes. There must be something I can do.

Mother turns her attention back on me. Her hair is pinned up now, her oval face clear enough for me to spot a hint of concern.

"Your breakfast is getting cold." She opens the door a bit wider for me to enter, but my appetite is absent. Her eyes soften.

"I know you want to help, Alira, but Ilesha will have several people at her bedside these next couple of weeks. There isn't much else you can do."

"Of course there is!" Quivering rage spills like hot melted wax. "How can you not think that? How can you be so complacent?"

She's silent, frozen, and listening.

"The pomegranates are dwindling, the hot spring is fatally hot, and isolation has left us convincing ourselves that this is as good as it gets. I just don't believe it. Not anymore. Something needs to change."

Her arms drop from the door. It clicks shut as she steps down from the stoop to stand in front of me. She places her hands on my shoulders and I can feel it; Something stirs within her, too. Her eyes are full of determination.

"If you want change, you must speak to the elders."

2

HUNTER

WITH BERILO BUSY teaching and Mother permitting me to skip school for the first time ever, I don't waste any time. If I do, confidence will fade into uncertainty and I'll miss out on my only chance to convince anyone that life here, in the House of the Earth Queen, has the potential to be so much more.

The sun burns into my back as I cut through the prairies, ignoring the footpaths. The wind pulls at my hair, tugging an unsecured braid loose. When I cross the creek, it soaks the hem of my skirts. By the time I find the path again, I'm a proper mess.

The courtyard is close now, just past a row of trees. I set my chalkboard down and take a few moments to fix my hair. As I do, I review what I've written.

Upon its slate surface is a list of all the ways our house could improve. It feels light in my hands when I pick it back up, but the words that are scribbled upon it have heavy implications that flurry through my mind, pulling me deeper into cyclone of thoughts.

Fire is out of the question, but there are other elements,

13

other houses apart from our own, and if the elders permit me, I can—

I cross beneath the row of trees and stop in my tracks.

The courtyard is like a beehive. Countless villagers buzz around, their incessant chatter louder even than the water streaming from Persephone's Light. A gathering of girls perch on the fountain shrine's southern edge, ensuring every last beam of sunlight bathes them in a tender glow. They sneak glances at the boys clustered in the outskirts, whose raucous laughter cuts through my thoughts and unravels my mind.

School should be in session, and yet everyone is here. Ms. Ilesha's fall must have been too last-minute for anyone to make proper arrangements. With school canceled, this is where everyone decided to go.

I pick up my pace with a new set of worries. Berilo will be at the Slate today and I need to be ready to face him.

The closer I get to the building, the more claustrophobic I feel. There isn't a single person here who wouldn't roll their eyes at anything I have to say, regardless of its importance. In their eyes, I'm too different to be one of them. Flint, at least, has black hair. I have nothing that ties me to the earth. Nothing except my mother.

I look behind me. I should have grabbed Gemma for this. People listen to her. She's pretty. She's normal.

But no, this is too important to put off. I keep walking toward the community center, ignoring the furtive giggles of the girls as I pass.

The building looms over me, as wide as the courtyard, with the same sod roof of phlox and thyme that covers most dwellings in the Earth Queen's realm. Beautiful clumps of red and purple ivy spill over its edge, clinging stubbornly to earthen walls.

The house insignia decorates the heavy slate door, shimmering in the sunshine. I push and wince as it creaks open, feeling like I'm invading a private sanctum.

Black floors are so thickly polished that they scatter even the faintest light. At night, they pull light from lanterns filled with oil from pressed sunflower seeds and paint the room in warm brushstrokes. On days like today, though, the skylight is opened wide and a collection of mirrors pull its light in every direction. They all intersect at the center of the room, where the house messenger, Jade, sits.

Her braids are frayed and her tired eyes are rimmed in purple. Somehow, she doesn't seem to have noticed I'm here. Instead, she's hovering over her desk with intense scrutiny.

Chalk marks down the moon phases in a calendar of events. The entire week is a cramped white mess and I shrink into myself as I remember why.

One week from today is the single most important event of the year: the Harvest Festival. There's no way the elders will have time to see me, even if they wanted to. I step back, thinking maybe I can leave before she notices me, but I'm too late.

Jade glances up from her work, and her furrowed brow loosens.

"Alira, right? You're Dhara's daughter?"

"Yes, ma'am." I lift my chalkboard to my chest, hiding its contents. Then, worried I've drawn attention to it, I drop it back down to my side.

"It's been forever since any of us have seen Dhara, is she doing well?"

She's only asking out of politeness, and besides, anything that comes out would be rude, if not downright hurtful.

Mother is always well. She does the same things every day. She seems to like her life of solitude and doesn't want friends.

It's a harsh truth, so I simply nod instead.

Jade smiles kindly. "That's good! Unfortunately, if you

were looking to speak with the elders, they don't have any availability this week. I can send for you when the schedule opens up."

"Oh, okay."

As her eyes return to her work, mine begin to glaze over. Tears threaten to spill and my throat tightens. It's stupid how emotional I am right now. Jade is one of the nicest people I know. She didn't even say no. She just told me it would be a while. Before it can get any worse, I turn away and whimper goodbye.

I walk past Persephone's Light with my chalkboard hanging limply at my side. The courtyard is bustling with activity now. Groups have formed at each corner to play a variety of games from marbles to hopscotch to fiddlesticks.

A couple of boys are playing a game of catch between them, tossing a weighted wool ball back and forth over the shrine. If an elder saw them, they'd be in big trouble, but it's as Jade said; the elders don't have time.

I keep my head down to avoid attention, gripping my chalkboard tightly as I pass. They don't seem to notice me, but I remain tense. Just as I'm about to step out of the courtyard, I hear one of them yell, "Go long!"

The sound of boots grinding on packed dirt becomes louder and louder until rigid leather clips my shoulder and knocks me to the ground. All the air in my lungs falls away with my chalkboard as I try to catch my fall. Dirt scrapes my hands and a blinding heat climbs up my arm, but I keep my eyes glued to the ground. I don't want the boys to take this opportunity to laugh at me.

"Sorry, Alira, I didn't see you there."

His voice is like dark maple syrup, rich and intoxicating.

There's only one boy in all the villages with a voice like that. Familiarity draws my eyes upward.

Burnished brown eyes bore into mine. A mop of shimmering curls hangs over them.

"Clay."

He takes my wrist and pulls me up in one strong movement. He's taller than I remember, but he's still wearing his usual leather jacket, and when I utter his name, I find he still has that same boyish grin.

Blood rushes to my cheeks. I glance toward the other boys and he follows my gaze, tossing the ball back to them before refocusing on me. His hand twitches toward mine when he sees it's scraped, already hot to the touch, but he thinks better of it. I dust off my skirts and pretend I don't notice.

"What are you doing here?" he asks.

I roll my eyes in reply. Everyone's here; it shouldn't be too much of a surprise. Then again, he knows this is the last place I would ever want to be.

My mind is buzzing, wondering why he's even bothering to be friendly with me. I look down at my hands, counting the months it's been since I last talked to him like this. Ever since his fight with Flint last spring, Clay has been out of sight and out of mind. He broke up with Gemma, sat in the back of the classroom, and was too focused on his final year of school to try to amend things.

Maybe that's just an excuse I made up for him, but Flint refused to expand on what exactly their fight was about, and it must have been big, because none of their fights ever lasted this long before. I think about asking Clay, looking back at him as he picks up my chalkboard from the ground.

My chalkboard full of notes that only the elders should see.

"What's on here?" he asks, his brows furrowed.

"Nothing!" I shriek. I reach to snatch it back, a moment

too slow. He backs away just out of reach and my hands close on nothing but a wisp of fall breeze. His eyes sparkle with mischief.

"If it really is nothing, then you won't mind me reading some."

He turns away to read the notes. I cross my arms and wait impatiently; there's nothing to do now but wait for him to judge me.

"What on earth is this?"

"It. Is. No. Thing." I repeat, "Just give it back, please, so I can go home."

"Does Flint know about this?"

He asks about Flint as though they just saw each other yesterday, as though they are still best friends.

"It looks cool," he says.

I do a double take.

"You're serious?"

He hands the chalkboard back to me and I take it warily.

"There are definitely things we could be doing better. This house could use some innovators. I think it's really admirable."

"Admirable?" I try not to blush.

"Yeah! Are you going to tell the elders?"

I shrug in an attempt to play off my disappointment. "I tried, but I have to wait until after the festival."

"Why don't you just tell them at the banquet?"

I hadn't even considered it. Each year at the Harvest Festival banquet, the elders present their annual speeches and open themselves up to questions as everyone eats. Normally, no one has questions, so they just watch us like hawks. I shudder at the thought.

"I don't know if they would want to listen to me."

"They kind of have to."

His warm laughter loosens me up. I no longer cower, but

stand straight in his presence. Even so, I still can't decide. It seems like the best option, but it's far more than I signed up for. I can handle talking to the elders in the secrecy of their hearing room, but out in front of everyone as they eat? My stomach flutters and it's hard to breathe.

"Alira?" He steps closer, smelling of leather and woodsmoke. As he does, a cloud passes under the sun, shrouding us in shadow. I take it as a sign.

When the Harvest Festival arrives, I'll be ready to present my plan to the elders. All three of them. I will be the one to bring this house out of the dark and into the light.

I spin around, running in the direction of home, and leave poor Clay in the dust.

3

ELDEST

WHEN THE HARVEST FESTIVAL ARRIVES, my fears are heavy on my mind and my stomach swirls in denial. Every inch the sun falls closer to the horizon brings me moments closer to speaking with the elders. I shift my weight to the balls of my feet, bouncing up and down to keep myself calm.

I've avoided this feeling all week, keeping myself busy with harvesting sunflower seeds, grinding wheat, and processing food in the hot spring, all while rehearsing my speech.

I haven't told Mother or Flint about my plans, though they've certainly tried to ask. All they know is that I want to speak with the elders. They have no clue what I'm about to propose. Only Clay knows.

As the line to the banquet table crawls forward, I shift my focus away from my impending humiliation and try to consider how each elder will respond. Arani will be the easiest, and Berilo will snicker at whatever I say. That's easy enough to handle. But one look from Demeter will corrode any confidence I've built. I'm hardly prepared for it.

The only consolation for my swirling mind is the smell of

20

the harvest. The air around the courtyard is saturated with spiced pumpkin pie, pickled beets, mashed potatoes, and most importantly, meat. I take a deep breath. The smell of bacon intermixed with berries and cheese is enough to make me salivate.

Clay's family must have caught a boar this year. There's a good chance they smoked it in their smokehouse, infusing it with hickory or maple or apple.

If I die of embarrassment tonight, an apple-infused boar will bring me back to life.

I turn to ask Flint if he can smell it, but his eyes are sharp and focused on something else. His hair is slicked back, his gray linen shirt tucked into his pants. When he catches my eyes, I let the question die on my lips. I already know the answer. He, just like everyone else, has fasted for two whole days, but I doubt he'll even touch the boar knowing it's Clay's.

It's his loss. The second I finish my business with the elders, that boar will be the first thing to touch my tongue. The anticipation gnaws at my stomach. I'm not the only one.

Most can hardly contain themselves, sneaking through the line to join friends near the front. The girls wear their finest skirts, ranging in color from mustard and peach to violet and rose red. Light braids and delicate flowers weave through their long, raven-dark hair.

I wear what Gemma helped me pick out: a cream-colored blouse and a sorrel-brown skirt. Two scarlet bows hold my braids in place. They fall limply at my collarbone, like marcescent leaves clinging stubbornly onto their dormant trees.

"These colors make you look more earthy," she claimed, though I doubt it will make a difference.

I find myself bouncing slower as the line progresses, eventually matching the rhythm of the lyre. Jade plays it at the far corner of the courtyard, plucking the strings with ease. Her hands drift down the instrument, guiding the gentle melody back and forth to symbolize Persephone's slow descent into the Underworld. It is a song I know well, having taught myself the instrument, but the skill is wasted on me. They'd prefer someone like Jade.

Whispers spread down the line and overtake Jade's melody like wildfire. Their tones are hushed and surprised, and it's only as we get closer that I can make out the words.

The pomegranate bowl is empty.

So, what Gemma said is true; the merchants are absent. With winter coming, it's unlikely we'll see them again until spring.

When I look at Flint, he seems perplexed. I can't help but wonder how this will affect his maturation ceremony. His birthday is this winter. If there's no juice, how will he choose his path?

I listen for more whispers, but suddenly the line has shortened and the food splays out before me. The pomegranate bowl is filled with its replacement: tomato juice.

Gross.

I move along the table and consider passing it by, but Mother shoots me a warning glare from her place in line. I sigh, annoyed, and take the ladle, hesitantly pouring the thick pulp into a small cup.

My distaste is shared. As I move down the line, I spot a small child tipping their cup over before taking their seat. Several villagers have only filled their cups halfway and more than a few cover their cups with their hands in secrecy.

When I finally take my seat, the sky is a deep orange against Persephone's Light. Built at the center of the four villages, the fountain shrine radiates warmth from the hot spring, protecting us from the brisk breeze that sweeps through the courtyard. Steam dissipates into the air around it as water is drawn up to the Earth Queen's fingertips. She walks lightly on her toes, holding the world tenderly in her outstretched hands. Water pools in her palms before trickling in an endless stream down into the depths of the fountain below.

The elders sit below the shrine and the setting sun bathes them in an eerie glow. With everyone seated, Jade strums one final, poignant note of depth.

The speeches are about to begin.

Berilo stands first. He smiles wide, his gleaming white teeth contrasting his slate-black hair. His mere presence makes me sick to my stomach.

"The Harvest Moon will soon rise, but before it does, I'd like to thank you all for contributing to this year's festival. If the banquet table is any indication of how bountiful our harvest has been, then I dare say our prayers have been answered." Applause erupts from several tables as he sits, and I let a shaky breath escape me. Next to him, Arani, smooth and elegant, takes his place.

Her hair is strikingly different from that of anyone else: yellow like dried hay. It shimmers as it reflects the setting sun. Unlike me, the villagers treat her kindly. Perhaps it's because she had to prove her lineage to earn that seat.

"Harvesting a bounty of this size is no small undertaking," she says. Her voice is soft, but the courtyard carries it like a song on the wind. I lean into her words.

"I know for a fact that many of you have worked very hard, not just to prepare your own households for winter, but to help your fellow villagers as well. If anyone is still in need of any resources for the coming season, please see me or Jade. But, for now, it is time to relax and celebrate."

Arani sits and more tables cheer, including my own. When we stop, there is a brief moment of silence.

One child, thinking this is the cue to eat, inhales a

spoonful of potatoes. I smile as his eyes dart around the court-yard with swollen cheeks. They rouge as he realizes no one else is following his lead. He lays down his spoon as Demeter stands to speak.

Tonight, her dress bleeds red against the fading sun as the moon rises into place. Her lips turn up into a wry smile and she regards each table, one by one. Her words are sharp and final.

"As always, we elders will be here to answer any questions and concerns you may have. Let the banquet begin."

Flint's spoon is in his mouth before the eldest is fully seated, earning a toxic glance from Mother. Normally I would laugh, but I am already out of my chair, trying hard to keep myself at a steady walk as I approach the elders.

As the villagers' eyes remain fixed on their plates, the elders watch me. Berilo frowns, Demeter regards me with curiosity, and Arani's eyes brighten.

"Alira." Arani smiles. "What a pleasant surprise. Welcome."

All three wait for me to speak, but my throat feels clamped shut. I bow to each of them and take a deep breath, stealing a moment to grab at the flurries in my mind and organize them. When I return to stand, my speech is clear in my head.

"I have a couple of questions." I start, "First, about the pomegranates."

The eyes of all four villages bore into my back at the mention of the absent fruit.

Arani's smile fades. "The merchants have been absent and have not been heard from since the spring. Until then, we are preserving the remaining pomegranates for maturation cere-monies," she explains. Her voice, though still soft and melodious, is less bright and more calculated now. Demeter and Berilo do not challenge her answer. A spike of confidence surges through me.

"I may be able to help with that."

Arani tilts her head slightly, curiously.

Curiosity is good. Anything that isn't utter dismissal is a win on my part.

"I have a request, but more so an offering. As many of us saw last week, Ms. Ilesha was injured in the spring." An eerie silence falls over the courtyard. Ms. Ilesha, they realize, is notably absent.

"Prayers are encouraged," Berilo assures, though Arani's frown is unconvincing.

"Even if she is okay," I point out, "she will not be able to provide for herself for some time. The Earth Queen may provide what we need, but I wonder if we are using her gifts to their full potential. Perhaps we could avoid this or even improve our odds in case something like this happens again. That is why I'd like to offer to travel in search of answers. Other houses may have knowledge that we can use while still staying true to our beliefs."

Whispers erupt all around me. The mention of the other houses stirs them. Our pride has kept us caged here, convinced we have everything we need, but if we can learn from them, then maybe we can make things easier.

Either way, the elders are still listening and no one has stopped me yet, so I stick in one last thought.

"Maybe I can solve the merchant problem, too, or at least identify the cause."

They sit there, so still and unmoving that I worry I've forgotten something. But then Arani speaks.

"Every villager is a valued member of our house, but Ms. Ilesha is our only teacher. Perhaps this could be a good opportunity for you to explore that as a career choice, as well as bring the merchants back."

"I disagree." Demeter's voice is not harsh. It's casual and

defined. Even so, it cuts through me like a slate shard. My cheeks feel crimson as she sets her slicing gaze on me.

"I believe the pomegranate problem will solve itself in time. If you wish, you may pursue teaching without experiencing the world abroad. Ms. Ilesha will be fine."

I feel like a shy little mouse stunned by the cat that is Demeter, but cat claws retract as Berilo lifts his hand, a gesture meant to quiet the whispers that hiss around me. His cruel smirk leaves me feeling sticky.

"Perhaps this could be a good thing. You may find your place out there, somewhere you truly belong."

His subversive tones are normally ruinous, striking doubt into my heart, but he's right. If I leave, I'll no longer be an outcast. I can just be Alira.

Demeter, however, does not give in easily.

"This problem is not a simple one. There are many houses and the world is large. It's a monumental task no one has attempted since Carnelian."

"Since what?" I ask.

"Dr. Carnelian was a traveling academic," Demeter says. "He took to the Travelers' Road nearly a century ago to discover the lands of Rhizole, to meet its varied people and to learn from them. However, much of what he learned was considered far more than what the elders at the time deemed necessary. His notes and teachings were largely ignored and subsequently lost to time."

"Well, if he could do it," Arani notes," I don't see why Alira can't."

"Alira is not equipped for the journey," Demeter replies, cutting ever deeper.

"Perhaps she needs a traveling companion, then," Berilo hints.

Ha.

It seems Berilo has found a reason to cleanse this house of the impure. I peek at Flint, surprised to find him eating Clay's boar.

"Yes, a traveling companion would ensure success," Arani agrees.

The courtyard is enveloped in silence as everyone waits for a final decision. Demeter's eyes soften and she nods.

"It seems I have been outnumbered, but you must understand that this is no small undertaking. You must find a traveling companion within a week, otherwise you will freeze on the road, and for that I will never forgive myself."

"I understand."

And just like that, I've won. The elders have granted me permission to leave. I can travel and learn and, when I return, I'll have earned my place.

I bow before picking up my brown skirts and backing away, sucking in all the air that I was too anxious to take in as I make my way back to the table.

Now that the show is over, most of the villagers have returned their focus to their food. I can't imagine any of them are sad to see me leave. In fact, they may not even care. I'm just one less mouth to feed.

It's Mother I worry about. She's pensive when I sit, chewing on her food and staring at the fountain shrine as though she's praying to it. When I look at Flint, he rolls his eyes and shakes his head before returning to his food. My actions went far and above what they expected, and I'll have to answer for it later.

Past Flint, on the far end of another set of tables, is Clay. I catch him watching me with a smirk on his face. He turns away just as our eyes meet. I want to thank him, but it will have to wait.

Looking down at my plate full of food, the emptiness in

my stomach becomes a ravenous hunger. Everything looks delicious and I have to keep myself from shoveling it all into my mouth at once. I take a bite of boar meat and feel all my worries drift away. The faintest hint of apple touches my tongue. I savor every bite knowing that this will be my last village feast for a long time.

4

FIRESTARTER

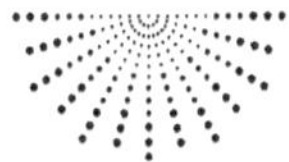

THE MORNING after the Harvest Festival, I wake up to silence. Mother's lumbering footsteps are particularly absent, and I jolt up when I realize I may have overslept.

The last time Mother let me sleep in was two years ago when I was sick with a head cold.

I scramble out of bed and tug on my skirts. When I get upstairs, the kitchen is empty. I call out, but no one answers. Then I notice the morrow bread pot is gone. In its place is a chalk note in Mother's delicate handwriting.

Alira,

I do not disagree with your ideas, but there are things we will need to discuss. I need time to collect myself. In the meantime, you need to focus on finding someone who is willing to join you. Time is running out.

Love,
Dhara

. . .

Dhara. The use of her given name betrays just how important this is to her. I trace my finger carefully along the edges of her words, wondering how much sleep she lost over this.

There's a part of me that expected her to react this way. Perhaps that's why I refused to tell her my ideas. I didn't want her to be the one to hold me back. Now I realize my fears were unfounded and I've clearly struck a chord.

I pull on my boots and head outside. The hard part is over, but she has a point. Demeter said I would need to find a traveling companion in just one week.

Flint has to come with me.

I follow the mud-slicked path to the barn. The patchy fields that surround it are muted sepia against the periwinkle sky. Each day, what is left of summer and vibrant autumn becomes subdued in the promise of winter.

When I open the door, the sheep perk up, and the chickens cluck softly in mild surprise, but Flint remains still. He sits on a small wooden stool, milking a ewe.

"Did you see the note?" I ask.

After a long pause: "Yeah."

"And?"

"How do you expect this to go?" He tries to sound curious, but there's a hint of frustration. Milking should be a thoughtless task, but today his eyes remain fastened on his work.

I decide to help him, taking up the extra pail and kneeling beside a second ewe. She turns her head to lick flyaway hairs from my face as I begin. I try to make my words casual, as though my entire plan doesn't hinge on what he does next.

"Well, if you really want to know, I expected Mother to be reserved, but I also half expected you to want to come along."

"What?"

The angry surprise in his voice is unprecedented. My milking hand jerks slightly, causing the ewe to stamp her foot and shift with unease. Quickly, I set a steady hand on her back to reassure her.

"I . . . figured you would want to come," I repeat.

"No." There is no pause. There is no question. There is no room for negotiation, and yet I sneak a glance up at him just to be sure. His jaw is tight even as his hands remain soft.

"Aren't you sick of being treated like an outcast?" I ask. It's almost a whisper.

"I've accepted it," he replies.

"We don't have to. Accept it, I mean. If we go and bring back the pomegranates, they'll treat us better."

He stops milking and pushes back his stool, skidding on packed dirt. It sends the chickens into a brief frenzy. He stands and turns toward me, his eyes narrowed.

"You really believe that?" He asks.

I shrug. "I mean, why wouldn't they?"

"I'm not going." He takes the pail of milk and sets it on the table with a surprising amount of control. I should take it as a hint of finality, but instead I stand up from my stool and follow him, setting my pail down beside his.

"Why not?" I ask.

Flint doesn't reply. Instead, he moves to the door and begins coaxing the sheep out of the barn. The chickens are quick to follow. When it seems like he's about to leave, I make my final plea.

"Flint. Please. Mother won't let me go if you don't."

As soon as he turns to face me, the last ewe scurries past him and out the door. His piercing blue eyes look angry and, surprisingly, hurt.

"You need to understand something, Alira. If you go on this trip, you've got a long teaching career ahead of you when you come home. But what will I be coming back to?"

I open my mouth, only to close it again. I have no answer for that.

"It's my future, too."

He abandons me there, leaving the barn and veering toward the orchards. Pebble isn't far behind, bolting from her perch on the front steps and carving a path through the herd to catch him.

It's not just about coming home to a career. It's about making the lives of the villagers easier. It's about making *our* lives easier. But he doesn't care about that. The inconvenient fact is that I happen to have a lot to gain in all this, but it's starting to dawn on me that I'm the only one who does.

I snatch a broom sitting along the wall, taking up the task of cleaning stalls despite it being an evening chore. The work is the only thing keeping guilt from prying me apart.

He might have a point after all. Whoever comes with me on this journey needs to have a motive. They need to be just as passionate about this as I am, and yet there may only be one teacher's role available when we return. What could I possibly offer them?

With the cleaning done, I put away the broom and step outside. A brisk breeze pulls at my hair, chilling my neck. Pretty soon, autumn will make way for winter and someone will have to be here to feed and milk the sheep. In the spring, the garden will need to be reseeded, the sheep will need to be shorn, and Mother can't do it all by herself. It is clear to me now. Flint must stay.

When I find Flint in the orchard, he is lying beneath the apple tree, a half-bitten apple in one far-flung hand. Pebble lies next to him with her head laid across his chest, something she only does when he's stressed.

"I understand you have to stay. I'll find someone else to take me. Maybe at the end of all this there can be two teachers."

"Okay," he says.

I start to leave.

"Hey."

When I turn back around, he's sitting up against the tree. "I'm sorry I stormed out. I know this is important to you."

"I pushed too far," I admit. "I didn't stop to consider that Mother needs you."

He puffs up at the thought of being needed and resumes his leadership role.

"Anyone who wants to go with you will need to pass my test." He instructs, "You can't just go with anyone. It's gotta be someone I trust."

I roll my eyes. "The only one you trust is yourself."

Rather than returning to the house, I keep walking all the way to the center of the four villages. There's a house behind the community center. It sits on an allotment that borders the western and northern villages. The path to the front door is etched in chalk from just two weeks ago, before I knew what my future would hold. On each side is a garden bed filled with flowers that I helped plant. It leads all the way to a slate door.

I lift the knocker and set it down tentatively three times before standing back and studying what else has changed since the last time I was here.

The two oak trees that grow along the northern edge of the allotment have leaves of goldenrod yellow. A single string is strung tightly between their trunks, laden with dried flax. Soon, it will be processed into linen fibers, woven into fabric, and delicately sewn into beautiful skirts and blouses.

The door opens.

Gemma pulls me in, her hug warm and reassuring, before

stepping back and studying me with wide-eyed accusation, "Alira! What in the Underworld took you so long?"

"Let's do some cloud watching," I say.

"I thought you would never ask," she swipes her jacket from the door and leaps across the threshold.

After we've settled into a small depression in the grass above her dwelling, I tell her why I'm here and she laughs. It's delicate and tender like lace. When her eyes find mine, she realizes how serious I am. Her smile fades.

"Do you know how to start a fire?" she asks.

I stare at her blankly.

"Neither do I," she admits. "The only people dealing with fire here are boys, as stupid as that is. You'll need to go with one if you don't want to freeze to death."

"I could make a fire . . ." It's a weak protest.

"Making a fire is only part of it." She says, "I know we're a bit sheltered, but things aren't all roses out there. There's going to be some thorns, too."

I pick up a rock on the ground, thumbing it thoughtfully. Names run through my head, names of boys who would be happy to see me freeze to death. Only one name pops into my head, a name she won't want to hear.

"What about Clay?"

Her lips curve down into a sharp and unmistakable frown before she averts her gaze. I know what her answer will be, but I've run out of options.

"That boy is trouble," she bites her lip, her eyes soft.

"He's a flirt, I know, but he's like a brother to me," I argue. "Besides, I'm not his type."

"Ha!" She barks out a laugh. "He doesn't have a type, Alira. You may not look like the other girls, but you are a girl. He's not blind."

I blush, unable to imagine myself with anyone, let alone Clay.

After that, I consider the conversation over. We return to cloud watching until the sun's warmth fades. All the while I run through the names in my head, trying to let go of Clay's.

~

I can't ask Clay to come with me. Even if he wanted to, the mere act of asking him would be a betrayal to Gemma. I drew up a request on the community board, but no one has shown up. Soon, word will spread that I'm not leaving after all. At this point, I'm starting to believe it.

After five days of obsessing, pulling at cuticles, and picking at dirt-scrape scabs, I resort to doing something productive instead. I sit at the kitchen table with a shirt that had been balled up in a corner of my room for months and pull a finely chiseled needle and thread in and out of the fabric of the ripped armpit.

Gemma taught me how to sew. She always says that sewing makes her feel closer to the people of our house, especially when she sees villagers wearing items she worked on herself. On days like this, it's nice to imagine feeling needed like that, as though my work provides something of substance to others.

Most villagers see a sheep and its wool and have no attachment to it whatsoever. It's the fabric, the yarn, the clothes on their back that they want. I provide the dirty, raw goods, and Gemma makes them beautiful enough to be wanted.

The knocker raps on the door and Pebble barks, darting into the room and pacing the small space between the kitchen and the door.

I don't have the heart to leave my work. After all, it's probably Jade coming earlier than expected to tell me the elders heard that I had been unsuccessful, or that they simply changed their minds.

"Quite, Peb." I order. She sits and watches me, her tail thrashing with anticipation as Flint exits his room and answers the door. I keep my head down and focused on my work. I don't want to see Jade's face when she tells Flint the bad news.

"Clay," Flint quips, "can I help you?"

My eyebrows rise in confusion but I try to keep my eyes averted. I wonder if he's here to make amends for their fight. I sneak a glance over and he scratches his head nervously.

"I was hoping to speak with you in private," Clay says.

Gemma has theories about why Flint and Clay stopped talking, but her theories are always so romantically fantastical that they're hard to believe. According to her, the reason the two boys fought is because they were fighting over her. There's no other reason Clay would dump her so quickly afterward.

I, on the other hand, know for a fact that Flint has no interest in Gemma, so the idea of them fighting over her sounds impossible. It's a dead end.

Flint studies him warily before answering, "Very well."

He grabs a light jacket and slips outside with Pebble close behind.

As soon as the door is closed, I drop everything and follow the sound of their voices, moving along the wall until they stop in a corner by a small window where I can only see their boots. I duck around and sit beside it, focusing hard on the murmurs that penetrate the naturally insulated walls.

It's useless. I can't make anything out. When I try to listen for changes in pitch, Flint sounds completely monotone against Clay's urgent pleading. All I can guess is that this is an apology visit—a long awaited one, to say the least. The good news is that no one is throwing a punch.

The door opens and I jump. Mother enters the kitchen and quickly assesses the situation.

"Spying again? I thought you would have grown out of that habit by now." She lifts the bag of flour she traded with the neighbors and sets it on the counter. I silently remove myself from the window and return to the table.

"Do you think he's here for you?" she asks.

"I don't know. He could just be apologizing for being an arse."

"That's possible."

The door opens and Flint is back inside. He sets a package wrapped tightly in wax paper on the table.

"Clay brought dinner," He says flatly.

Clay hovers in the threshold looking like a lamb who's been kicked by their mother.

"Would he like to partake?" Mother asks.

"No," Flint replies.

I watch Clay as his armor of confidence falters.

"I should be going."

The door clicks shut and then he's gone.

Flint sets the table with plates and utensils and Mother sets out three cups of milk. I, however, remain still, studying our meal. As I shift closer, the smell of grilled venison wafts up and I begin to salivate. I close my eyes and inhale the blissful aroma.

Gemma would never want me to ask Clay to come, and there's a good chance that this is no more than an apology steak, but if there's even a sliver of a chance that Clay came to ask Flint for permission to join me, then I need to know.

I unwrap the steak. It's thick and grilled to perfection. Judging by the size of it, he never intended to join us. This is a gift.

I cut the meat into thirds. It's still hot, fresh from the fire. As we sit down to eat, I study Flint carefully. He chews slowly, silently, staring off into nothingness. After only a few bites, I find myself gripping my utensils so tightly, an indent forms in the palm of my hand.

Mother smiles. She knows me.

"I hope you thanked Clayton for the steak," she says. He nods silently. I decide to take a different approach, testing him.

"This is *so* delicious," I gush. "Perhaps I should thank him myself."

"That won't be necessary," Flint replies.

Mother returns to her food, but I stare at him, unable to eat

"You're being rude," I blurt out.

Ice shard eyes turn on me, sharpening. "The conversation was private, no need to dig around for information."

"If I am the subject of the conversation, then I have a right to know," I shoot back.

"He wanted to talk to me in private, Alira, what does that mean to you?"

"Enough," Mother warns.

Silence permeates the meal once more. I do not eat; my steak is getting cold. Flint tries but cannot seem to. Mother is the only one who eats without concern. She chews each morsel of meat knowing that the silence will break in three, two, one—

"Fine." Flint breaks the silence. Mother smiles to herself.

"Clay has given me two choices, well, three if you count the one where I say no. Either I allow him to join you on your journey, or he assists Mother with the chores so that I can join you myself."

"And if you refuse?" Mother asks.

"Alira will have to find someone else," Flint answers.

My utensils clatter to the table in frustration. "What's so bad about Clay coming with me?"

Flint makes a face that I cannot decipher. A mix of fear, embarrassment, and uncertainty.

"It's not like he's asking for my hand in marriage. He's just as interested in this stuff as I am. In fact, he's the one who encouraged me to try to talk to the elders at the banquet."

Flint's eyebrows furrow in confusion. Clearly, Clay did not explain himself well. Typical.

"Why didn't you mention him?" Mother asks.

"Because I knew Flint would be like this! Ever since their last fight, they've barely said a word to each other. Flint won't go, Gemma says I need to take a boy, and there's no one else in this village who wouldn't abandon me on the road the first chance they get, so Clay is my only hope."

Flint grips his cup with such force that I wonder if it might break. In one sudden movement, he rises from his chair, drops his dish into the wash bin with a loud clatter, and retreats into his room.

"Tsk-tsk," Mother chides. "You've hurt his pride."

"What else am I supposed to do?"

After dinner is finished, I spend the rest of the evening in my room. Two seed oil lamps cast light upon my chalkboard as I scrub out my previous notes and make a list of all the boys in the village. I try to order them by how willing I would be to travel with them, but very few top the list. Terran is one, but he's Gemma's ex as well. Clod isn't bad, but he's one of the most dim-witted people I've ever met.

I get about halfway down the list before two strong and certain knocks sound at my door. It could only ever be Flint.

"Come in."

He walks down the steps and sits across from me on the woven wool rug. I make no attempt to hide my list from him.

"If I'm being honest," he says, "I think I just don't want to accept that you're leaving. I definitely didn't expect you to leave with him."

"Would you rather it be anyone else?"

He glances at my chalkboard, then averts his gaze.

"You can still come, you know," I say, but he shakes his head in quick reply.

"I can't leave Mother. I have to stay."

"Flint, you sound trapped."

He drops his head, proving I'm right. Just as I yearn to leave this place, he must want something more, too. It's not fair for me to be able to leave if it means he's obliged to stay.

"Whatever you decide to do should be for you." I say, "If that means joining me, then join me. If that means staying here and taking Father's place, do it. If it means carving an entirely different path for yourself"—I pause as his eyes flit up to mine—"you should be free to pursue that."

"Thank you, Alira," he whispers.

He leaves the room and I'm left feeling giddy.

Problem solved.

5

ACUITY

"So I have to warn you . . ." Jade says. Her tightly woven black hair glows orange as she leads me and Clay down the candlelit staircase to the basement of the community center. "There is quite a lot for you to sort through. I've done my best to index everything over the years but it's been a monumental task."

"We'll make do," Clay says. He sounds optimistic. In fact, he's been a beaming light of positivity ever since I told him he was permitted to join me on the journey. He seems genuinely interested in learning about the other houses. It's not something I expected from a boy who almost failed his final year of classes.

At the bottom of the stairs are two doors: one to the school classrooms where Ms. Ilesha gives her lectures and one to the archives. Jade reaches into the pocket of her skirt and pulls out a black key. Inserting it into the hole, she tugs on the knob, pulling hard before twisting the key just so. The lock clicks open and the door swings away to reveal the archives.

I expected to see the seed oil lanterns that are hung upon the wall, but the mirrored windows are rare. The volcanic glass

41

required to make them is a material that only the merchants can supply. Placed at specific angles within a narrow tunnel, they can bring sunlight into an otherwise dark place. When Jade steps aside, they reveal the countless boxes that we will have to sort through.

"This looks like a project," I say rhetorically.

"There are aisles in the center of the room containing all the information that I have been able to index so far, but I fear it won't be of much help to you."

"Why not?" Clay asks, stepping toward the first stack. There's nothing decorative about it. Each one is no more than a simple wooden box with a single drawer. I peek around him as he opens one up and see thin terra-cotta tablets lined up closely together.

"These boxes contain census data. They're filed by year. Careful, these ones are heavy." She gestures to a separate aisle. "Those are filled with paper, much lighter to sift through, but they are primarily for storing birth, death, and marriage certificates, as well as blueprints for projects such as smokehouses, underground dwellings, and kilns."

If all the boxes are like this, it's unlikely we'll find what we need.

As if to answer my unspoken question, she gestures toward the wall. "Those are the boxes I have yet to sort through. Some of them may be helpful, but I can't guarantee anything."

"Even a little bit helps," Clay says, his voice thick with determination. He closes the drawer and walks with purpose over to the wall.

"Very well, let me know if you have any questions. I'll be at my desk," she says, leaving us alone in the archives.

I step up to a box next to Clay. His focus and determination would normally motivate me, but the word *monumental* is starting to sound quite fitting.

"Do you think this is worth it?" I ask. "We only have a few days. I feel like we could be spending this time doing other things."

"Information we find here can only serve to help us. As of right now, all we have to go on is what the merchants have told us, which is very little because no one asked. We don't know how long it will take to find a house, much less what we can expect when we get there."

The goal is to find anything related to Carnelian's travels, but even the elders said that his teachings had been largely ignored and lost to time.

Clay opens his first box. It's dark against the brick walls. The drawer opens with a loud screech, like nails on a chalkboard. I cringe instinctively before looking for his reaction.

"This is . . . not good," he says. He takes out a wad of papers and hands them to me. They stick together, ripping as I peel one away from the next.

"Why are they like this?" I ask.

"Being set along the wall like this means they may have been exposed to water damage. This isn't exactly the best place to store things."

As we sort through each one, we discover little of value. The papers that aren't destroyed are falling apart, smudged, or consisting of vague scribbles with no context.

We do find a pamphlet of Carnelian's titled *Lyres of Rhizole*, but the only page untainted is the one on which he describes Persephone's lyre. A rough sketch shows its general construction and fine script describes the historical context.

Persephone's lyre is an instrument that originates from the House of the Earth Queen. Though legend depicts the instrument as carved from gold, this material is no longer deemed acceptable. Instead, lyres are carved from wood or tortoise-shell and strung with kitstring ranging in number from seven to thirteen. It is an instrument reserved primarily for ceremonies. Common hymns include "Persephone's Descent," "Persephone's Return," "Aril Eternal," "Blooming Asphodel," "Hound of Hades," and other various lamentations. Its design is similar to that of the House of—

When I turn the page, it tears easily. Ink bleeds through and the rest is unreadable. Disappointment fades into resignation. As intriguing as it might be, lyres won't help us. I set the pamphlet aside and move on.

After several more disappointing ventures, I wander to the back of the room and sit on the first thing I can find. Clay continues for a while before slumping against the stack in front of me.

"Maybe we are wasting time," he says. "I just find it hard to believe there's nothing of value left here."

I don't want to give up. I want to find *something*. Seeing his optimism fade out like a candle with no air is the last thing I want. If it means sorting through hundreds of papers and their boxes, it will be worth it.

"Let's search a few more."

As I stand, his eyes widen.

"Alira, look what you're sitting on!"

I leap up and find a piece of paper folded neatly on my box. It has a waxy sheen to it.

Clay snatches it up, his face beaming with excitement.

"It's a map! Carnelian must have coated it in wax to prevent it from getting damaged. It's genius!"

His happiness is contagious. All of the effort suddenly feels worth it. I turn back to the box I was sitting on.

"What in the Underworld is this?" I ask. It's different from the others. In fact, it's not a box at all. I try to lift it, but it's stuck to the ground. Clay sees me struggle and sets the map aside, then pries it off the floor. It doesn't have a drawer. Rather, it opens upward, revealing two discs and a knob. It shimmers blacker than Flint's hair, maybe even Mother's.

"It might be a machine," he says.

"What's a machine?"

Clay presses the knob and the discs begin to spin into each other, creating an odd whirring sound.

"Sometimes the merchants come by with stuff like this and people can't stand it. I'm surprised Carnelian was allowed to keep it."

"What does it do?"

The whirring continues until he presses the knob back down.

"There should be some kind of— Ah! There it is." He flips a switch and the discs begin to spin backward. A distant voice echoes back through the mysterious machine:

Sometimes the merchants come by with stuff like this and people can't stand it. I'm surprised Carnelian was allowed to keep it.

Clay turns it off.

It seems so simple, and yet it can do something unfathomable. It can take our words and spit them back out.

"Does my voice really sound like that?" Clay asks and I laugh.

"Not really." I touch the dark material. It's hard and cold, like Mother's favorite pot.

"It might be useful." Clay says, "We can record people's answers to our questions and play them back later if we forget."

Curious, I move to the box next to it. If the machine and

the map withstood the water damage, the items in this box should be safe as well.

Inside are spools, *a lot* of spools. Clay huddles next to me, causing goosebumps.

"These look like what it records the information on." He takes one out and reads the inscription.

"It looks like some of them are already full." He sticks one into the recorder, but it doesn't budge. Taking it back out, he blows on it and a cloud of dust rises.

"They'll need to be cleaned before we can use them." He says, "I'll see what I can do tomorrow." He glances at the light coming through the window, giving the room an orange sheen. "It's getting late and we won't be able to do much by lantern light alone. Here, take this map up to Jade for packing. I'm going to check a few more boxes before I leave." He hands me the map and I stare at it for a moment. The paper, despite lasting all this time, still feels fragile in my hands.

"Okay."

I walk out of the room with a strange feeling. On one hand, we got exactly what we came for, and on another, we found items so mysterious, so unprecedented, that it makes me wonder what we'll find on the Travelers' Road.

When I enter the main hall, Demeter is standing next to Jade's desk, giving her instructions. I try not to interrupt and stand quietly by until Jade waves me over.

"Did you find anything good?" Jade asks.

"Not too much, but more than expected. Clay will be bringing more up. I just have this." I lay the map down on the desk and Demeter stares at it in bemused disbelief.

"That is quite serendipitous," she says. She takes it up and unfolds it carefully.

"How so?" I ask.

"Your father brought this map to us," she answers.

"My father?" No one ever talks about him. Not even

Mother. The people of our village don't even know his name. I'm not sure they care to.

"It was curious, indeed. He didn't say where he got it, but I doubt anyone asked. Carnelian's signature is clearly marked. See?" She places it down on the desk and points to the lower left corner of the map. It's slightly smudged from use, but sure enough, a large and intricate "C" curves around it.

"Huh." I stare at it, unable to sort through the questions that rush through my mind. This piece of paper is the only link I have to my father. It's something I never imagined I would find and something I never knew I wanted. He left us. He left Mother all alone. I should hate him, but all I want at this moment is to snatch it back, clutch it to my chest, and cry.

But Jade grabs it first.

"I'll have this packed with the other supplies," she says.

I stop by Ms. Ilesha's house on the way home. It sits just above the hot spring, the absolute center of all four villages. From here I can spot hillside dwellings in all directions. I feel like I'm in the center of my own little bubble, and that bubble is quickly expanding.

Ever since Ilesha slipped into the spring, I've wanted to come and see her, but being on the verge of death meant no one was allowed into her home without express permission from the healers. Besides, with festival preparations and the stress of finding someone to travel with, I knew I wanted everything sorted before I finally talked to her.

I tap a finger lightly on the door and it swings open.

"She's had me perched at the window all day waiting for you to come," the healer says. I recognize her. Her name is Tierra.

She's one of the nice ones. Even before she graduated with

Flint, Gemma and I often saw her studying botanicals in the gardens of the courtyard.

I smile back politely, relaxing when I see Ms. Ilesha behind her.

The professor's face lights up, her voice full of excitement, a magnetism that pulls me through the threshold.

"Alira! My bright and shining pupil. Look at you! You are going places, girl!"

It occurs to me that she may be loopy from her pain management. I look to Tierra and she stifles a giggle. When I turn back to Ms. Ilesha, she is patting the empty spot on the bed beside her persistently.

"Sit! Sit! I simply cannot contain my excitement. Do you know how boring it is, sitting in this bed all day long being waited on hand and foot?"

I have no clue.

"This will be a fantastic opportunity to strengthen the curriculum. I'm almost happy I slipped into that hell-pond."

I can't help but smile at her brashness.

"Oh! That reminds me. Tierra, dear, would you be a doll and grab that big red book from the shelf, please?"

Tierra sweeps over to the bookshelf and plucks out the biggest book of them all, handing it to me directly. It's no mystery what this book is. *The Queen's Acuity* details everything we know about earthen energy, including our customs and lore. It feels heavy in my hands.

"The other houses have not seen our kind in a very long time." Ms. Ilesha notes, "It may be wise to practice your teaching skills on them."

The frayed fabric that binds it brushes against my fingertips.

"Did Dr. Carnelian write this?" I ask.

"No, Carnelian specialized in information pertaining to

the other houses, and all we have of his work is in the archives."

I sigh disappointedly. It's a shame his life's work was largely ignored. There's a fairly large chance my work will suffer the same fate, but to be honest, I'm just happy to be able to get away.

I wonder if Clay feels the same.

"I worry . . ." I whisper, "I worry that by bringing Clay, I'm taking away any future he has planned for himself."

Ms. Ilesha smiles. "Well, I'm sure he's fully aware of what he is doing by joining you. Clay is very intelligent. He may struggle in academics, but it is more due to a lack of passion than an inability to succeed. He's often bored with the subject material and so I'm not surprised he is looking elsewhere. He may very well become a good teacher if he finds himself drawn to the information you collect. When you return, he will be free to choose to be a teacher or to take up his family's tradition and remain a hunter."

A weight is lifted off my shoulders. Flint will remain to help with Mother. Clay's brothers will assist in the hunt, and when we return, he will be free to do what he really wants. Everything feels like it's falling into place.

I rise and bow deeply.

"Thank you very much, Teacher."

"You're a teacher now. Go. Learn. Conquer."

6

CITRINE

I THOUGHT that once I found a traveling companion, Mother would open up, but she remained reserved. Up until now, she has continued to act as though I'm not leaving at all. It isn't until my last day that she fulfills her promise to me over a cup of tea.

"The most important thing you need to know is to be careful of vagabonds."

I try to mimic her relaxed demeanor, but her sudden warning has me digging my elbows into the table.

"What are vagabonds?"

As she sets her cup down, her eyes catch mine and the depth of them scares me.

"They're outcasts, thrown from their families and their houses. They live in the wilds in packs of three or four and lurk near the roads for easy pickings. On a good day, they'll merely question where you're headed." Her smirk turns sour. "On a bad day, they'll threaten you for anything you value as your own."

I must seem terrified. She reaches over and pats me on my cheek.

"Don't worry, they're tamer than they look. Usually all they want is food, so if you happen upon them, use your manners and share."

"How do you know about them?" I ask. It isn't like her to know such things.

"Your father was one," she says, smiling to herself, "or is one. Who knows these days?"

I perk up in shock, almost spilling my tea. "What? You never said anything about him!"

"Well, why would I? He left us."

There is anger underneath that mask of hers. It feels like a warning, but I need to know more.

"Well, why did he leave? Do you know?"

She shakes her head. "Every time I think about it, I get more frustrated and lose a week of sleep, so I'd rather not."

I look down into my cup, sorry to have thrown salt on the wound. For a few moments, we sit in silence. I sip my tea quietly and she sits lost in thought. Her thumb begins to rub at her ring. It's warm and yellow and hard like the recorder. She reaches out to take my hand from across the table, squeezing it lightly. When I look into her eyes, they are misted and out of focus. Her mind has been pulled into the past.

"I just have no idea. He was so happy here—at least I thought so, until you came."

I flinch, pulling my hands away as though burned by her words.

"I don't understand."

"I know, and I don't want you to dwell on it."

I thought I wanted to understand my father. I thought that knowing more about him would make me feel less like an outcast, as though having blue eyes and lighter hair would make it worth it if my father was a half-decent man. The map was a link to him that I didn't know I wanted, but if I'm the reason he left Mother all alone, I want nothing to do with him. I want even less to do with myself.

"All in all, I lucked out," Mother says. I look at her like she's insane.

"How so?" I ask.

"Well, you and Flint were far better behaved than I ever was," she remarks.

"Really?"

"When I met your father, I was running away from home. It was something I did quite often.

"It was the first time I had run into the vagabonds. They looked at me like I was a piece of meat, but your father took care of me. They wouldn't dare touch me if he was around. Hellhound, they called him. You'd think he'd be a terrifying monster of a man with a name like that, but it was quite the opposite. He was quiet and subdued, with a softness not many cared to see. But when it came to protecting others . . ."

I don't interrupt her. If I do, she could stop altogether.

"My father searched for me whenever I ran off, and my punishments got worse and worse. When I got pregnant, that was the final straw. He wouldn't have me bearing a child with a vagabond. Father chased me barefoot, all the way to the spring and said if I took one more step southwards, that he would never forgive me. Your father wanted to kill him. But it almost went the other way around. So much for being a hellhound."

"So you left."

She nods and my heart breaks for her. My hand squeezes hers this time. All my life I had questions. I still do. This is the closest I've come to understanding everything.

"I was lucky to have an elder's help. They certified our marriage and offered us this allotment. The future started to look bright for us. But then he left. I'll never know why."

She rises to place her cup in the wash bin and I stand as

well, thinking the conversation has ended. Then she comes to stand in front of me.

"I want you to have this." She reaches into her pocket and takes out a ring. It's nothing like hers. It's black like volcanic glass, with a bright and cloudy yellow crystal set in the center. Looking into it is like trying to see through a blizzard. It's beautiful and rare.

"This was a gift to me from your father. He gave it to me shortly after you were born." She takes my hand and slips it onto my finger.

"Alira is an Old World name. It means truth, clarity, beauty. These are the qualities of quartz crystal."

"Quartz," I say; the word is strange to me.

"He probably stole it," she jokes, "but it is meant for you."

I look up and find her holding back tears. I hug her tightly.

"Thank you."

"What kind of mother would I be if I didn't encourage you to pursue happiness?" Even so, I can tell it's difficult for her. First Father left. Now me. It's no wonder Flint feels pressured to stay.

After we've finished our tea and cleaned up, I head to the barn for evening chores. Flint's already there, milking the sheep, as I hang over the barn door.

"Did you know Father was a vagabond?" I ask.

He glances up from his work and grins.

"Congratulations. You're an adult now."

That night, I dream of warmth. It's like the spring, but different. Colors light up the back of my eyelids; purple, blue, orange, yellow, and it becomes so bright and blinding that I wake up in a cold sweat.

The dream dissipates as the door slams above me and feet

fall heavily upon the floor. I get up quickly, and rather than putting on my usual skirts, I pull on a pair of thick brown pants, fastening one of Flint's belts around my waist. I tug a long-sleeved black shirt over my head. It skims over my curves as I tuck them into my pants. Mother made it for me in the days leading up to my departure. She said she wanted to make sure I had dark clothes. When I asked her why, she said it was common sense.

I worry this whole trip is the opposite of common sense. One last sliver of doubt creeps into my mind, tainted by the heated dream from overnight. I close my eyes and the bright light that stained my eyelids is gone. All that's left is darkness.

It's time to go.

I shuffle up the stairs and find breakfast is already on the table. There are three settings and I wonder if I'm still dreaming.

"Good morning, Alira." Mother used to keep her back to me in the morning, too busy to spare a glance. Now she smiles warmly. If my leaving depresses her in any way, she doesn't show it.

Even so, I doubt that means she feels good about it.

Flint walks in shortly after I take my seat, and for the first time in a long time, we eat breakfast together, all three of us. We talk about trivial things, like the weather and final preparations for winter. Before long, we're all donning our coats and walking on the path to the community center.

Things fall quiet for a time. A certain tension holds us together, like a taut string. I wonder if they will say anything at all between now and when I leave, but when the community center comes into view and the crowd that has formed is easy to see, Mother turns around. Flint, too.

"I know I said I'd support you," Mother says. She presses her lips thinly together and turns her eyes skyward, an attempt to keep tears at bay.

I close the gap, hugging her tightly. Her arms wrap around me.

"You've done more than enough already," I say. She chokes back a laugh.

"Of course, but if you don't come back . . ."

"She will." Flint says, "She has to. I can't handle you myself."

The joke earns him a weak slap on the head.

"Go on, now," Mother says, as if shooing a rabbit away from her azaleas. "I don't want you to be late."

The crowd that hovers in the square is not large, but it is comforting. The few that showed up happen to be the few I care the most about. Ms. Ilesha is the first person I see. She leans heavily onto a walking stick, watched closely by Tierra. Gemma's family chats idly with Clay's, though Gemma seems awfully uncomfortable. When she sees me, she perks up and abandons her mother's side.

She lunges into a hug, holding me close as she whispers in my ear.

"I'm really happy for you, Alira. I'm happy you were able to find someone."

"I wanted it to be you."

"Me too." She backs up, smiling wickedly. "But I found a way to make it up to you."

Gemma reveals from behind her a pair of new traveling boots, newly sewn. I'm in awe of their beauty. I snatch them up and drop to the ground to put them on.

"This is amazing!" I squeal, wiggling my toes against the fresh leather.

Gemma pulls me up with a grin.

"In the absence of skirts, you are a woman in need of new boots, so that all the boys can swoon when they see you."

She winks. Her skirts billow around her as she spins to walk away, and as she does, I can't help but notice Clay watching her go. He comes to stand next to me, away from the crowd, but before he can even utter a word, the sound of horse hooves strikes the path behind us.

Jade leads a large chestnut horse toward us. He is harnessed to a covered cart that holds all the items we painstakingly packed over the last few days. Food, traps, blankets, even some holy spring water for trading. As the horse comes to a stop in front of me, he blows hot air onto my face. I reach up, placing my hand tenderly on his muzzle. He sighs, nuzzling into my hand. He is beautiful.

After a moment, I step away, giving Jade room to turn the cart around to face the road ahead. As she does, the slate door of the community center swings open and the three elders enter the courtyard.

Demeter walks ahead of the rest, as is customary. Her dress billows behind her, a striking shade of red, with a warm yellow sash tied around her waist. The rich autumn leaves that litter the ground around her seem pale in comparison. Arani follows close behind, wearing a bright blue that matches the color of the sky. Berilo, last to settle at the fountain shrine, has his black hair slicked back and wears the same mossy green suit he wore to the festival. The crowd falls to a hush. The ceremony begins.

"Alira and Clayton," Demeter bellows over the courtyard, "you have expressed an interest in obtaining knowledge for the purposes of improving our humble house. For this, we admire your curiosity, courage and, most of all, loyalty."

Clay stands beside me, his shoulder perilously close to mine. I feel shivers when he shifts his weight and pray to Persephone that he doesn't notice. I know Gemma is watching closely.

Arani's voice rings out and brings me back into focus.

"Your agreement is as follows." She gestures to Jade, who

holds a soft clay tablet in her hands, one that has not yet been allowed to cure.

"Alira and Clayton will journey to the other houses, learning their ways and adapting that knowledge to our own. This contract will be enacted on a rolling basis, whereas after each house, Alira and Clayton will return here to debrief and share what they have learned. When enough knowledge has been obtained and/or all the houses have been studied, Alira and Clayton will be permitted to return and take up roles as chief professors, implementing their findings and curating a new curriculum."

Cheers spread amongst our small crowd and Jade approaches with the tablet. The words etched into its surface are deep and real. I take the etching needle and carefully inscribe my name before handing it to Clay.

"To aid you on your journey, we offer you a gift." Demeter gestures to Berilo. On cue, he steps up to us, handing us each six pomegranate seeds. I haven't seen pomegranate juice since the Strawberry Moon, but I can't remember the last time I saw seeds.

Berilo smiles at me and it almost feels genuine, probably because he's getting exactly what he wanted. I smile back. I'm getting what I wanted, too. When I return, he'll be stuck with me, forced to treat me with the same feigned respect he affords Arani.

Demeter removes a small leather-bound book from the pockets of her dress. It's red with gilded yellow marks on its binding. It's a beautiful book, one that matches *The Queen's Acuity* in craftsmanship. She opens it and begins reciting a portion of a poem from within:

> *Eat these seeds,*
> *For they will give you strength,*
> *Warming you on the coldest nights.*

At the sound of the book snapping closed, Clay and I both consume our seeds. Each one bursts in my mouth with surprising flavor.

"Safe travels." Demeter bows. Berilo and Arani bow in unison behind her. Then the crowd bows, too. I look to Mother and Flint and wave goodbye once more before clambering into the cart beside Clay and leaving the only home I have ever known.

Farewell, Persephone.

PERSEPHONE'S CURSE

If she fails to break the soil,
Return to me her soul,
Then bold will be her mother's child,
And coal will be Rhizole.

—Dr. Carnelian

7

TRAVELERS' ROAD

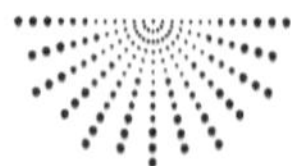

THE REALM of the Earth Queen is far behind us. Green pastures of rolling hills slowly make way for the cover of trees. Their leaves filter the sun's rays in splendid shades of red and orange and yellow, casting a warm glow on the road that stretches before us.

My chest pounds with excitement. My breathing is hardly controlled. Each time I turn my head I see something new. Birds cross ahead of our cart in frenzied excitement. Their songs coalesce into a symphony of melodies, all different and yet delightful when strung together. Squirrels chitter amongst the branches of the trees. They scramble down the trunks and scour for acorns littered about. I even see the white flash of a deer as it flicks its tail and leaps away into a thicket of thorns.

Soon enough, though, the animals catch wind of our travels. It's as though they all whispered amongst each other news of our arrival and subsequently hid themselves in the darkest depths of the forest. The road stretches onward and I begin to yearn for some direction other than straight.

Turning in my seat, I open the cloth covering that separates the front of the cart from the inside. The map is folded

60

up neatly and tucked between the recorder and a box of jars. I pluck it out and open it wide to read.

Its simplicity is concerning.

"How are we supposed to glean anything from this?" I rotate the map left, then right, trying to orient myself.

Clay laughs and the horse skips a step from the sound of it. We bump shoulders briefly and my cheeks burn. I scoot just a smidge over to convince myself it won't happen again.

"Make sure north is pointing up first, then reorient."

I try to follow his simple instructions, but the map still seems useless. I sneak a glance sideways, hoping he is too busy driving the cart to judge me, but instead his deep brown eyes are reading my confusion easily.

"The sun is to the left of us," he explains. "It is still rising. The sun always rises in the east and sets in the west."

"I know that."

I inspect the map again, but I still don't have any context. I get frustrated, tightening my grip and causing a minor tear in the delicate paper. I bite my lip and pretend it was always there.

"There is no east. All it shows is north."

"Dr. Carnelian assumes we know what a compass is. East is to the right of north, and west is to the left."

"So, north is up?"

He nods.

"And south is down?"

"For the purposes of this map, yes. We will follow the path south along the stream." He points to a squiggly line on the map, tracing it downward. "Then we will follow it to the river, where some sort of water village should still reside."

"I feel dumb." Rolling up the map, I stash it behind us for later.

"Don't." Clay says, "The only reason I know any of this is because I hunt."

When the sun is high, we stop for lunch. Clay leads the horse to a thicket of blackberries before joining me in the grass beside the cart. I set a quarter loaf of morrow bread and two jars of pickled eggs between us.

"He's really well behaved," I note.

"He's well trained." Clay explains, "I recognize him. He's one of two horses that regularly transport goods between the villages. Different scenery, same work."

As if on cue, a squirrel rushes out from behind a tree. Its fur is ash and stone, with black markings along its nose and feet. At the sight of our horse, it skids to a halt and spins around, skittering back the way it came.

The horse, meanwhile, continues to graze.

"Well trained, indeed," Clay says, biting into his piece of bread.

"I feel like there should be more animals around."

"It's the helenium, probably." He points to a patch of meadow on the other side of the creek; their paper-thin petals and whirling stigmas remind me of coneflowers.

"Most animals avoid it—it's poisonous. That's why I had the horse graze on that thicket."

"I never knew you were an expert on plants," I prod.

He laughs. "I'm definitely not. But knowing where to find animals is my thing, and you won't find them here."

I'm almost disappointed. It would have been really cool to see something I'm not used to. I've seen foxes, groundhogs, and deer in the fields before, but forests are new and intriguing to me. I want to see the beasts that hide within them.

"It's better this way," Clay says, predicting my next question. "Wild animals are rarely kind."

I finish my bread and pick out the last egg from my jar. Its tangy flavor is sharp on my tongue. It tastes like winter.

As Clay hitches the horse back to the cart, I look through our supplies.

"Do you think we packed enough?" I ask. Clay climbs back up to the front of the cart and I walk around to climb in myself.

"I think we packed too much," he answers. He holds out his hand to help me up and I falter. Common courtesy feels alien to me. Not even Flint has the decency to help me most of the time.

After a moment of hesitation, I take his hand. He pulls me up easily.

"Thank you," I say, looking away. I worry my face is too red.

"Of course." He picks up the reins and we begin again.

"I wonder what kind of food they eat in the other houses." he says, "Got any guesses?"

I pause to think, looking to the river for ideas. "I bet the Water House eats fish and uses water to wipe impurities from everything else."

"That's actually really believable," Clay replies.

"What about you?" I ask.

"I bet the Sun House dries all their food outside. Meats. Fruits. All of it."

"But what about winter?" I ask, "Wouldn't it freeze?"

"No," Clay says, "from what I've heard, their house doesn't get winters."

We continue on like that for some time, quizzing each other on what we think we'll find. As the sun begins to fall in the west, Clay intermittently holds his hand up to the horizon, using his fingers to measure the time left before we need to stop. With the wind picking up, it's likely that we'll sleep in the cart. The thought of sharing such a small space with Clay doesn't bother me, but the thought of sleeping near him does. The heat that rises in my cheeks at the thought is more than any autumn breeze can cool in a single blow. I try to hide it with more banter.

"So are you going to tell me why you decided to come? Because Gemma is convinced it's to take a pass at me."

"Do you believe that?" he asks, guiding the horse along a bend in the road.

"No," I reply. It just doesn't make sense.

We turn the corner and a dim glow becomes visible in the distance. I squint to get a better look at it.

"Well," Clay says, "I really just—"

"Is that a house?"

The dim glow flickers through a window of a tall wooden structure. Smoke rises eerily through an opening at the height of the slate roof's ridge.

I remember what Mother said about vagabonds, but she never mentioned this. The vagabonds live in packs in the wilds, not in wooden houses on the Travelers' Road. I can barely imagine who would want to live out here in the open. It doesn't make much sense.

"This might be a nice place to stop for the night. Looks homey to me." Clay begins to slow the cart down.

"Wait." Fear seeps in. "What if they are dangerous?" I grip the edge of my seat, watching the smoke waft over the forest behind the house like a dark and foreboding cloud.

Clay, seeing my panic, quickly pulls the cart over and faces me. He is searching me up and down for a way to reassure me, but how can he? What is the worst-case scenario and how can we avoid it? I don't know the answer to either of those questions and it terrifies me.

He watches me as my mind flutters, laying his hand on my shoulder for comfort. Normally, I would shrink away from him, but his hand is so warm in the cold fall air that I start to sink into it as his voice steadies me.

"If they were dangerous, this road would not be fit for

travel. Merchants have spoken of the stream before, so they must know of this cabin." The stream follows parallel to the other side of the road across from the house. It's true, there was a stream on the map, and if the merchants speak of it, then it's safe.

A patter of raindrops smacks onto my head. The sun is getting lower, now shrouded in cloud cover as a storm rolls in. Trees sway as wind gusts through, whisking away the brown leaves that clutched to their branches and sending them spinning through the air.

"The goddess has given us a sign," Clay jokes. Seeing my face, he gives me a halfhearted smile and picks up the reins.

"Fine," I relent, "you knock. I'll stay in the cart."

Clay grins, turning up the charm as he pulls the cart up in front of the cherry tree that sits at the front of the house. A small evergreen stands beside it, a spindly-looking thing. He swings from his seat in one smooth motion before strolling up to the door and knocking. I peer from the cart nervously, half hiding from view. I keep my shaking hands close to the reins just in case things go sideways.

Clay doesn't seem concerned in the least. His apparent ease with taking risks begins to weigh on me. Isn't he supposed to be protecting me?

The door opens, revealing a tall woman wearing a thick woven sweater and dark pants. She rolls up her sleeves at the sight of Clay, revealing muscular forearms as she crosses them against her chest. Her eyes are narrow, her face stern. She keeps the door closed slightly, eying Clay with uncertainty.

It's probably best for me to get down, to show the woman that we aren't a threat and that Clay isn't alone. I jump down from the cart and a sharp pain shoots up my legs, causing my knees give out. I lurch forward with my hands splayed out to catch me as I fall.

"Oh, there's two of you," she says. Her tone is bleak,

giving me a bout of anxiety. I want so much to turn around and go back to the cart, but the steady rain falls harder. The sun is completely shrouded and the moon will be no different. The best I can hope for is for this storm to pass quickly.

I stand and bow to the woman. "Sorry to bother you like this."

The woman nods, not bowing back. She turns sideways, keeping an eye on us as she calls inside.

"Well, Joe, looks like we've got some carpenter ants."

"Ants?" I ask. If all we are to her are tiny little insects that are destined to be swatted and squashed, I can't imagine feeling welcome here.

A man, presumably Joe, appears in the door behind the woman and chuckles at my question, "My sister didn't mean anything personal by it, right, Jane?"

He smiles when Jane shrugs in reply. He's taller than her, with wide shoulders and a thick brown beard tinged with red. He holds a book against his chest, bound in linen fabric.

"You must be lumberjacks." Clay turns to me in explanation, "They rely on wood sourced from trees. It builds their home, lights their fires, and is a valuable resource for them. My father and I have met some north of the villages."

"Ah, I sense a hunter in this one." Joe's laugh is deep, vibrating my ribcage. "Come in, it's getting dark and wet."

Clay strolls in but I hesitate on the threshold, sensing tension. The woman pulls Joe aside to exchange words in a harsh whisper that I can't discern over the sound of the rain that pours behind me. Joe makes no attempt to lower his voice along with hers.

"Jane, it's raining. Not everyone is a vagabond, they're just youngins. Now go put the horse and cart out back so the real vagabonds don't get all excited."

Jane rushes behind us and out the door. I glance at Clay,

wondering if he heard, but his eyes are scanning the various trinkets sitting on the fireplace mantel.

"That there is my father's hand," Joe says, pointing to a wooden sculpture. "He made it when he was about your age."

To sculpt a hand from clay was easy enough, but to sculpt from wood seemed infinitely harder. If you take too much clay, you can wet it and patch it with more material, but with wood, every line is final.

The entire house feels like a work of art. Hardwood floors, a fireplace of stone, and stairs that go up rather than down. There's a large resting area beside the fireplace with a short bookcase dividing it from the kitchen. A *proper* kitchen. There's a round table for four people, a wood stove, and knives far sharper than Mother's slate shards.

"We were just about to eat dinner before you came," Joe says, placing his book on the mantel. "There should be enough for everyone. Let's sit."

I barely eat the food. I'm so intrigued at how fire and wood somehow complement each other that I start asking questions instead.

"So wood really is all you need?" I ask.

"It's the main ingredient, sure, but there are others," Joe explains. "Wood is a trade resource, as well as a raw material for many other trade goods, but it doesn't feed us. We get most of our food from the forest and Ma started a vegetable garden as well. Before she died, of course."

Joe is eager to share this information between each bite of steak, but his sister is quiet. She doesn't seem as angry now, at least. Perhaps this is simply their sibling dynamic, with Joe making up for her lack of charisma with his need for attention. He reminds me of Clay, in that way.

"And Pa, well, he worked himself so hard he died of a heart attack just about two years ago."

I try to offer condolences but he brushes me off.

"We've done our grieving," he says. "We honor them each day with honest work."

Still, it seems rude not to offer some sort of sentiment.

"In the House of the Earth Queen, we scatter the ashes of our loved ones onto the sacred ground surrounding the spring."

"Lumberjacks have no house," Jane replies, cold and sharp. It leaves me wanting to stay silent for the rest of the meal. But Joe refuses to acknowledge his sister's rude remark.

"Our loved ones are buried with the seed of their favorite tree, never to be cut or burned. Mother resides in the cherry tree and Father in the pine."

"That's beautiful," I glance at Jane for a reaction, but her eyes are fixed on Clay.

"Are you sure we can stay?" I ask.

"It's no problem at all," Joe replies. "We will do what we can to help. Tonight, you can sleep in the main room by the fire."

Jane breaks her silence. "You, boy, can help gather wood when dinner is done."

Clay seems happy to help, despite Jane's grumpy demeanor, and Joe doesn't give her any attention at all. I suppose this is just who she is. There's no use dwelling on it. I decide to direct my questions at Joe after we clear the table. He's happy to comply.

"So you trade wood?" I ask.

He laughs. "Wood by itself isn't worth much. It's paper that gets us by."

"Paper?"

"Oh yeah, I could go on for days about paper."

I don't doubt it.

Clay, upon hearing the exchange, interrupts us. "Let me go get the recorder."

He leaves momentarily and returns with the slick black

machine, which he sets down on the table for me. He turns the knob and the spool begins to spin.

"Hey, fancy piece of machinery there," Joe admires.

"You've seen machines before?" I ask.

"Of course, and you haven't?"

When I shake my head, Joe laughs. "You ants really are stuck in your anthills."

Blood rushes to my cheeks.

"Machinery has many uses, and can assist in completing many kinds of tasks," Joe says, "but they are rare."

I study the recorder on the table. Its black coating shimmers in the firelight. I wonder what else machines can do, and where we can find more.

While Jane and Clay set up an area by the fire for sleep, Joe launches into an explanation of wood and pulp and paper.

"Chopping down a tree is one thing, but shaving the bark off, cutting it to size, and grinding it down into smaller pieces is a whole chore. It's one I partake in every day. Thankfully, Pa had the foresight to trade a nice piece of furniture to a sun merchant back in the day, so we have a quality grinder out back that makes the work much easier."

"What did you do before that?" I ask.

"We didn't make paper before that. It was just too much work, and Jane and I were too young to help. Pa sculpted and built furniture instead."

"I see."

Back home, most furniture is made of stone, heavy and unmovable. Only bed frames and the occasional chair are carved from wood.

"The grinder is good, though. It really gets the wood down to a pulp. Jane likes to do the last couple of steps but"— he peeks around me to look at her and thinks better of it— "basically she uses a wooden frame and mesh cloth to separate the fibers from the pulp, and then we heat it up and squeeze out the remaining water. Press it, dry it, cut it, the whole nine yards. She even got into bookbinding."

He pulls out a small booklet from the bookshelf and hands it to me. It's light in my hands. Twine knots up the spine, holding the rough pages together. When I open it, Joe's small scribbled handwriting covers the page, as though every inch is valuable. The words are etched in a way that chalk and slate will never match. Only someone skilled in holding a quill pen can write like that.

It reminds me of Carnelian's map, folded and tucked away in the back of the covered cart, must have been difficult to make, and would be even harder to replace.

"Honestly, we don't really need to trade for much of anything, but papermaking keeps us busy. We've got a full library now. It's mostly Pa's books; notes on carpentry and papermaking experiments and all that."

"Did you make that one?" I point to the book he set on the mantel when we walked in.

"That's one I traded for. The merchants know I'm a sucker for a good story. Books are hard to make, but finding one with a good story inside is even harder."

Reaching back into the shelf, he digs out a notebook identical to his own and hands it to me.

"Here, take this. You're going to have lots of stories to tell when you're done with your quest."

I take it and hold it, admiring its uniformity. It feels like I'm holding the fleece of a black sheep.

I can't waste any of it. Everything word will be meaningful and important henceforth and forevermore.

Wind whistles outside and rain pelts at the windowpanes next to the door. When our conversation ends, I turn off the recorder and move to the fireplace, where the sleeping area has been set up for me and Clay.

"If you have time tomorrow," Joe says, "we can show you how to make paper all on your own."

Joe heads upstairs, not noticing me smile uncontrollably. This entire quest is coming to fruition.

I set myself down on the floor where a pile of blankets curls inward. I pull them over my chest, first one side, then the other, wrapping myself in a warm cocoon.

I've barely laid my head to rest and I'm already eager for morning to arrive. The fire crackles beside me, warm and bright. The flames become mesmerizing, luring me in like a moth. I stare at them until my eyelids feel heavy.

What a lovely day it's been.

"You look happy," Clay observes. He lies across from me on the other side of the fireplace. His dark eyes dance with the same flames, mesmerizing.

"I am."

"Goodnight, Alira." My eyes close in reply.

8

SPLINTERING

I DREAM I'm back at Persephone's Spring. Hot steam rises and sweat beads off of me. A hand taps my shoulder. I spin around and see the girl, jeering. Her eyes are pits so dark and deep that they cannot reflect light. I teeter at the sight of her and slip. My foot falls in, steam rising as the skin bubbles, boiling off. I want to scream.

I jerk up from my dream wide awake, but my eyes feel like they're glued shut. I pry them open and forked flames lick up the walls and across the floor, reaching for my feet. My vision blurs from the smoke and I panic. I open my mouth to scream and curl into a debilitating cough.

To think that the hot spring was as dangerous as fire was foolish. This is everything the elders warn our house about. This is why fire is so heavily restricted.

It is an element of uncontrollable and inescapable destruction, and now I'm going to burn with it.

I'm moving. Backward. My blanket cocoon is dragged across the splintering floors. Cold air rushes through the door, stoking the flames as I'm pulled out of the cabin and dropped onto the dirt. I still can't open my eyes.

72

The horse whinnies nervously close by. The cart must already be out front. I hear someone trying to make space in the back. Then a simmering pain spreads down my foot.

I force my eyes open, look down, and scream.

The blankets that swaddle me are spitting fire. I scramble out of them and into a pair of muscular arms. They lift me up onto their shoulders and load me into the cart. I lean forward, coughing violently as someone sets their hand on my shoulder to steady me. When my eyes adjust, I look up.

Jane looks back.

"Where is Clay?" I peer behind me and find Joe stamping out the charred blankets. The cabin behind him is engulfed in flames of red and orange and blinding white, but my brother's best friend is nowhere to be seen.

Joe tosses the blanket into the cart and rushes around to the front. It shifts with his weight as he climbs in.

I turn back to Jane. She's staring at my foot. I ask again, louder, more frantic, "Where is Clay!?"

The cart begins to move.

"Don't worry about that," she replies. She takes my foot and begins to wrap it in cloth, but I retract it immediately.

"What? How can you say that? Where is he?"

"I don't know," Jane admits.

She tries to take my foot back, but I'm scrambling to get out. I launch myself away from her and fall onto uneven ground.

"Alira!" Jane calls out.

"I need to find him!" I cry out. I get up and stumble toward the house. The pain in my foot is numb but I am weak; I trip and fall.

Jane's hands wrap around my waist. I struggle against her.

"He wasn't inside. We don't know where he is."

Tears coat my eyes. Burgeoning flames of red, orange, and

yellow blur into one large mass. Even if Clay were right in front of me, I wouldn't be able to see him behind the tears.

Joe walks briskly past us. A machete glints in his right hand.

"I'm going to find him now. You go on ahead," he says.

"What's the machete for?"

Jane picks me up with surprising strength and sets me back in the cart. Despite her attempt to be careful, my foot bumps against our supplies and a splintering pain takes my breath away. I cry out weakly before darkness overtakes me.

The sun is a dagger in the dark. It pierces through a crack in the cloth covering the cart and jabs at my eyelids until I remember.

Where is he?

I swipe at the cloth and push it aside. The forested path has receded to one side of the road. On the other, prairies stretch as far as the eye can see. They're warm and colorful, leaving the sky muted in comparison. Crimson asters, goldenrods, bluegrasses, and beautiful oxeye daisies paint the landscape in rich, broad strokes. The stream winds through it. It's wider than before: a clear sign that we're moving forward.

We shouldn't be. The only direction we should be going is back. We can't go on before finding Clay. I can't.

I have to go find him. I have to go back.

I calculate every move I make, inching my way toward the edge of the cart and lowering myself carefully to the ground. I set my good foot firmly onto the road and lean against the cart to look around.

I need to tell Joe and Jane to turn around. I have no clue how long I've been sleeping, and if we keep moving, Clay will fall even farther behind.

I spot an opening in the brambled tree line that seems like a good place to start. I step out confidently only to stumble and gasp in pain, clutching for the stability of the cart.

I look down at my foot, red and inflamed. It's bandaged loosely, as though Jane was trying not to wake me. Hopelessness creeps up on me. I can barely stand on my own with these burns. The lumberjacks are all I have now. If I can't convince them to turn around . . .

A new fear creeps in, one in which they ignore my pleas to turn around and go home or, even worse, they decide to leave me here all alone and take the cart for themselves.

I hear a faint rustling of leaves and panic. I climb back into the cart, pushing myself up against its side just as voices emerge from the opening in the trees.

It's Jane's voice I hear through the taut fabric that separates us.

"There's simply no other explanation."

"That's preposterous, Jane. The Earth House doesn't even use fire, and they aren't vagabonds."

"The boy is a hunter, he uses fire," Jane points out.

"That just reassures me that he is smart enough to get out of there," Joe retorts.

What was she insinuating? Why hadn't we turned around? I reach for the fabric but Joe's voice cuts through the air. It's stern and sharp. I recoil at the sound of it.

"Their mission is clear. I do not see any motive here. Regardless, we have to keep moving. I don't know how serious her burns are and the healers at the outpost will have to assess them. We can send someone out to look for a cause, or we can cut our losses and rebuild."

I let out a deep breath. Joe seems safe. He clearly has a plan. Jane has no intention of going back for Clay, but Joe does—just not until my foot is healed. I look down again at the bandages. They're so loose that they've unraveled. The ends fall away to reveal tender skin pocked with small blisters. I gently press a finger to them and wince in pain.

Without proper treatment, the wound could develop complications. All I want to do is turn around and find Clay, but without knowing how long that would take, it would be a massive risk. Joe knows this. I need to accept it.

"Fine," Jane snaps, "if you want to believe their little story, that's your choice. I am not tying myself to them."

"No one asked you to."

The cart lurches as Joe climbs back into the cart, causing it to rock slightly side to side. Jane groans and her footsteps fade as she walks away.

I stick my head out of the cloth that separates me from Joe. His stern grimace softens when he sees me. "You're awake."

"How long until we get to the outpost?" I ask.

"On a cart with three people and only one horse? A couple of days."

Clay can survive days. He can hunt.

"Do you believe what Jane says? About Clay being suspicious?"

"No." His eyes are determined, his voice certain. I find myself trusting him completely.

I let out a soft sigh of relief knowing that I can rely on Joe. When all is said and done, we will find Clay. I know he'll be okay until we make it back. Still, the knot in my stomach remains. I want to know what happened to him, I want to know why he wasn't there and if he truly is okay. I watch Jane, who sits by the widening stream, staring at it with such intensity that it's difficult to tell whether she's angry at Joe, Clay, or herself. Joe follows my gaze, answering before I have the courage to ask.

"My sister doesn't trust anyone. You two came at just the right time to avoid all that rain, but she doesn't see it that way.

She doesn't see signs or have faith. Our parents' deaths made her cynical. We've spent much of our lives isolated, even more so since our father died."

Jane's eyes are dark and brooding. I try to imagine what it would be like if two teenagers had shown up at my home. How would I have greeted them? Visitors aren't common, and those looking for a bed are even less so.

I suppose Flint would have been suspicious, but I think we all would have been happy to have some extra help with chores. Clay's family hosts merchants all the time and he's never had anything bad happen before.

But if a fire had come out of it, who would we have blamed? How could the fire have been prevented in the first place?

Jane finally gets up and begins to walk back to the cart. As she climbs in, a thought occurs to me and I can't help but blurt it out.

"Build earthen," I say.

They look at me in confusion.

"Earthen homes don't burn."

They are both silent as they ponder the possibility, but to me, it's the only answer. If lumberjacks didn't limit themselves, they would probably still have a house right now. This is my chance to make an impact. Originally, my goal was to invoke change within my own house, but now I see the full potential of my work.

Lumberjacks aren't bound by house rules. They can build earthen and still burn fires, so long as they build a chimney to disperse the smoke. The heat of it could warm a home in winter and thaw a rooftop garden. Their belongings would never be burned and their home would remain intact regardless of weather. The possibilities are endless.

I close the cloth divider and grab the notebook Joe gave me. Taking a quill pen, I feverishly write down a checklist for building their new home. Ink splotches onto the paper as I write.

Ms. Ilesha taught a dwelling-construction module last year. I know the steps and the materials by heart. All that is required is the knowledge of how to build the chimney within it, which is something only Clay will know.

My stomach drops and I look out the back of the cart, wishing he would appear where the road meets the horizon.

He's not gone. He's out there looking for us, looking for me. For now, making this list is the best I can do to keep me sane.

When I place the notebook down, I notice just how many valuables Joe and Jane were able to save from the fire. There's a wooden frame for making paper, and some of their cloth mesh is folded inside it. It's delicate and frayed where they ripped it for use as bandaging.

Beside the frame is a wooden box carved intricately with flower blooms. I open it and inhale sharply. A bright yellow ring lies inside. It's nothing like mine. It's smooth all the way around its edges, polished to perfection. I realize it looks just like Mother's. It must be a wedding gift of some kind.

I close the jewelry box carefully. I don't want Jane thinking I'm as bad as she assumes Clay is. I drag my eyes away and take inventory of our remaining supplies instead.

Our boxes of food are still full. Cotton is stuffed between each jar to prevent breakage. Three are missing, though I'm not surprised. Joe's probably hungry enough to eat twice as much food at any given meal. The next box is covered by Clay's deerskin tent. I lift it and my breath hitches.

Claw traps.

Clay was going to use these for hunting. I don't know how he'll catch anything without them. He may have other ways of finding food, but the more I dwell on it, the more it feels like the odds are stacked against him and there's nothing I can do about it.

I shake it off. If there's nothing I can do, then I need to focus on something else. I shift my gaze over to the next box, but my eyes catch on something between them. I breathe out a small sigh of relief when I see Carnelian's map still tucked where I left it, right between the box of traps and the box of spools. But something is missing. Something important.

The recorder.

I check every nook and cranny, lifting the charred blankets, and find nothing. The last time I saw the machine, it was in the cabin, just before we went to sleep. There's no way anyone bothered to pick it up. It's gone.

My heart shudders and my chest tightens. Without the recorder, we won't be able to listen to Carnelian's recordings. We never even had a chance. The spools are practically deadweight now, but I can't bring myself to toss them out. I hope and pray another machine will turn up eventually. Just like with everything else, all I can do is wait.

9

CLAW & BONE

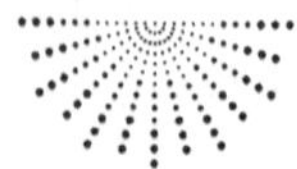

FOR THREE DAYS WE RIDE, stopping only to graze the horse. Every now and then I soak some cloth with holy spring water and rewrap my foot. It's painful at first; the shock of water on tender skin feels like it's being burned all over again. The nerves are sensitive. Joe says that's a good thing.

It feels rather ironic that the spring can so easily scald and heal. What we have is meant for trading, but there's more than enough. At least, that's what I tell myself.

Joe and Jane take turns driving the cart, keeping the horse at a brisk and steady pace. They don't talk much. Joe decides where to stop for the night, Jane decides what to eat for breakfast, and neither truly knows how much longer before we reach the outpost. Carnelian's map isn't quite to scale. All we can do is follow the road and watch the stream widen each day, growing much larger than the mere brook that flowed through the villages.

Joe and Jane sleep outside in Clay's deerskin tent, leaving me sleepless in the cart. I peer out of the cart and watch the stars. There are clusters of them that gather in the night sky. Mother calls them constellations, but she only knows how to spot one: the one that Father showed her. She points out the body, then the arms, always so proud to recognize the constellation of Persephone.

It's only ever visible in spring or summer, but there are others, clusters of stars with stories that I may never know. Seeing them now assures me that Mother, Flint, and even Clay are sleeping under the same night sky. It's a comforting thought that guides me into a restful sleep.

In a space between sleeping and waking, Clay's eyes flicker in the light of the fire. A dull orange glow stains my eyelids. For a moment, I wonder if the whole thing was a dream, that we're still at the cabin, sleeping by the fire. Soon, the sun will break over the horizon and Joe will teach me how to make paper from trees.

I try to roll over, but my foot bumps into a box. I jolt awake and whimper in pain, cradling my foot in my hands. The cart isn't moving, and the glow outside isn't a fire.

Where are we?

Slowly, my memory drifts back. Clay is missing. Joe and Jane are taking me to the outpost. Their home burned down and no one knows why.

I'm awake now.

I listen for Joe's familiar snores, but all I hear is a restless cricket.

I peak through the cloth covering that separates the back of the cart from the front, but neither of them are there. Scrambling to the other side, I lean out and search for the source of the light on my left. Two tree stumps sit on each side of a stone walkway that leads up to a plain wooden door marking the entrance to another roadside cabin. There is no house inscription.

These are lumberjacks.

When the night breeze blows, the faint smell of bacon hits my nose. I can't tell if I'm making it up or not.

Something is off. There's no fire. There's no smoke billowing from the chimney. Only lantern light slips from the window.

Joe and Jane are nowhere to be seen. I lean out farther to look around, but my finger scrapes the wooden railing and the yellow quartz ring Mother gave me slips off. I swipe down to catch it but am too slow. It falls away and lands on the ground below, rolling on its edge under the cart.

I don't know where we are, or whose house this is, or why I smell bacon, but I need to get that ring back. It's a desperation that I cannot control.

I quietly climb out, an impressive feat on my part, but immediately drop to my hands and knees when the pain stabs at my burned foot. Crawling under the cart, I feel around blindly for the ring. Frustrated at the errant light that shines from the cabin, I hold a hand to my eyes to block out the light, forcing them to adjust to darkness. When I pull my hand away, everything is clear.

There.

Right next to the horse's hoof, next to the front wheels and shrouded in shadow, the ring lies flat against the ground. I crawl into the shadows and snatch it up.

Then the door opens and I freeze. My eyes swivel to the door and all I see are two sets of bare feet.

A primal fear grips me. If I move, they'll see me. I don't want to be seen.

The feet shift and a woman speaks. Her voice is tired and annoyed.

"I doubt there's anyone there. He was adamant that it was just him and his sister. I'd rather not waste time. Let's go back inside."

The woman's feet turn around and I take my chance. I push myself up against the wheel of the cart, deeper into shadow, tucking my knees deep into my chest. My ring is gripped tightly in a fist. The sharp edges of the crystal dig into my palm.

"She said otherwise," a man snaps back. His feet move closer to the door, stepping past the threshold and out onto the stone path.

The horse nervously paws against the ground, sending dirt up into my lungs. I press my elbow up to my mouth tightly to avoid sneezing, biting my sleeve.

"Let's see, shall we?"

I shut my eyes and pray.

The man walks around to the back of the cart, leaning in and shifting it with his weight. I squeeze deep into the wheel, willing myself to stay absolutely still and silently thanking Mother for making me wear dark clothes on the Travelers' Road.

He peers into the cart where I was sleeping just minutes before and sighs in frustration. He shuffles through what's left of Joe and Jane's valuables.

"No girl." He huffs.

There's food, though.

The cart is full of jars packed to the brim with pickled eggs and vegetables, even some sheep's cheese Mother made. Is that not of use? I can't understand why they would only want me.

"I told you," the woman says, "even if there is one, she's probably a skinny little thing. Let's go, we still have work to do."

He walks away and I open my eyes. They were shut so tight that everything around me blurs. The door clicks shut and I exhale a gust of air.

Who are they?

What are they?

Where are Joe and Jane?

So many questions build in my chest and I still don't dare move. My eyes flicker around, looking for options.

The door creaks open again. Fear grips me just as tightly as it did before. The man's bare feet shuffle through the threshold, dragging something, someone, away from the cabin. It isn't until he turns the corner that I see Joe's limp body. The man pulls him into darkness and returns with empty hands.

"That lumberjack is too used to the warmth," the man jokes. "If the beating didn't do the job, the cold air will."

Again, the door clicks shut.

Nothing is right. Clay is lost, Joe is in danger, and Jane is nowhere to be found.

The glowing black boxes dim out one by one, thrusting me into complete darkness. I dare not move. I can only hope and pray they go to sleep soon.

Persephone's constellation is all that soothes me.

I sit unbearably still, twirling my ring on my finger to calm myself as I wait for the barefoot strangers to fall asleep. Two hundred twirls later, a single snore reverberating from the second story window turns into two. This is my chance to do something.

I stretch and pins and needles radiate up my leg.

"*Come on,*" I whisper. I squeeze it, smack it, anything to wake it up. Finally, the pins are replaced by a bitter cold. I roll out from under the cart and consider my options.

If what the man said is true, then I don't have a lot of time. I have to work quickly.

I raise myself with my good foot and lean against the back of the cart, looking for something, anything, that could help us get out of here fast. Five claw traps sit in the closest corner, wrapped in linen cloth. I take one out carefully. If they scrape too loudly, I'm done for.

There's no avoiding it anymore. I have to put weight on

my foot. A full ache turns into a stinging pain, stabbing me with each step I take to the front door. I bite my tongue so hard that it draws blood. I can't stop. This is the only way.

I thank the Earth Queen that Clay had the sense to show me how to set this thing up before leaving the village. I lower onto my knee, giving my foot a rest, and begin. I work excruciatingly slowly, ensuring any noise I make is timed with the rhythmic snoring above me.

I feel better knowing there's something between us and them. If things go badly, this will save us. If it works, that is.

I can barely get up so I stay low, crawling around to the side of the cabin. Over the past hour, my eyes have adjusted to the darkness of night. The moon is shrouded in cloud cover, but I can still see the shadowed outline of Joe, lying motionless under a cracked and crooked window.

"Joe." I shake him weakly, then harder, putting all my weight into him. One eye, dark and tender, remains squinted shut. Even with good feet, there's no way I'd be able to drag him or lift him into the cart. There has to be something here that can help. I get up, using the window frame for support, and as I rise, I see Jane.

She lies limp on a bare wooden floor, surrounded by several chairs strewn about a wooden table. Her legs are bare. Her shirt is torn.

My eyes glaze over as I understand the depth of the pain that she has endured.

If that man had found me, would I be lying next to her?

I need to do something.

I can't lift both of them, but I could use something inside to wake them. I scan the room for anything remotely useful. It's rather barren, I realize, with just the table set up across from a cold stove. The plates are still sitting atop the table, but the glasses have tipped over. Water drips into a puddle on the floor.

It gives me an idea.

I lean against the wall as I make my way back, lowering to a crawl when I reach the front of the cabin. In the cart, I find exactly what I need: a jar, emptied of holy spring water. I take it to the stream and dunk it in.

The water that rushes between my fingers is shockingly cold, but that's the point. I fill the jar to the top, seal it up, and make my way back to Joe.

The snores are obnoxiously loud even as the wind whistles in the trees. Regardless, I feel like I'm racing the clock, like one wrong move will be the end of everything.

When I get back to Joe, I try to stop and think about what I'm going to do. I frantically cycle through all the ways this could go. A lot of them are bad. Their injuries have set our course in stone. If there was ever an inkling of an idea that we might turn back around for Clay, it's gone now. We have to get to the outpost as soon as possible. The only way to do that is to wake Joe up.

I pull him from the ground and pivot him so that he's up against the wall beneath the window. The jar is ice cold in my hands, and I shake as I remove the seal. Then I pray.

And splash it in his face.

He lurches forward with a gasp and the force of his body almost propels me backward onto the ground, but I toss the jar aside and hug him tightly.

"It's me. Stay quiet. They're sleeping."

Every second is dangerous. I took a gamble waking him up like that. He could have pummeled me in confusion, but as I hold him, his tense muscles loosen; his heartbeat slows. His breathing slows, too, and I tear up a little when he starts rubbing my back, just like Mother used to.

I lean back to inspect him. His left eye squints against the swelling, but he smiles and his hand reaches for mine. We're both so cold, but somehow he's already warmer than I am. He wraps both hands around mine.

He shouldn't be the one reassuring me right now. We have to hurry.

With barely a whisper, I find the words I need to say. "We need to get Jane back to the cart. Are you able?"

He nods silently. I move aside and he rises to his feet, only to grip his leg in pain. I yearn to help him, but I can barely even help myself. After only a moment, he collects himself and begins to walk.

A snore rips through the silence and Joe freezes. His face twists and contorts. I no longer recognize him.

"I could kill them."

It's not a whisper but a gruff, primal growl that has me thinking he really could.

"We don't have time to test that theory."

Please don't test that theory.

He takes a moment to weigh his options, but when his eyes find mine, he softens. "Let's go, kiddo."

I lead him to the front. We both limp, me on my burned foot and him on his bad leg. I tug on his sleeve at the front step, pointing to the claw trap I set. He smiles at me proudly, just for a moment, before facing the door.

He does not move.

Can he do this? Am I asking too much?

A snore cracks through the night and Joe's muscles tense up. He reaches over to the knob and opens the door quickly. When it's wide open, he hesitates for only a moment before stepping over the claw trap and disappearing into the void of darkness.

I leave the door wondering if there is more that I can do. One trap should be enough to get us out of here, but I want to make absolutely sure.

Just one more trap, I tell myself. *We can afford to lose one more.*

I take a trap from the cart and rush around to the back of the cabin. I look into the window and sigh in relief when I see Joe has successfully picked Jane up and is making his way back out the door. I keep moving forward until I get to the back of the cabin, setting a trap on the corner. I kneel low, making quick work of it.

As I get up, something knocks into my head. My hand jolts to stop it, worried I'll make noise. I can't see what it is, so I use my hand to feel it.

From taut string hangs something hard and round. There's a crack at the top where the string slides through. It weaves in and out of two holes the size of an egg and comes out through jagged edges that feel like teeth.

It has to be a skull, but I don't remember deer skulls being this round.

It isn't until the cloud's shift and moonlight glints against bone that I realize why the man wasn't interested in our food.

We are the food.

I don't crawl, I don't walk, I don't freeze. I run. I burst forward and my shoulder clips another bone. This one is long, like an arm. It swings and whacks against countless more, hung across the length of the string from the cabin to the trees. They rattle like dominoes falling in a line.

The snoring stops.

Adrenaline is like lightning through my veins. I sprint for the cart, my foot barely stinging with each stride. When Joe sees me, he hoists himself up into the cart, takes up the reins, and calms the horse as chaos ensues.

Footsteps barrel down a wooden staircase and I can feel what's coming. I keep my eyes locked on Joe. The door opens and I'm almost to the cart.

And then I trip.

I try to get up but my knees give out. I roll onto my back and see the cannibal smile wickedly from the door. Her hair is a matted mess of gray curls. Her eyes are a dark and endless void.

"You're mine," she growls. She takes a step and then—

CRUNCH

As the claw trap clamps around her foot, I am frozen in fear on the ground. Her mouth opens in pain, but I cannot hear. I cannot see anything else but her bloody foot lifting up and stepping over the threshold as she continues to approach me. I can't look away. Each step is death and I can't remember how to move.

Strong arms wrap around me and hoist me up from behind.

Joe tosses me in the back and launches himself into the cart.

"*Hyah!*" he shouts at the horse and it breaks out into a gallop.

The woman reaches out and grazes the railing of the cart, but she stumbles and falls to the ground. She watches us leave with eyes full of grief. At first, I figure it's due to their lost meal, but as the man closes the gap between them, I feel her fear. His ax glimmers in the moonlight as he stalks toward her.

I turn away before the screams begin.

10

OUTPOST

FLINT USED to read me fairytale stories as a child, but I didn't believe in them. Myths of wild beasts and ravenous monsters were more intriguing than terrifying, and I had all but forgotten the dark tales of men who feasted on their brethren because I assumed they could never be true. It's hard to fear something you can't see.

But last night? I can't unsee that.

A mountain range reaches up from the horizon, grasping at clouds. They're easy to see now that the deep woods are far behind us, a welcome distraction from the nightmares that came to life last night.

After we made our escape, Joe and I switched places; he didn't trust himself to drive through the night, and neither did I. After a quick lesson on steering the cart, we continued on, stopping frequently to check on Jane in the back. She's wrapped in the same charred blankets that burned my feet just four days ago.

"What happened?" I ask. It's the second time I've done so. The first time was shortly after we made our getaway, but Joe said he had to focus. He was tense and full of anger, as though replaying the events in his head. I decided to leave him alone. This morning, as the stream continues to widen, he seems calmer.

"To be honest, I don't remember a lot." He brings a damp cloth to his eye. "We thought they might let us park the cart there for the night. It seemed like a good idea since they were lumberjacks, too, but now I'm not sure what they are."He stares out at the tree line to the west.

"The man was strange. He invited us in for stew and asked inappropriate questions of Jane. Jane can fend for herself, but she's my sister. I told him to quit it and he started pounding on me. I don't remember anything after that."

He sighs. "Jane has endured too much. That man, he did things to her. I can tell."

"Joe, you can't blame yourself for this," I point out. "You saved her, I couldn't have done it myself."

"I should have known something was off. They asked if there were others. I said no, and Jane didn't contest it. I think we both knew we were taking a risk. I wish we had just bypassed them, but the smell of food made my stomach lurch and I couldn't help myself." He rubs his stomach absent-mindedly.

"I heard the man say that Jane mentioned me."

Joe winces at the thought.

"Did they look for you?"

I nod.

"You're a survivor, Alira."

He reaches over and rubs my back reassuringly and I can feel tears welling up again.

I look down at the reins in my hands, "I just wish Clay were here."

"Things would have gone very differently," Joe says.

He's right. What occurred last night was probably a best-case scenario. If it had been me and Clay, alone, he would have had the same nonchalant demeanor. He would have walked up to the door and knocked without a second thought, all so that we could sit at another dinner table and meet Joe and Jane's fate. I shudder at the thought.

The best I can do is send someone out there to find Clay before he finds the cabin. She may not be around, but her partner might. I have to send someone to find him.

"Oh, there it is!" Joe points to a bridge up ahead where the river splits, turns, and bends. Across the bridge is a stable and, next to it, the outpost.

"We should switch places," he says.

"What? Why? I'm fine driving."

"No." He grabs at the reins in front of my hands and pulls the cart to a stop. "There's going to be a lot of men here, and I need you to let me do the talking. I don't want them getting the wrong idea."

"And what exactly is the wrong idea?" I ask.

"Just trust me, okay?"

I roll my eyes and we switch places.

As we get closer, the river becomes deafening. Water rushes down the mountain and under the bridge before heading south, where the forest begins again. Our roadside stream is a babbling brook in comparison.

Stalls line the path up to the outpost and I peer in to look for other horses, but there are none. It isn't until we pass an opening between the stalls that I see a fence and a herd of horses grazing in the rolling fields beyond it.

"Haigh, you need a bed?" I whip my head around to the man standing in front of the cart. His narrowed eyes are green and his hair is pale honey. Rugged men sit behind him on the stoop of the outpost, smoking cigars. Their hair ranges in color from grizzled yellow to auburn red.

They're all staring at me.

"We need a healer," Joe informs him. "We ran into a lot of

trouble on the road and we'll need to send someone out to search for a friend."

One of the rugged men pipes up, "Why didn't y'all do it yourselves?"

"Because we're all injured and the cannibals are in the way." Joe replies.

The man's eyes widen and glance at me before darting away.

"All right, come on in. We'll have a healer come and check in on y'all."

Joe jumps down and circles to the back of the cart as a girl about my age comes out from the stalls. Her hair is bright like sunshine, braided loosely. She's pretty and clean. I run my hand through my hair, trying to remember how long it's been since I've had a proper bath.

I glance back at the rugged men, dirt clinging to their sunburned skin. They're looking at her now, not me.

"Clara." The man turns to her. "Bring the cart to Marshall and help him clean out the stalls when you've finished."

The girl nods silently, waiting for us to head inside before taking the horse and cart away.

I walk ahead, holding the door open for Joe. He carries Jane with both his arms, keeping her wrapped in two blankets to ensure she's fully covered. Together, we enter the outpost.

A large oak desk stands against the wall on the far side of the room. It's smooth and polished, with a single large book splayed open on top of it. Joe waits patiently in front of it and I do the same. To our right, several tables of varying sizes are set out with plates and forks and knives. Real ones, not slate shards.

"Hello!" A woman walks in from the door behind the desk. Her eyes are like the river and her hair is the color of flax, but her skin is a warm olive tone that makes me seem sickly next to her. She's even prettier than Clara.

"My name is Lynn. Please write your names in the ledger here, and I'll show you the way to your rooms." Her eyes lock onto Jane. "I can also show you to the infirmary if you are in need."

I step up to the book and busy myself with the task of writing all our names in my neatest handwriting as Joe responds.

"The man out front said a healer would come by to check her out."

Lynn rolls her eyes. "Of course. Wade is always contradicting me. I'll lead you to the infirmary since he has no clue how this operation works."

She sweeps away from the desk just as I finish writing my name. Joe follows, his limp barely noticeable. I wonder how hard he's trying to hide it. I wonder why he bothers.

As we continue down the narrow hallway, floorboards squeak underfoot. A cat darts in front of me, weaving between my feet and almost tripping me up. It meows incessantly.

"Don't mind Mr. Meow, he's just looking for more food," Lynn explains.

Joe uses his free hand to reach into his back pocket. He takes out a small piece of hard cheese and nicks off a piece, letting it fall to the floor. Mr. Meow pauses to gobble it up before returning and repeating the ritual.

"Since you're new," Lynn says, "I'd like to assure you that we accept most items as payment, and we don't ask for it until you leave. Please focus on healing while here." She spares a look at me specifically as I, unlike Joe, have been favoring my burned foot openly.

We enter the infirmary at the end of the hall. The room is white, but a lantern flame paints it in an orange glow. A woman sits in the corner with a book, her straight red hair pulled up into a messy bun. She jumps up at the sight of Jane and helps Joe set her down on the bed.

There is no greeting, there is no welcome. She takes one glance at me and my wrapped-up foot before skirting across the room and sticking her arm elbow deep into a wooden cabinet.

"Cut or burn?" she asks. Her voice is smooth as water.

"Burn," I reply.

She takes out two glass bottles, one wide and clear with a jellylike substance, the other skinny, filled with tiny, ovate pebbles. She shakes one out onto her palm and walks over to me. She gently takes my hand and places the wide bottle in the palm of it.

"Aloe gel for burns. Stay off your feet and reapply dry bandages daily." Then she takes my other hand and drops a pebble inside of it.

"A pill for the pain. Swallow it."

"And you"—she turns to Joe—"Stop hiding that limp and sit down."

I stare at the two items she's placed in my hands. They both seem odd to me. Tierra might know what aloe is, but the pill is like nothing I've ever seen. I place it on my tongue and chew it once, grimacing at the bitter taste.

I should have swallowed.

I glance back at Lynn. She takes my arm gently and guides me out of the infirmary, closing the door. I follow as she leads me away from Joe, and the imaginary string that's held us together become taut. She stops at the door to an empty room and tucks a stray hair behind my ear.

"No need to worry about them, sweetheart. They're in good hands now. She might take a while, but he'll be released quickly. Dinner will be served at sundown. Come to my desk if you need anything."

She floats away, stepping on each wooden floorboard with measured grace. They don't creak under her feet. I watch in awe before turning away.

The room is small, but it has what I need. A soft mattress with a puffy quilted blanket sits upon a wooden frame along with a pillow of unknown material.

Wool? Or feathers?

I push down on the pillow with my free hand and smile to myself.

Feathers. So many feathers.

I look down at my hand, still clutching the bottle the woman gave me. After all we've been through, this is the first place that feels utterly safe.

I climb into the bed and push the covers aside, unraveling my bandages. I apply a small amount of aloe to the burns. It's cool and soothing at the same time. When I'm done, I rewrap my foot and lie down.

I've had plenty of time on the ride to think. I've worried endlessly about Clay and Jane and Joe. But lying in bed staring at the ceiling of the outpost paints it all in a different light. I worry, yes, but there's an inkling of hope. Maybe it's because, for the first time in five days, I feel truly safe.

My eyelids feel heavy, and when I try to lift my head, it just falls right back into the pillow. The pill casts a haze over me and the pain in my foot fades.

"Just a little nap," I say. And then I'm asleep.

A creaking floorboard from outside my door jolts me awake. I'm so groggy that it takes me a moment to remember where I am. I look around the room of oak and pine and stone. Dust particles dance in the light that filters through the window and geese call to each other as they fly south.

I've slept through dinner, I realize.

In fact, I slept through the entire night.

Joe will be worried, but I don't want to get up yet. My

entire body is sore, as though I've been lying here for days. Slowly, a dull ache presses at my stomach, and I get a fizzy feeling in my throat. I haven't eaten since the morning before we reached the cannibal cabin. A rabid grumbling eats into my sides. I can't ignore it anymore. I have to get up.

I push my blankets aside and sit, almost knocking the bottle of aloe over in the process. I pick it up and remove my bandages carefully. My foot doesn't seem as red as it did before, but there's lingering pain. The skin that was burned has since flaked off, slowly being replaced by new, tender skin. If I can keep up the aloe treatment, it won't take long at all for it to heal up completely. The pain pill seems to still be working so I skip another dose and put on my boots for breakfast.

I walk over to the dining hall where several travelers sit at a table. They're all blond or gray-haired. None of them look like Joe, so I try to find a table for myself. Just as I veer away from them, one of them calls out to me.

"Hey! Come sit with us! We don't bite!"

I glance at Lynn, sitting at the front desk, and she nods reassuringly. She knows what I've been through. If she thinks they're safe, then I'll trust her judgment.

I take a seat at the end of the long table and my stomach growls again. The table erupts with laughter.

"The ant is hungry!" one man jeers.

Ant? How could they know that?

"Alira, is it? Lynn was talking about you. The girl with the burned feet. How did that happen, anyway? Didn't your mother tell you not to sit too close to the fire?"

The table laughs. I peek at Lynn again, wondering if she made some sort of mistake in trusting them, but she's disappeared from her seat.

"If you're heading to Neró, you're going to need to get used to fire," another informs me.

"Neró?" I ask.

"What did I tell you all about pestering new guests?"

Lynn appears beside the table, balancing several plates on her arms. The men quickly get up to help her, setting the plates of ham, eggs, bread, and potato slices in the middle of the table. One of them takes my plate and loads it up before taking food for himself.

Lynn turns to me, a look of apology on her face.

"Sorry, hun, but your lot is a fine story to tell. Burned feet, drugged women, and limping lumberjacks."

Drugged?

"You both missed dinner," she adds. "No worries, you needed rest."

She leaves to fetch a pitcher of milk, then pours some into all the cups before returning to her desk.

Was Jane drugged? If so, how long will it take for her to wake up? And if Joe missed dinner, is it because he slept in? I need to ask him what's next. I need to know what the plan is for finding Clay.

But right now, I'm salivating.

I look down at my plate and find the aroma intoxicating. The eggs are barely cooked, their yolks bright orange and threatening to spill onto the bread. They're far from the hot-spring eggs I'm used to. When I cut into one, the yoke spills out and the bread soaks it up. I bite into it and moan in delight.

Then I try the potatoes. They aren't boiled whole or smashed the way Mother makes them. Rather, they're sliced into thin slivers that break easily when I try to stick my fork in them. They smell of rosemary and garlic and salt. I pop a whole forkful into my mouth and burn my taste buds in the process. My mouth hangs open as I try to let hot steam escape, prompting the same man who filled my plate to shove a glass of milk in front of me.

"Easy, lass, slow down."

I chug it and the other men laugh. I don't care. I shovel the last of the eggs up, chug the milk, and take the bread to go. It's no time at all before I'm up and out of the chair and place my plate in the wash bin near the door to what I can only assume is the kitchen. I pivot from there and walk directly to Lynn.

"Who knew an ant could eat so fast?" a man says behind me.

The table erupts into another bout of raucous laughter that lingers even until I get to Lynn's desk. She bends over a list of food inventory items, but quickly notices my presence. She smiles.

"Could you show me to Joe's room? I'm worried about him."

She nods, setting her quill down next to her bottle of ink, and leads the way down the long hall of doors. Mr. Meow tries to weave through my feet, but I know better than to bother feeding him like Joe did. Lynn stops abruptly just two rooms down from mine. I almost bump into her.

She knocks once, then again, listening intently for a response, but there is only silence. She calls his name through the door, but there's no answer. Anxiety creeps up into my chest.

She sighs, taking out a key and unlocking the door for me. It swings open.

The light of the window settles on an empty bed because Joe isn't in it. He's crumpled into a ball on the floor, shirtless and wet with sweat.

"Joe!"

I run to him, falling to the floor and holding him close. He's hot as Persephone's Spring.

"Water! I need water! It worked last time!" I shriek.

But Lynn is frozen at the door. Her eyes are glued to Joe.

Luckily, the man who gave me milk shuffles by to see what all the noise is for and bursts into action.

"Misty! Get over here!"

He runs down the hall. I latch onto Joe's body, refusing to let go, pushing my head against his chest to listen for his heartbeat. It's slow and shallow.

A hand settles on my shoulder. "He will be fine, but we have to take him to the infirmary now."

Misty. Her hair is a rich burgundy in the light of the morning sun. Her eyes are kind, but her hand is firm.

I clutch at his shirt, unwilling to let go.

"I don't understand—he was fine! He just had a limp!"

Two more men come in and scoop Joe up and away from me. My hands are empty fists, nails digging into skin as I force myself to rise and follow them to the infirmary, where they lay him down in the bed next to Jane.

Misty gets to work immediately, wiping the cold sweat off of Joe's body. The men leave with a look of pity pinned on me.

"I suspect that the drug Jane was given was also given to him," Misty observes. She sets her damp rag aside and covers him with the blankets.

"Drug? What drug? He was fine!" I sit heavily in a chair across from the beds and bury my head in my hands. She brings a chair over to sit across from me as Lynn hovers at the door.

"We don't know yet what the drug was. It seems that the effects were delayed for him. Tell me, Alira, what really happened?"

Bringing my mind back to that night is like getting sucked into a bottomless spring. I look at Jane, then Joe. The sight of them unconscious pulls me in until I'm back at the cabin, feeling string and following it down with my hands until I feel bone. They decorate the back of the cabin like trophies.

I can no longer hold back my tears.

"We stopped at a cabin; we thought it was lumberjacks, but it was"—I sob—"cannibals."

"Oh, hun." It's all Lynn can muster.

"I was asleep in the cart already so Joe and Jane went in alone. Joe said they had some kind of stew. I . . ." A gag rises in my throat. The smell of bacon doesn't seem so appetizing anymore.

Misty takes my hand, sitting next to me, and rubs my back in small circles as I gasp for air between sobs. Her voice is cool and soothing.

"Listen, you woke him up, put him to work, warmed him up, and kept him hydrated." She explains, "The pain pills I provided must have reacted to whatever they gave him. If you hadn't checked on him . . ."

"What about Jane?" I ask. She's a ghost beside her brother. It's an improvement from the last time I saw her, but she's not awake.

"You were able to keep her warm, but you were not able to wake her up. She also had some slight head trauma and bruising."

"I need them to be okay. I can't do this alone. How long until they're healed?"

"I've been able to reverse the effects on Jane and she should wake up in the next day or two, but Joe will probably take a bit longer." She glowers at him. "Men are always trying to be tough."

"This is all wrong. First Clay, then the cannibals, and now this?"

"Clay?"

"Yes." I perk up, wide eyed. "We lost him on the road and couldn't go back after the attack. He'll be trying to catch up to us, but I need someone to go back and find him before he reaches the cannibals."

Misty's blue eyes spark. She glances at Lynn, who spins on her heels and rushes down the hall, almost tripping on Mr. Meow.

"Lynn will send someone to find him." Misty says, "There will be no extra charge. There is no bartering life or death."

Tears of relief spill down my cheeks. "Thank you."

"In the meantime, you should get some rest. You've had a rough go of it."

"Please tell me I can work in exchange." I beg, "I can't sit around all day."

Her eyes soften and she nods. "It can be arranged. Be sure to take care of your foot. Don't overwork. You can find Marshall in the stalls tomorrow morning. He'll give you work to do."

I bury my face in her shoulder, and she holds me for a moment before I break away, drying my tears and telling myself everything will be okay.

11

FISHER

THE WIND OUTSIDE is cold and harsh, biting at my face. My hair blows wildly around me as I walk slowly toward the stalls, careful to keep my bandages in place.

Early this morning, before breakfast, I grabbed some holy spring water from the cart, added it to the aloe and gauze on my foot, and gave a bottle to Misty, hoping it would help Joe and Jane. She smiled kindly, but her eyes remained hardened. I worry endlessly.

I spot the man I was told to meet, Marshall, gathering tools for cleaning the stalls. He, too, is blond.

"By the Goddess, who are you?" he asks.

"Alira."

"You don't look like an ant."

"Is it really that obvious?"

"Lumberjacks get plain names, and your name isn't a River Goddess name," he explains.

"River Goddess?"

"Yeah, when you cross that bridge, you enter the House of the River Goddess."

The name rolls off the end of his tongue. All this time, I

had been calling it the Water House. I wonder who the goddess is, if they're anything like Persephone.

I shake myself out of the urge to ask questions that no one has time to answer.

"Misty said I could get some work from you."

He scoffs.

"You a farm girl?"

I nod.

"Good." He tosses me a shovel, "There's another batch of taters due to be harvested. Leave what you harvest in the kitchen. There's an entrance in the back. When you're done, you can help Clara in the coop."

I perk up at the mention of her name—the girl I saw when we first got here. I want to know more about her.

I follow the path around the side of the outpost to the back where the fields are. I make a beeline for the potato mounds. Small cloth flags mark the rows that are ready for harvest. I stick my shovel in and begin. It's grueling work, but slowly, the fear and uncertainty I've felt this past week falls away. All there is is dirt and crop and sky and earth. It's the happiest I've ever been to have work. Chores used to be boring and monotonous, but now it feels therapeutic.

Someone is out looking for Clay. I stayed up last night by candlelight trying to figure out where exactly he should be by now. We traveled for four days without him and slept here for two. Six days without Clay has felt like a century, but it will be over soon.

I assume the horse moves at least three times as fast as anyone at a normal walking pace. Our stops along the way slowed us down, but he will have made stops as well, sleeping each night and hunting for food. He should only be halfway between where the fire was and here. That means he's close to the cannibals, but not there yet.

We still have time to save him.

The thought keeps me sane, knowing that he will be saved from the danger we all faced. I hope I get to see him soon. If he is halfway, then it will probably take them two days to find him and another two to bring him back. By then, we will be all healed up and ready to move on.

With the last potato plopped into the bucket, I pick up the shovel and pail and lug them over to the back door where the kitchen is. I set the shovel against the wall and the pail on the counter before dusting off each potato and setting them aside for storage. As I do so, I notice my ring.

The shimmering black band pulls in all the light it can grasp. Its clouded yellow gem is orange in the dim light of the kitchen, like the innermost edge of a sunflower.

This ring is the only reason any of us are still alive.

Perhaps Persephone does approve. Perhaps she is watching over me. I pray silently that she watches over Clay as well.

When I step back outside, the mountain is shrouded in a cloudy mist that hides the city built into the side of it. The men call it the grand city of Neró: a haven offering anything you could ever need. I ache to see it.

My eyes drift to the chicken coop. I must keep working. If Marshall sees me slacking, I worry he won't want me working and, so far, working is the only thing keeping me from falling apart.

I walk to the front of the coop, open the door, and slip inside.

Clara has her back to me, picking eggs. Her hair is just as beautiful as it was that first day, bright and rich like sunflower petals. She wears a light blue headscarf the color of the sky and she wears pants, like me.

"Do you need help?" I ask.

She spins around, scaring a chicken out of its nest. It tries to slip past me, but I scoop it up by its chest, securing its legs and tucking its wings in before handing it back to Clara. She takes a relieved breath before accepting the bird and returning it to its box.

"I prefer to work alone," she says, "but you can watch if you'd like. I could use the company."

I turn a spare bucket over and sit. The chicken coop is larger than I realized. There are boxes that wrap around the exterior wall and an open area in the middle for the chickens to walk on.

"It's warm in here." I say, wiping at the sweat that's begun to bead on my forehead.

"It's the wool." Clara explains. "We insulate the walls with it."

"Oh! We tried that once."

"Did it work?" She asks.

"Uh. . . We didn't get that far." I reply. "Some foxes got into our underground coop, and we were going to rebuild one like this, but the elders forbade it. They said it was unnecessary. So now they live in the barn with the sheep.

"Huh." Clara replies. She remains focused on her work, holding each chicken up carefully with a gloved hand as she reaches for the eggs beneath them. But the short reply lingers, and I tug at my shirt sleeves, searching for a way to fill the silence.

"It seems like it works great for you, though." I add.

"Yeah. We don't have sheep, but a merchant told Lynn to try it a few years ago, so she bought some and had Marshall put it in. It does the job." Picking up the last egg, Clara turns to me. "Earning your stay?" she asks.

"Unfortunately, yes. We were just passing by, but things got complicated. We didn't intend to stay this long."

I adjust the bucket for comfort, bumping my foot and wincing in pain. I think of my pain pills, sitting on the table next to my bed. I could use them right now.

"You're with the two in the infirmary, right?"

The pain continues to radiate up my foot, making it impossible to speak, so I simply nod.

"I heard about all the trouble. I can't imagine. I've been wanting to study healing, to travel and help people on the road. Your story is exactly why I want to do that."

I perk up, and the pain in my foot dulls. "That sounds like an amazing idea. Are you going to do it?"

She shakes her head. "Marshall and Lynn might let me study healing if I'm lucky, but they won't let me travel alone after the way Bay disappeared."

"Who's Bay?" I ask.

"Sorry, I've gotten ahead of myself." She smiles awkwardly. "I'm Clara." She holds her hand out and I stare at it blankly. After a moment, she stuffs it in her pocket.

"Sorry," she says, her cheeks red. "Handshakes are a common way to greet people in our house, but you wouldn't know that."

To greet people?

"Oh! I'm sorry. I didn't realize. In our house, we bow," I explain. I hold my hand out. "I'm Alira."

She smiles, taking my hand and squeezing it with a light shake before letting it go.

"To answer your question, Bay is my brother. So is Marshall. Lynn's my sister, and Wade is our cousin. We all run the outpost together, but Bay liked to travel alone and . . ." She pauses, as if wondering if she should be telling me this.

"I think you could still do what you want," I say.

She tilts her head curiously. "How?"

"There was no way the elders would have allowed me to go on the road alone. I had to find someone to go with, first. Maybe you could find someone to go with you. Someone like Misty?"

"Perhaps." She doesn't seem sold on the idea. Her eyes narrow. "How did you end up with lumberjacks?"

My cheeks redden. No one's asked me that question, yet.

"I was traveling with my friend, Clay, and we stopped to rest at Joe and Jane's, but then their cabin burned down. We lost track of him during the fire, and with my burned foot, we couldn't turn around to find him."

"Oh no! Do you think he'll be okay?" she asks.

A surge of emotion rolls through me and I try to tamp it down, "I hope so. Lynn sent someone out to find him."

She nods, relieved. "That's good. I'm happy things are looking up. I think you've done enough this morning. You should eat and rest that foot."

I look down to see my bandages peeking out from my boot. I was able to ignore the pain, but getting up, it rushes back. The first thing I'm going to do when I get back inside my room is take another one of Misty's pills.

I turn to leave but her hand catches my arm.

"Hey, thanks for the advice. I'll ask Misty what I can do to help. I might as well start somewhere."

I give her a reassuring smile. "Of course."

Joe and Jane surprise everyone by waking up the next day. Joe wakes in the morning, jumping right out of bed and acting like nothing happened. He gets a harsh talking to from Misty about hiding his symptoms and he apologizes profusely. He tries to give me a wink but I don't entertain him.

"You both saved my life, and I will never be able to fully give you the thanks you both deserve, but I will try."

We spend the morning catching up on what's happened since he collapsed. When I tell him that Clay is getting picked up, he beams.

"That boy deserves a nice steak when he gets here and a strong apology."

Jane wakes in the afternoon. Her mind is muddled at first, but when the memories start returning, she falls apart. She sees me and takes my hand tightly.

"I'm so, so sorry." She squeezes each word out between heaving sobs. The strong woman who once looked at me with daggers in her eyes is cracked and broken.

"What are you sorry for?" I ask. "You've done nothing wrong."

All it does is make her cry even harder. Misty sets a steady hand on my shoulder.

"I have to do some final tests, and she may be in perfect health, but it will take her some time to process this. Go tell Lynn to ready a room for her and get some food for yourself, too."

I nod and walk away.

I get to the dining hall early enough to avoid the men. They've been good about giving me my space ever since Joe collapsed, but tonight I want to eat alone. Lynn isn't at her desk yet, so I go to the table by the kitchen and help myself to the crock of soup and plate of bread that sits atop it before finding a table in the corner. It all feels rather automatic to me. I can't stop thinking about Jane as her hands grappled mine in desperation. I can't understand why she would feel sorry. She got the worst of it.

I remember what the cannibal man said, about Jane mentioning me. Is it as simple as that? Either way, it doesn't matter in the slightest. She fought for her life. If the roles had been reversed, I don't think I would have sold Jane out, but fear is a strong and terrifying demon to face head-on like that. It grips you and makes you do crazy things.

Slowly, the men filter into the dining hall and take up their spots at the main table. It doesn't take long for their laughing to become unbearable. I take my bowl to the wash bin and find Lynn has returned to her desk. I need to update her on Jane.

"Hi, Lynn."

Lynn peers up from her book and smiles at me. As I open my mouth to speak, her gaze drifts to the tables and she sets her book down in shock.

"Oh no," she growls, scrambling to get up from her chair. It's the most ungraceful thing I've seen her do during my entire stay. She rushes over to the table and the men quiet at the sight of her. They all seem terrified. All except one.

"Fisher, why in all of Rhizole are you here?"

Some look on in astonishment, others smile at her ferocity. Fisher doesn't seem too concerned, though. He takes the time to chew on his bread before answering her.

"What's the problem? I said I would go. No need to nag."

"I told you to go *two days ago*."

He shrugs. "I don't remember you saying anything about a deadline, but it's mighty brisk out there and I don't handle cold well."

"Well, I'll make note of that next time a boy is dying and needs a pickup." She turns to the others and growls, "I need someone to find this boy. *Now*."

The men scramble and it takes me a moment to understand.

Someone was supposed to go out for Clay. That someone was Fisher.

I look at him, his smug face, feeling like he didn't do anything wrong and like Lynn can't boss him around. He's the one who told me not to sit too close to the fire.

Everything inside me burns and I feel just as hot as Lynn's face. I walk up to the table wondering how long that smirk will last after I'm done with him.

"Have you ever seen a cannibal?" I ask.

His face twists into confusion. "What kind of question is that?"

"I saw one on the road. Two, actually. They're living in a cabin feasting on anyone who wanders by. The lumberjacks and I escaped. But because of you, my friend will die."

It's a lie. Clay will be fine. He has to be. But when my deepest fears spill out of me, it feels like the truth.

Fisher's eyes widen. He stands, trying to defend himself. "Hey, now, I didn't know it was that serious, miss."

Lynn jabs at his chest. "You know how dangerous it is out there and you didn't think that this would be important? I told you there was a boy who needed to be picked up. I told you not to take *any* pit stops. I told you to leave as soon as possible. And what did you say?" She jabs him twice more. "'Yes, ma'am.'"

All the color drains from his face as he looks out the window. Gusts of wind pick up wisps of snowflakes that melt as soon as they hit the window.

"I'm gonna go out for a little trip," he says, his voice trembling.

He slips past us, grabbing his jacket from many by the door. He tugs it on in two quick movements and tugs at the handle, opening it up to walk out, only to find the way is blocked.

A man with frosted gray hair stands on the threshold. One hand is half-raised as if to knock. The other holds firmly onto something bulky slung over his shoulder. He hands it to Fisher, who staggers at the weight, falling to the floor as his knees give out.

The heavy thing rolls onto its side and several layers of cloth fall away to reveal Clay's red face. His eyelashes are coated in frost. They flutter as he wakes.

"Clay!" I run to him, falling to my knees and pulling him up close. "What happened?" I ask. He feels frail in my arms.

Seven days. Seven days did this to him?

Or was it the cannibals?

He mumbles an answer and I wonder in shock for a moment if I've heard him correctly.

Fisher is scrambling back up onto his feet, but everyone else is just staring in shock. Only the gray man speaks.

"Are you all dumb or something? This boy needs help!" His voice rasps and deteriorates into a shaking cough. He curls forward and Fisher tries to help him up with a panic in his eyes that must match mine.

"Move out of the way!" Misty's voice rings out and parts the crowd that has formed around us. She takes one look at Clay, then at me. She shouts some orders to the men at the table, but I can't be bothered to listen. The whole time I'm holding Clay, wondering if what he mumbled is the answer to all my questions.

"Jane."

12

THE CHASE

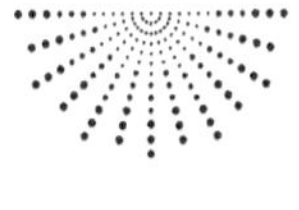

CLAY

ALIRA HAUNTS MY DREAMS, but Flint turns them into nightmares.

"You're probably the only person I can trust to protect her as I would," Flint had said. *"And you must protect her,"* he added, *"or I'll kill you myself."*

With that, Flint had officially given me his blessing. It was a brotherly trust we hadn't shared in months.

But respect was something else entirely. That was something that would have to be earned back, and I fear I've already lost the chance. I promised to protect Alira.

I failed.

A tree branch breaks with a baritone crack and I jolt awake. I don't waste any time. Every day that passes pulls me farther behind.

I stand up from my makeshift bed and grab my bag with one hand. The fire I built last night has long since burned out, reduced to ashes. I don't bother cleaning it up. No one's following me. Quite the opposite, really.

The wind picks up, kicking up the ashes with a gust that whistles through the trees behind me. I shiver, pulling up the collar of my oversized coat as I set the bag down and kneel at the bank of the stream. I take out what I need and unwrap the gauze that clings to my hand. Then I plunge it into the ice-cold water.

It's still painful and swollen, but all I can do is wash it for now. I splash my face in an attempt to wake up before rewrapping and heading on my way.

Right now, Alira is in our cart, stolen by the lumberjacks who had seemed so welcoming to us.

Hindsight is so unbearably clear. I chuckle to myself, scaring a robin from a patch of grass next to the road. I can't help it. This has been exactly what Alira feared.

They took our cart at the cost of their childhood home. I smirk at the thought. Was it even their childhood home? Joe seemed genuine, but that could have been an act. Jane, on the other hand, is clearly a maniac. What happened that night has me wondering if I can trust anyone at all.

I replay the night's events over and over, as I have every day since the fire. I worry that if I stop, the facts will get mixed up in my head. I don't want to forget anything Jane did.

Alira wanted to keep moving, but the rain was coming. Besides, it was a chance to show her what I was good for. I've met lumberjacks before, in the forest north of the village where my father and I hunted each spring. They're all rather independent, but never inhospitable.

My ego took over. I wasn't as cautious as Flint would have wanted. I didn't really consider the possibilities, just strolled right up to the door and knocked.

How cocky of me.

When Jane opened the door, she called us carpenter ants. I brushed it off as a joke, but it was the first red flag of many. She looked at me like I was a puzzle to solve and I played into it for flirtatious fun. Now I couldn't be more repulsed.

Arriving precisely at sundown that night may have seemed

odd, I'll admit, but Joe didn't seem to mind. I latched on to being right, throwing caution to the wind. If anything, I thought Joe would be the threat, but his extroverted optimism quickly allowed that fear to dissipate.

As Joe delighted in orating the process of papermaking for Alira, I assisted Jane in collecting firewood from the stockpile and setting up a space to sleep for the night. She studied me closely as I wandered around the space asking about paintings and keepsakes that decorated the shelves. I was aloof, charming, all the things village girls would have loved. And yet all it amounted to was more suspicion.

Alira, of course, fell asleep almost immediately. I, on the other hand, found myself restless. It was too hot.

I left the fireplace and escaped outside. The rain had stopped falling and the wind had died down. It was the perfect fall night. So perfect, I almost wanted to go back and wake Alira for it. I should have.

I wandered around back to the large shed where Jane parked our cart. I cracked the door open and greeted the horse inside with a pat on the shoulder. It didn't take long for me to cool down enough to go back inside, but when I did, I noticed a door was open that was previously closed. I wondered if a fall breeze through an open window might have opened the door, so I wandered over with the intent to close it back up.

I paused in awe. The room was a library filled to the brim with books. Shelves covered every inch of the walls, even the space between the ceiling and the window, below which Jane stood, cast in the eerie glow of the fire.

"Come in," she said, so I did.

Stepping inside, I took the opportunity to peruse the books that lined the shelves. They were bound in a variety of fabrics: linen; cotton; leather. When my gaze returned to Jane, her eyes pierced mine.

"Something of mine is missing."

"I'm sorry to hear that. Would you like help finding it?"

She chuckled as if I were joking. My face reddened, and for the first time ever, I was unsure of what to do. Then she turned and walked toward me, leaning in to hiss into my ear.

"I don't believe you," she said. "Your story, your quest. My prized possession is gone, and you have just left to attend to your cart. Coincidence?"

"I was just hot," I said.

Her eyes scraped over me like nails on a chalkboard. "What else did you take?"

"Take?"

My ego and disbelief betrayed me, painting me to be uncaring or unfazed by the clear threat. I tried to correct it. I stuffed my hands in my pockets, turning them inside out for her, but she barely offered me a glance. Instead, she took a step through the doorway and closed it behind her, jamming it from the other side. Unable to comprehend the situation, I walked up to the door.

"Jane? Surely there is a misunderstanding. I didn't take anything. We just need a place to sleep."

The sound of her footsteps faded away. I checked the door, tugging at the knob, but it was thoroughly jammed. I looked around the room for options but found none. I was trapped in there unless I could figure out what Jane wanted.

"Jane?"

I listened closely through the door, wondering if I should yell. It would have woken Alira up, but that would have put her in danger. I was the one Jane wanted.

The light of the fire slipping under the door became stronger, brighter. My feet suddenly felt very warm. I looked down, realizing that Jane had placed a stick of fire under the doorframe, allowing it to lick around the edges. The flames strengthened, eating at the wood.

"Are you crazy?" I raised my voice in a panic.

"Quiet," she hissed from her side of the door, "or she goes, too. Tell me where it is and we can pretend this never happened."

"I have no clue what you're talking about."

She huffed in displeasure.

"Come on, *ant*, just spill it. Then the fire won't have to spread."

She sounded desperate. Did she actually want to follow through on this? I tried to reason with her.

"You don't have to do this, Jane."

There was a pause. Was she considering it?

"Don't call me Jane. You're a stranger and a thief. I bet I'll find it in your cart." Her footsteps faded away.

I looked around with options dwindling. Yelling would have put Alira in the crossfire. I couldn't risk calling Jane's bluff.

The flames under the door became stronger and deeper in color. I could no longer sit and listen. I had to do something. At this rate, the cabin would burn down in its entirety. For what, I wondered, to scare a petty thief? It all felt exaggerated and overdramatic.

Eventually I abandoned the door altogether. The door-knob began to emanate warmth. Even if I unjammed it, opening the door would only feed the fire. I had no clue how big it would get.

I turned to the window, which at this point seemed like my best chance. As I walked up to inspect it, I realized that it, too, was jammed.

I rifled through the library table stacked with books and notes and freshly packed paper. The glass would not be difficult to break, but it would require something heavier than a book. After fishing around and finding quills, ink, more paper, more books, and a watch, my hands caught something. I pulled it out, inspecting my new find. It was a hammer.

Out the window, the moonlight revealed the absence of the horse and cart from the opened shed. Jane was either hiding evidence or preparing an escape. The grass surrounding the cabin gave off an orange glow. Did Jane only burn the door, or had she planted seeds of destruction elsewhere?

There was no time to figure her out. I brought the hammer heavily down at an angle onto the window. Glass shattered, jagged around the edges. Wind blew in, cooling the sweat I didn't realize had begun to dribble down my forehead. I looked behind me, watching the flames dance over to the bookshelves. The wind stoked the flames and they crawled ever closer.

I had to get out, grab Alira, and find somewhere safe. I tapped out each stubborn piece of glass that clung to the window frame and climbed out, but lost my grip and fell to the ground. I took a sharp inhale as a piercing pain shot through my hand and up my arm. A jagged piece of glass had embedded itself in my right palm. I got up, stumbled forward, and turned around.

It was amazing how quickly the fire had spread. How much time had I wasted at the door, begging Jane to listen? How much time had I spent looking for a tool to make my escape? I could not help but wonder what prized possession had been so important for Jane to have gone on such a disastrous tirade. Had she really thought me a thief or had she just been looking for an excuse to burn the place down?

Suddenly, a scream cut through the air. Alira was awake, and her scream was coming from outside. Something in the house collapsed in front of me, forcing me to move. Slipping around the side of the house, I stuck to the shadows of the trees. In the front, the cart began to move, but Alira tumbled out. She called for me and I took a step forward, only to freeze as Jane jumped down and pulled back into the cart.

Then came Joe, furious and red from the heat. He rushed

past them, straight toward me, as though he could see me through the flames. He held a machete in his hands, half-raised as he approached.

"Clay!" he roared.

Shit.

Shit shit shit.

I ran into the woods, scared for my life. I was sure Jane had already convinced Joe of my thievery and, if not, perhaps she had convinced him I started the fire in the first place. I laid low for several minutes as Joe rushed around the perimeter of the cabin, yelling my name and swinging his machete whenever something, anything, got in his way.

Then, silence.

When I finally peeked out of the shadows of the woods, the cart was too far for me to see.

I knew one thing for certain.

Alira wasn't the target. I was.

It was then that I made my decision. Let them take Alira and I would follow. If they take her where she wants to go, I will find her.

After the cart had gone, I raided the shed for supplies, finding the bag, the coat, three jars of clean water, and a first aid kit. I ran from the shed in time to see part of the cabin collapse upon itself. Then a tree fell behind me onto the shed. Staying any longer would have trapped me there and I would be dead.

Adrenaline had set the pace at this point. My feet hit the Travelers' Road in the direction of the cart, the river, and Alira. For days, I walked, one foot in front of the other, until I stumbled too many times to make any sort of meaningful distance at all. I ran myself into the ground before submitting to rest.

I worry she is latching on to those two as her new travel companions. I can almost hear Jane as she manipulates Alira into believing that I'm dead, or ensuring Joe believes I started it all. How easy would it have been to circle back the next day and find me?

There is another possibility, one I don't like to dwell on.

If Alira was burned in the fire, she would need medical attention, in which case they will be heading for the nearest outpost. The faster they travel, the longer it will take to catch up.

Suddenly, my boot kicks something with a dull *thunk*.

The jar rolls on its side down the road in front of me. It's one I recognize, one that I packed myself. It's uncracked, unlikely to have fallen from the cart. It's not the first one I've found, and honestly, it feels like Alira is leaving me a trail of crumbs. I smile at the thought, not hesitating before cracking the jar open on a nearby rock and emptying the contents into my shrinking stomach.

Pickled eggs never tasted so good. I let the tangy flavor sit on my tongue, savoring the flavor of home.

Alira's kindness toward me had always been confusing. Most girls in school fawned over me in the usual way, asking if I needed help studying or demanding I stay for dinner. That's how Gemma got me.

But Alira never showed any kindness with the expectation of something in return. Her kindness was genuine and sincere, never impaired by a long-term agenda.

After the festival I went to Flint on a whim. I knew he would be cold after our fight last spring, but I had to pursue it all the same. I just admire her so much. Her worldview makes me want to study the ways of the houses with her and maybe, just maybe, figure out if her kindness could be something more.

I shake off the thought. She has never given me that kind of inclination. I doubt this will change anything. For all she knows, I'm dead.

I secretly relish the thought of seeing her face when I find her. I want to see her recognition and relief turn into something more. It's not likely, but it keeps me warm.

After walking all day, lost in thought, I freeze at the sight of a cabin off in the distance. The hairs on the back of my neck rise immediately. I begin to walk a little quicker.

Did they stop here? I can't imagine Alira being comfortable with that after what happened last time. The cabin is intact, so Jane must not have tried any fire tricks.

I pause, unsure. Something feels wrong. I can't quite place it. I get the urge to circumvent the cabin entirely, leaving the road for the security of the trees. But in the search for Alira, I can leave no stone unturned. I need to question whoever is in that cabin and learn more about Alira's whereabouts and whether or not she is injured, sad, or heartbroken.

As I get closer, I spot two stumps. They frame the path to the front door, but they're cut jaggedly on an angle. It seems like sloppy work for lumberjacks. I step closer to inspect them before looking up and staring at the front door.

It's splattered with blood.

I step back in shock, feeling pulled in several directions. I open my mouth to call for Alira but nothing comes out. I should run, but my legs pull me forward. I steer away from the blood-encrusted stoop and do a perimeter check around the rest of the cabin. My training in animal tracking kicks in and I notice the grass growing sideways, as though something heavy was dragged through it. It stops at the windowsill, and I crouch low before peeking inside, only to find myself more confused and terrified.

Blood is everywhere and yet there is no one. Lying on the

floor in the barren room is a handsaw coated in dried blood and a claw trap clutching a rotting foot.

A human foot.

I scratch anxiously at my wrapped hand as thoughts swirl through my head. I could back away, pretend I saw nothing, and move on. But if I do that, I risk leaving Alira behind. She could still be here.

I need to practice caution. Where there's one trap, there's more, and if those traps are from our cart, then there could be as many as four of them scattered around this place.

I move with measured steps along the side of the cabin and turn the corner to the back of the house before freezing.

A string of white bones stretches from the house to the shed. They're scraped clean of meat and marrow, stripped of the pieces that made them whole. Normally, bones wouldn't bother me. I see them often enough. But these aren't deer bones.

"They're gone." A voice, low and sultry, weaves between the bones. My eyes drag away from them and settle on a woman sitting at a table facing away from me. She's hunched forward, but I can't tell what she's so focused on.

"Who's gone?" I ask.

"My meal."

A soft breeze tugs at me, urging me to leave. The bones that hang above her clink together weakly. My eyes drift down and I realize in horror that she's missing a foot. The stump that remains is wrapped in crimson cloth. Blood soaks it right through.

I should turn around and run, but her voice pins me in place.

"You think I'm a monster, but you hunters are no different. In your village, when a coyote kills a sheep, who's the first person the farmer calls?"

The woman laughs. It sends shivers down my spine and

goosebumps all the way up my neck. She turns toward me, her eyes like hollow discs, with dark and heavy circles and irises of volcanic glass. She looks sick.

Behind her is a skull, completely skinned but not quite white. The gaping hole on the right temple is surrounded by cracks that stretch in every direction.

"No. I am no monster. The only monsters here are people who wish for more. They take and take and take—an all-consuming greed that tears me apart."

It makes no sense. She sighs, tapping her long fingernails on cracked bone.

"Basil didn't understand either. He'd rather keep what little shred of humanity he has left. So Alder and I settled here and did what we could."

I didn't think it was possible, but she might be more insane than Jane. Why was she telling me all of this?

She smiles devilishly at me. "Regardless, there's just no way of knowing if they made it to the outpost in time."

She turns back to the skull, her dark laugh fading into the distance as I turn around and run.

If I'm being honest, that's the last thing I remember.

13

RIPLEY

CLAY

ALIRA'S DROOL is on my hand. I don't know where I am or how I got here, but I know she's here. This is not a dream. She's real and her drool is on my hand.

She's in a chair beside my bed, hunched over in a shallow sleep. Her pink lips are parted slightly. She's healthy and clean. Her hair is smooth and soft. I stroke it lightly, letting it curl around my finger and fall away.

A redheaded woman opens the door and I jolt in surprise. Alira lifts her head and the moment is gone like a wisp of a wind.

"Thank the Goddess you've woken up, finally. I was starting to wonder if you were drugged, too," the woman says.

Drugged?

When I turn to Alira for an answer, she's groggy, wiping drool from her mouth as she begins to take in her surroundings. Then she sees me.

"Clay!" Her smile spreads from ear to ear and I smile back, though it feels forced. I can't even begin to guess what hardships she had to bear without me.

"Don't get too excited." A girl appears in the door, her hair bright yellow. "He has a long rest ahead of him."

Alira's smile only fades slightly. "I'm just happy you're okay."

She gets up from her chair as if to leave but I grab her arm and bring her back next to me. She jolts forward, wide eyed.

"What is it?"

"I need to talk to you." I glance at the two other women. *Can I trust them?*

Alira looks worried and she should be. Even now, she's in danger.

She turns to the healers. "Can we have a moment?" she asks. They're hesitant but turn to leave.

Another voice croaks next to me.

"You'll just have to deal with me."

I follow the voice to a gruff man lying in the bed next to mine. He smirks at me with tired eyes.

"This is the man who saved you," Alira says.

His hair is grizzled yellow. He has an air about him, one of confidence and strength.

"Well then, I suppose I should thank you," I say.

"Can't thank me for something you don't remember." He chuckles, "Besides, you were already here. I just had to get you to the door."

He's right, I don't remember him. I don't remember much of anything after seeing the cannibal woman.

"I saw her. The cannibal." I turn back to Alira, gripping her arm with my good hand just a little too hard. I correct myself, moving to take my hand away, but she takes it back and holds it steady. She shakes her head in disbelief, "I can't believe she survived. The man was going to kill her with his ax."

I think back. I didn't see a man, but the cannibal mentioned a man, Basil? Alder? The memory is blurred. One thing is clear: She sat hunched over a skull with a crack drag-ging down the back.

"I think she managed to get the upper hand," I reply.

Her eyes hold mine, fraught with worry, "We tried so hard to send someone to find you before you could get there. I'm so sorry."

"We?" I ask.

"Of course. Jane and Joe are here, too."

So the skull, those bones, it wasn't them.

Realization hits me like a brick.

"That's where the merchants went."

"What?" Alira asks.

"The pomegranates!"

Alira's eyes widen in horror.

"We need to send someone after her," she says.

"No." I shake my head. "It's not worth it."

"But she's going to continue killing people!" she contests.

"Alira, her foot is gone. All that's left is a bloody infected stump. And the house is a mess. No one in their right mind will go near it. It's better that we just stay away."

She looks down, as if unsure, then nods. "Okay."

"Where's Jane?" I ask.

"Jane . . ." Alira leans in close. "You said her name when you got here. What were you trying to say?"

Oh, Alira, I wish I didn't have to say this.

"Jane started the fire."

Alira's hands break away from mine. Her eyes are like glass, as if reliving a nightmare. I try to sit up, using my hand for support, but wince in pain. I fall back into the bed heavily and stare at my hand. It's no longer wrapped, and the infec-tion is gone, but the scar remains.

"What happened, Clay?"

"I . . . tried to break out, but a piece of glass cut my hand. Hurt like hell."

Alira waits patiently as I realize I haven't told the whole story.

"She thought I stole something. She got so desperate to smoke me out that she ended up burning the whole place down. I barely got out."

"She told us she didn't know how the fire started or where you were." Her voice is cracked and weak. She grips my sheets in tight fists. Her voice darkens. "She tried to convince Joe you had started it."

Anger emanates off her like the heat of the hot spring.

"We're leaving as soon as you've gained your strength back," she announces. She gets up from her chair and bows to the man beside me.

"Excuse me." She opens the door to the two healers waiting patiently to reenter. They look at me curiously as she rushes past them.

She leaves too soon.

"Okay." The redhead steps back in, an air of authority about her. "Clara is going to check on you two every hour." She nods to the girl and leaves. As soon as does, the girl, Clara, turns to us. Her eyes are a stabbing blue as she gives her orders.

"I'm going to go get you both some food. After dinner, you must rest. We've had far too many instances of egotistical men around here and I'm not Misty. I'm still learning. *So rest.*" Her voice is clear and concise.

"Yes, ma'am," the gruff man says.

She closes the door behind her as she leaves.

I glance over at him. He's much frailer than I expected. His cheekbones are sharp against his skin and I can see the angles of his skull beneath short gray hair. His broad nose is lined with deep wrinkles and creases darken his narrow green eyes.

"Don't look at me like that, boy."

"Sorry." I avert my gaze, "I was just trying to remember you."

"No use forcing memories. There's a reason they stay hidden." His voice is gritty, his breathing staggered.

"What's your name?" I ask.

"The name's Ripley," he says. "Don't get too attached, though; I have a feeling I'm on my way down the river."

His voice is soft, his eyes kind, but his words sting.

"It wasn't me, was it?"

He laughs and his breath catches, deteriorating into a coughing fit. He curls over and I try to reach over to help him., but he holds up a hand, waving me away. He takes a moment before speaking again.

"I've been fighting this for a good long while."

I try not to show him too much pity. He clearly doesn't want it. It hurts, though. This man saved my life and yet he's convinced there's no way to save his.

"Do you know the cause?" I ask.

"I have my theories." He strokes the stubble on his chin. "For a while I felt it was just a part of getting older. I'm not the only one who thought so. But then the newer mums in our village began having issues, and the little ones started struggling, too." His voice hitches. I reach for the cup of water beside him, but he swipes it away, refusing my help. He takes a few long gulps before setting it back down.

"The elders of the village didn't want us leaving. Said it was a sickness to be contained. Then, a few weeks ago, they started advising the young mothers to drink from the rainwater storage. Can't remember the last time we had to use it."

"You're saying they think that the river is causing it?"

"It's merely a guess."

"So what now?"

"I was meaning to head to Neró to ask the elders there if they would perform some kind of evacuation. I thought I could get here before winter. They say it's going to be a bad one, you know. But I'm too weak to make the rest of the trip. Misty says I'll die if I go. I keep trying to tell her I'm floating belly up already. She's stubborn, that one."

"Alira and I will go. We'll make sure they know." It's the least I can do for the man who saved me.

"Then maybe there's hope for the villages after all," he says.

We fall quiet. The silence eats at me. I have no clue how to reassure a dying man. I open my mouth to try only to shut it again.

He chuckles lightly. "Don't worry, boy. It's not easy, but death is always kind in the end."

When the lights go out and everyone's asleep, there are no nightmares. I lie awake in weakened candlelight, thinking about my conversation with Alira to the tune of Ripley's haggard snores. They're intermixed with the wind that whistles through the cracks beneath the window. Rogue snowflakes strike the panes before settling on the sill.

When we were young, Alira used to follow me and Flint everywhere. She'd follow in our boot marks in the deep snow to keep from sinking in too deep herself, and only ever caught up to us when we were turning around to go home. Now it's the opposite. I've spent the entire time on the road trying to follow her tracks. Now that I've found her, it's too late to turn around. Now that I've met Ripley, it's not even an option.

I've already failed in protecting Alira. She made it through the fire, escaped the cannibals, and almost made it all the way to the city gates without me. But there are still dangers lurking, and all I've done is make it worse.

She was probably safer caught up in Jane's lies. I could

have let that narrative play out until we left, but now she knows. I handed her the match to light the flame without knowing the nearest water source. All I can do is get us out of here before the flames spread.

I kick the blanket off and swing my legs over the bed. I pause and look down at my body. Seven days of walking with nothing but the occasional jar of pickled eggs has left my shirt hanging much looser than when we left home.

I'm in no condition to be walking around, but it's the only thing I have control over right now. The faster I get better, the faster we can leave. We can go to the city and warn the elders about Ripley and the villages. At least then I can say I've fulfilled at least one of my promises.

I lean forward and stand on two feet. For a moment, I feel amazing.

Then the world begins to spin. The candlelight pendulates around Misty's chair and my head feels like it's being pulled to the floor. I widen my stance and grip the table beside me but it slides out of place. The candle clatters to the floor and I try to catch it. It's like a melting snowflake. The weight of the world pulls me down until I'm kneeling on the floor.

My head throbs, my hand stings, and candle wax drips beside me.

When the door opens, my eyes close and my nightmares begin again.

BLACK MOON RISING

Black moons pull the veil taut
Asphodels quivering

Cypress sways as the lyre plays
Death comes withering

Teeth snapping
Claws grappling
Silence always screams

Whatever you do
Do not intervene

—Dr. Carnelian

14

WITHERING

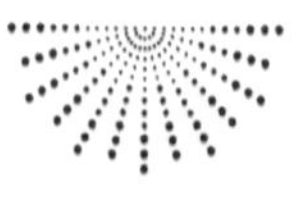

CLAY

I WAKE to Misty's withering glare. She reminds me of Jane, standing there with her face painted in distrust. I don't blame her. Clara warned us not to be cocky, but here I am.

I sit up in my bed, unsure of how I got here. "What time is it?" I croak through parched lips.

"Time to rest," Misty replies. She makes a pointed glance at the glass sitting on my bedside and I take it, drinking until there is nothing left.

"When can I get up?"

Her eyes narrow slightly. She rests her hands on her hips.

"You can't rush these things," she says.

"I know."

"I'm not sure you do."

I glance at the window as a chickadee lands on the sill. It hops atop the snow that's built up overnight, studying its reflection in the glass before darting away. Its tracks are faintly carved into the snow. It won't be long before they're buried beneath the next storm.

"I need to be ready," I say.

"You hear this?" she asks Ripley. He shrugs.

132

"You spent half a fortnight on the road with no proper rest, no proper medical attention. Your hand was infected, you didn't eat nearly enough food, and you walked yourself damn near into the ground. You'll be ready when I say you're ready."

"But we need to tell the elders about Ripley and his village."

Misty's eyes soften. She spares a glance at Ripley.

"I'd like to say he's wrong," Ripley says, "but the rainwater storage will only last so long. The acorn crop is thickly shelled, and the deer are fatter than they've ever been. We won't be seeing another rain till spring."

Misty leans back in her chair. The bun that sits atop her red head is lopsided, and her eyes are rimmed in dark shadows that hint at the long night she's had watching over me.

"So let Alira go with the lumberjacks," she says.

I shake my head. "I can't do that."

"Why not?"

Ripley coughs abruptly, a sound of shattering lungs and rasping breaths. I can't tell if it's a genuine cough or a product of trying to keep his mouth shut. Misty gives him water but there's suspicion in her eyes.

"I can't help anyone if they keep secrets from me." She looks at me expectantly.

I don't know what the lumberjacks will do if I reveal their web of lies. In fact, I'm surprised they aren't knocking down my door to keep me quiet. I told Alira. That was a risk. But nothing has happened yet. If I tell Misty, there's no telling what will come of it.

But if I can convince Misty that it's time to leave—that Alira can't go alone—then I can tell the elders about the water problem myself.

"It's Jane," I say.

Misty's eyes narrow.

"Jane started the fire that split us up in the first place. I don't know if she intended to burn her house down, but it felt an awful lot like the lumberjacks didn't want me around. Maybe they feel differently about Alira, but I can't take that chance."

"Joe, too?" she asks.

I nod. "During the fire, I was trying to find Alira, but Joe was walking around with a machete, yelling my name. I ran and hid, worried he'd kill me if I got within ten feet of him. I don't want to test the theory."

"Well, I do." She gets up and leaves the room before I can so much as utter an objection. Ripley merely chuckles, but my chest tightens with every second that passes.

Before long, Joe rushes in. He's a monster of a man, but with his flannel shirt tucked into his pants, he looks more like a stuffed bear than an ax-wielding maniac. He lights up at the sight of me.

"Clay! I didn't know you were taking visitors yet. Alira said you were looking rough."

Misty gives me a reassuring nod, but I bite my lip, unsure.

"Joe, I need to ask you something."

Misty pulls out her chair and he takes it, leaning in to listen intently to whatever I have to say. It's hard to imagine this man trying to kill me, but I need to be sure.

"Do you think I started the fire?" I ask.

"Of course not." He doesn't miss a beat. "You had no reason to."

"Do you think Alira did?"

"She was sleeping when I found her," he says.

"So who do you think started it?"

His brow twitches and furrows. He glances at Misty before answering.

"I don't like where this is going."

"I don't either." I say, "But this is what happened."

I relay the events of that night to Joe: escaping outside to cool down, the insinuation that I was a thief, the locking of the door, and the spreading of the fire that followed. His eyes never stray from mine.

When I'm done, his eyes drift down, fixed on my gauze-wrapped hand.

"I don't think it was her intent to burn everything," I say, a weak attempt at reassurance. "She sounded desperate to stop. But she wouldn't. Not unless I gave her whatever it was she thought I took."

"It didn't make any sense." He says, "Jane tried to convince me you started it, but to disappear and leave Alira behind like that? I went looking for you, brought my machete along in case you got stuck somewhere, but I don't blame you for running. For thinking us monsters."

"There's nothing that can be done about it now," Misty says. "You did everything you could, Joe. You just didn't know."

"I should have," he says.

"Look," I say, "I trust you. But I don't trust Jane. I need to know that Alira will get to Neró without Jane going crazy again."

Joe's eyes widen, searching mine. He looks like I've just told him I'm dying. I backpedal.

"It's just that I'm still recovering, and Ripley here was trying to get to the elders about the sickness spreading in the water villages, but he can't go, and well, neither can I right now. I'm going to have to rely on Alira."

Joe looks over at the Ripley, but he has no quippy come-back. He's already dozed off into a shallow slumber, free from coughing fits for now.

Joe leans back, stroking his beard. When he stands from Misty's chair, he is neither maniac nor stuffed bear. He is Joe.

"Alira saved both me and Jane. She didn't have to."

His eyes are hard with determination. "I'll keep Jane in line."

A tightness in my chest releases and I sigh in relief.

There's a soft knock at the door, and I know that the hard part is just beginning when I see Alira standing there with a bowl of soup. She sees Joe standing next to me and smiles.

"I brought you some food. How's everything going?"

Misty moves aside to let her through.

"Well, Joe and I were just talking . . ." I trail off.

"What about?" She take's Joe's chair and sets the bowl on the table next to me. I freeze. I'm not sure if I'm ready for this. Misty and Joe nod reassuringly.

"Ripley told me why he's sick."

"Oh?"

"Yeah, he said that the southern water villages are falling ill, and that he thinks it has something to do with the river."

She looks to Ripley, her mind fluttering from one thought to the next. Her blue eyes follow each idea as it darts by and I notice specks of honey and sage green stretching out from her pupils before waves of blue overtake them, rimmed in a dark teal that is utterly captivating.

Her bottom lip trembles. "What can we do?"

I stammer, briefly losing my train of thought. "We need to . . . tell the elders in the city about the villages. But . . . I'm not fully recovered yet."

"Well, when will you be?"

I glance at Misty for backup.

"It could be a while," Misty says. Alira looks at her in dismay. She looks to Joe, then me.

"I . . ." She hesitates. "I don't want to go without you. I can't do that again."

She looks at me in a such a desperate way that I almost consider saying yes. But Joe knows. I reach for her hand, holding it tightly as the words spill out of me.

"Alira, you've been through so much without me and I hate that. Every part of me wants us to leave today so that we can get ahead of the snowstorms and move on. But I'm not ready and we need to tell the elders about Ripley."

"You're making me go with Jane?" she says. Her blue eyes turn to ice.

"Joe will keep her in line, right, Joe?" I ask.

He opens his mouth, but Alira doesn't let him speak.

"I won't go." She says, "Not without you."

"Alira," I say and my voice falters.

"Someone else can go." She says, "Why does it have to be me?"

"Getting an audience with the elders is not easy." Misty answers, "But someone from the House of the Earth Queen is sure to get their attention."

Alira's hand breaks away from mine and a bitter cold replaces it. She turns to Misty, her voice splintering. "Can you just leave us alone, please?"

Misty nods, prodding Joe toward the door. He gives me one last look of pity before heading into the empty hall.

Alira turns back to me.

"I thought you were dead," she says. "I kept telling myself you weren't, but I had no clue what to do. It felt like I was being dragged by a leash. I just had no control. And then we stopped at the cannibal cabin and I. . ." Tears spill down her cheeks. I reach over with my gauzed hand and gently wipe them dry, tucking a strand of her hair behind her ear.

"All I could think about on the way to the outpost was how to get to you before the cannibals did." She sucks in a breath and bites her lip, holding back a gasping sob.

"You don't have to worry anymore," I say, my voice calmer than expected. "I'm safe."

She takes my hand again; her thumb begins to rub circles into my palm. I relax at her touch.

"Please, Clay, just focus on getting better." She whispers, "I want you to be better more than anything else."

I can't describe how it makes me feel when she looks at me like that. Something flutters in my stomach.

I give her a sly smirk, hoping my confidence will ease her mind. "It won't take me long. When I catch up, you can teach me everything you've learned, and we can continue on from there together."

She nods. "Okay."

She pulls her hands away from mine, standing and leaving before I can convince myself I'm wrong. I'm stupid and I want her to stay. I'm wrong and I want her to sit here and rub little circles on my hand until I fall asleep. I want to get up and follow her out the door, but I can't.

That would be wrong.

15

NERÓ

IF IT WERE UP to me, I wouldn't be leaving today. I would stay here and make sure Clay is fully healed before heading into Neró together.

But that's not happening.

"You should reach Neró well before nightfall," Lynn sets plates full of food before the three of us, "but you should take it slow. The snow hasn't melted yet and the road is bumpy as it is."

Joe doesn't waste any time. He scoops up a forkful of eggs and tips his cup of goat's milk back until it's half-empty. I begin to pick at the food on my plate, wondering what the food will be like in the city.

Jane doesn't touch hers.

"Anything wrong, Jane?" Lynn asks.

"Just a little nauseous. It will pass," she says, her voice dry.

"Okay," Lynn says, "I'll have Marshall prepare your cart for you." She walks away and leaves us to our meal.

"I hear the eggs in Neró are steamed," Joe says, his plate already mostly empty.

"Steamed?" I ask.

"Sure as the solstice," he replies.

Misty appears at the table, her hair pulled into a tight ponytail.

"Is Clay okay?" I ask, peering behind her toward the hallway. The door to the infirmary is firmly shut.

"He's fine," she replies. "I have Clara watching him while Marshall prepares your cart. I've been watching him myself and it's quite exhausting. Luckily, I think I've finally convinced him that staying in that bed is the only way he's getting better quickly." She shakes her head in disapproval. "If he leaves now, he'll be setting himself up for complications. I can't let that happen on my watch."

I nod weakly. I don't know what to say, but it feels nice knowing he's trying. Something about it makes my heart flutter.

With breakfast over, there's nothing left to keep us from leaving. I stand aside as Joe loads the last of our items into the cart.

"Those eggs really did a number on me," Joe says, patting his belly. "Why don't you sit up front, Alira? I'll take a nap in the back."

I know it's his way of making sure I get a front row seat to a view of the city, but the idea of sitting next to Jane makes me writhe. When I glance at her, she shrugs.

"The faster we get there, the faster we can move on with our lives," she says.

I haven't talked to her much. Ever since Clay walked in, she's been reclusive. I don't think she knows what Clay told me, so I keep my mouth shut. The last thing I want is to stir the pot. Once we're settled in the city, it will be easy to stay out of her way. But right now, I just have to suffer and ride with her up to the gate.

Most of the ride is steeped in silence. Neither of us seems adept at casual conversation, so neither of us tries. That is, until I see it.

"Holy cow, that's a *city*." I gasp.

I imagined it would be slightly larger than our village, maybe even the size of all four combined. Whenever I looked over the pastures from the outpost, the city was shrouded in fog. But now, Jane and I stare in astonishment at the city splayed along the mountainside. It towers over us, stretching ever upward until it reaches elevations barely visible from the road below. The river roars down its center.

A giant fish looms over us, sculpted into the facade. Its head and tail jut out, its scales shimmering in the light of the afternoon sun. The two men who stand at the entrance seem small in comparison. The gray-haired one leaves his post to greet us, strolling up to the cart with a confidence that reminds me of Clay.

"What is your business here?" His voice is ripe with authority. His eyes are slits, studying the cart with understandable scrutiny. Jane peers down at him.

"We are in need of a place to stay for the winter. My brother and I are lumberjacks, and our cabin burned down."

"What about you?" He shifts his gaze to me. I clam up briefly.

"I, uh . . . need an audience with the elders. There's a problem with the southern water villages."

He cocks his head to one side and regards me with curiosity before turning to the young man next to him and nodding, prompting him forward.

The boy stands just as tall as the older guard, but he's skinny and has jet black hair. He holds a chalkboard in his hands. His eyes are glued to it.

"Names, please." he says weakly.

"I'm Jane, this is Alira. My brother, Joe, is resting in the back."

The older guard chuckles.

"Just a bunch of lumberjacks," he says.

"I'm not a lumberjack," I interject, my voice sharp. He raises an eyebrow at me.

"She's an ant," Jane explains.

To my surprise, he smiles broadly. "We don't see many from the Earth Queen's realm here. Must be important if you've come all this way." He bows deeply.

Finally, someone who isn't so quick to call me an ant.

He peers around the covered cart and opens up the back. A snore erupts and he simply nods.

"Very well, head to the bed-and-breakfast just past the square." He turns to the young guard. "Go to the elders and report what we've heard."

"Yes, sir," the young guard replies. He turns and waves to a third man, who I hadn't noticed, standing beside the gate at the river's edge. Next to him is a mule harnessed to a circular post. He slaps its backside and I jump.

There's a loud creaking sound as the mule begins to move, turning the gears above him that lower a massive turbine into the river. When it hits the raging current, it begins to spin. The force of the water against the blades turns them, and that in turn pulls the gate up into the facade.

Jane scoffs next to me. "So complicated. They could have just used the mule to pull up the gate, or designed it to open out instead of up. Why use the river at all? Show-offs."

I ignore her, knowing this is just the beginning of what's possible. Soon, I'll learn everything there is to know about waterpower. As Jane lifts the reins, I turn to the guard.

"What is your name?" I ask. He smiles. His teeth are a dazzling white.

"Name's Delta, head gatekeeper. The boy is my son, Bradán."

I watch the young guard as he prepares for his trip up the mountain. He shirks off his coat and reties his laces. His black hair is far darker than Delta's grays, but otherwise they look very much the same.

Delta steps aside and the horse pulls against the reins. He's far more energized after his long rest and he seems just as eager as I am to see what lies ahead. Jane handles him well, keeping the cart moving at a steady pace.

The road that enters the city is cobbled stone mixed with dirt. It's packed down with heavy travel, unbothered by the raging water that flows beside it. Before long, the river twists away from us. A square courtyard comes into view, and just before we reach it, something red darts across the path.

A red fox pauses at the edge of the road, observing us. Its ears and feet are tipped in black, and its coat is dusted with snowy white hairs. A shimmering silver fish lies limp against its jowls. It stares at me, one eye blue and the other a ghostly pale. A shiver ripples up the nape of my neck.

"There's the square," Jane says.

"What?" I ask, looking away for only a moment. I try to focus but my mind is muddled. I turn back to the fox, but it's gone.

"The square, it's up ahead." Jane repeats herself for me.

The cobbled city square is similar to our courtyard back home. A large fountain shrine towers over the center, reminiscent of Persephone's Light. A statue of a woman sits within, her dress cascading down around her. She rests her head in the palm of one hand and gazes at the water flowing from a jug held in the other. Her eyes, at first, are vacant, but closer inspection reveals a loving gaze, as if the water she pours is actively feeding life into the city below. As the water hits the pool of water around her, it splashes upward, spraying a fine mist into the air.

Children play at its base, darting and dodging as they chase each other around its frosted edge.

"Oh, such cute little fishies," Jane calls them.

I'd much rather be called a fish than an ant.

The fountain's edge is carved into benches, on which a blond boy with brown earmuffs sits reading a book. His eyes rise to inspect the cart, following us as we move toward the edge of the square. I wave to him as we pass and his suspicious gaze softens. He waves back before returning to his book.

The cart lurches upon the bridge that crosses the river and I turn away to take the rest of the city in. Each house we pass has a slate roof, wooden barrels, and frosted gardens. They line the cobbled road beside the river, which runs down the mountain for as far as I can see. A faint fog hugs the houses near the top.

The cart jolts forward, almost throwing me off.

"Sorry, these mounds are larger than I thought." Jane says, pulling up the reins lightly.

I lean over the side of the cart and find a ridge of dirt about two feet in width stretching from the river's edge across the path and past the back of each house. All the houses have slate roofs, wooden barrels, and frosted gardens.

I strain to see just how far the mound goes. It splits a narrow path in half before disappearing beneath a soft slope. I spot farm fields beyond that, spotted with sheep and horses and even a few foals.

The farmlands disappear behind a line of homes, and before I can find another opening, Jane's pulled the cart in front of a house on the side of the main road. I look up at the sign that hangs over the front door.

Tranquility's B&B

A woman walks out, gracefully stepping down each step as

she balances a jug in her arms. Her hair is light blond, set in a delicate fishtail braid that slides over her shoulder and settles at her waist. She calls out to us that she will only be a moment and then steps around the side of the house to a barrel and turns the spigot. Water gushes out and into the jug. Then she turns to us.

"Sorry 'bout that, bad timing I suppose." Without a free hand to shake, she opts to curtsy instead. She does so slowly, expertly.

"I think that was great timing," I reply, jumping down from the cart. The woman smiles and I'm starstruck.

"My name is Tranquility, but you can call me Quill. I run the inn here."

A young boy with red hair bursts from the door and weaves around Quill to greet us. His face is dotted with freckles and his smile is wide.

"Hi!" He waves emphatically. "I'm Kai. I can take your cart for you."

Joe jumps down from the back of the cart, rubbing his eyes before turning and freezing at the sight of the little boy, who stands no higher than Joe's waist. Kai peers up at him in awe and I smile, holding in a laugh.

"Uh, hi." Joe waves to Kai sheepishly.

"Yes, hi." Quill seems to be tiring of her jug. "Did Delta send you?"

Jane nods in reply.

Quill bends down to Kai. "You remember the knot I taught you for tying up the horse, right?" He nods excitedly and takes the reins from Jane asQuill leads us inside.

The first thing I see upon entering the inn is a staircase. Its banister is intricately carved with waves and fish. Artwork climbs the wall beside it; faint paint on white canvas. I'm almost certain it's Kai's. It has a childlike quality that makes me smile.

"Coats go on the rack behind the door," Quill says. She sweeps around the staircase and opens a hidden cabinet beneath it. "Dirty clothes can go in here. Laundry is done daily."

"Daily?"

Back home, we washed our laundry once a week, as it was such an annoying chore. I can't imagine having to do it every day.

As Joe and Jane take off their jackets, I'm left standing in awe as my eyes drift over the rest of the room.

"This is the great room," Quill says. "Feel free to relax here at any time of day. We have plenty of activities available for the winter months."

The space is large, with cloth-lined loveseats set beside bookshelves and a table on each side of a massive fireplace. One table holds a chessboard and the other an unfinished wooden puzzle. Atop the fireplace mantel is an arrangement of pottery carved with curving interconnected lines that resemble scales. A fish sculpture juts out from the wall above the fireplace in precisely the same way as the fish carved into the city gate. Its scales shimmer in the warm glow of the fire.

I could get used to this place.

"Alira, get over here."

I turn and realize the others have moved into the next room through an archway at the far end of the staircase. A sign hangs above the threshold:

Food is where the heart is

The entryway narrows as a solid oak countertop juts out from the left side of the door and turns left, following the wall along the length of the kitchen. Quill is already on the other side, pouring her jug slowly into a tall glass implement as she continues to explain the daily schedule for us.

"Dinner is always at six, though if you miss it, I can whip up something for you."

The water slides down the glass cylinder, slipping in and out of a porous limestone before coming to rest at the bottom.

"You filter your water?" I ask.

"Yes." She smiles kindly. "The rainwater is very clean, but the slate roof can get a bit dirty over time, so we run the rainwater through limestone. It does an amazing job of filtering the water of impurities. I typically boil the water as well before letting it cool for consumption."

"Back home, we don't have to filter our water," I explain, "because it's already boiled at the hot spring."

She smiles at the thought. "That sounds very convenient."

I don't mention that the work involved in retrieving the water is backbreaking.

"Does that make you from the House of the Earth Queen, then?" she asks, her eyes flitting to Joe and Jane.

"She is," Joe answers.

"I'm here to learn about the other houses." I explain, "We've been isolated for a long time."

"Well the city is a very friendly place. I'm sure you'll have a lovely stay." She sets the empty jug aside and opens the countertop upward to exit. It sets back down with a satisfying *click*, something Mother's slate countertop could never have managed.

"On to the bathroom."

On the opposite side of the main door is a short hallway capped by a wooden door with a sign that reads *Unoccupied*.

"Please keep in mind there is only one bathroom, and to always flip the sign to *Occupied* when you are using it."

"How does it work?" I ask.

"There's running water and plumbing in Neró, so you can take a shower, run the sink, and use the latrine." I try to peek my head in before we move on, but Quill moves awfully fast. She begins to walk up the stairs to the second floor, but Kai bursts through the front door and passes right by her, spinning around at the top to face us.

"Did ya meet Tayn yet?" he asks. His face is bright with excitement.

"No, hun, he's out today, remember?" Quill laughs. She catches up with him and turns to explain. "Tayn is another patron currently staying here. He's a merchant from the House of the Illuminator."

"The Illuminator?" I ask. "I didn't realize their house had a name. We always just called them sun merchants. I'd love to meet him."

"That's good. He loves company," Quill replies.

I count the rooms on each side of the spacious hall. There are eight total. If Tayn is the only other patron, there will be enough for all of us. Even Clay.

"I'm going to my room now." Kai opens a door on the left and adds "I have my own room, you know."

"Practically a grown man," Joe jokes to Kai. "I'm sure your father is proud."

Kai shrinks, his face turning red. Quill stiffens.

"We don't speak of his father," she says; her tone sounds distant.

I glance at Joe, worried we've crossed some sort of line. Instead of apologizing, he kneels down in front of Kai.

"Well, I'm proud. You seem like a brave boy."

Kai beams at the compliment and I sigh in relief. He handled that well.

After Kai shuts his door, the tour continues.

"Are there other patrons staying here?" I ask.

"Not at the moment. Winter isn't usually busy, what with the lack of travel. When the Spring Festival comes around, this place will be packed to the brim."

I wonder if we will be able to stay for it.

Across from the stairwell is a large room with two beds.

"Jane and I can take this one," Joe says.

"Very well," Quill replies.

"Are you sure, Joe, there's plenty of space!" I say.

"Well, I wouldn't want to take space from other potential patrons, should they decide to show up."

Jane is quiet, but her glares are all I need to confirm my theory. This is just another way for him to keep an eye on her. For my sake and Clay's, I'm thankful for it.

As they settle into their room, Quill shows me to mine. It's all the way at the end of the hall.

"You'll be happy with the view, I think," she says.

The bed is freshly made, and the desk is a soft wood with rounded edges. It's decorated with a vase of lavender and, beside it, a stack of notebooks. I look up through the window and see the city square.

Everything is perfect here.

The doorknob creaks as if she's about to leave, but there's so much more to say.

I spin around. "Wait."

She pauses in the doorway, her blond brows raised.

"Can you save a room for my friend, Clay? He's still healing at the outpost."

She relaxes. "Of course, hun. I'll make sure there's a room for him when he comes."

"I don't know how payment works," I say, my eyes dropping to the floor. "We have plenty of holy water and Joe and Jane have their paper frames but—" When I look up, she has closed the gap between us, rubbing my arm with her hand.

"Everyone offers something unique." She says, "If you are here to learn about our house, and to teach us of your own, that is more than enough for me. As for Joe and Jane, I'm sure they will be on their way soon."

I shake my head. She doesn't understand. "Joe and Jane's house burned down. They have nowhere to go."

Her hand pauses on my shoulder.

"But maybe their next home can be an earthen home like mine. Then it won't burn."

She smiles. Her eyes are soft and motherly.

"You need not worry about them. They'll be happy here until they're ready to move on."

With that, she leaves me to myself, closing the door softly behind her.

16

SIONNAN'S HEART

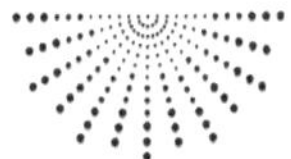

I WAKE in the early morning feeling unbearably hot. The warmth of the fire in the great room seeps up the stairs and into my room, heating my toes and interrupting my dreams.

The rain that poured steadily through the night is gone. I get up from bed and shuffle toward the window to find all the snow from the last storm has washed away. The clouded pale light of dawn paints the city of Neró in blue and gray. Cobblestones glimmer around the fountain shrine and a shadow hovers on its edge.

I squint and recognize the studious blond boy I saw when we rode in. He sits with his legs crossed and his arms leaning on the fountain edge, as if patiently waiting to watch the sun rise over the city. Curious, I slip on my boots and escape out the door, sneaking down the stairs and out into the open air.

Back home, Mother would try to take advantage of quiet early mornings by rushing off to the spring to fetch the tea water for the day. Sometimes, on mornings when sleep evaded me, I would join her. But the river rushing along the cobbled road is by no means quiet. It roars down the mountain just as loudly now as it does any other time of day. The water pools in shallow pockets, reflecting the city around it. I almost want to sit along its edge and waste a little time.

The sun is starting to creep up on the horizon, lending a soft light to the city. Each step toward the fountain is a rediscovery. I study the way the stones are laid upon the path and pause on the wooden bridge, watching the fish swim just fast enough to stay in place against the push of the current. I continue on, and a flap of wings draws my eyes upward. A flurry of bats rush through the air for one last meal.

When I look back toward the path, the fountain is in front of me and the boy is still sitting along its edge.

His eyes are turned away, staring into the fountain depths. He's taller than I thought, and lean. Veined wrists peek out from his sleeves. I try to make a point not to stare.

"I was told you're an ant. So tell me, do ants always wake up with the sun?"

I answer with a question of my own.

"Do fish sleep at all?"

He smiles and his eyes rise to meet mine. They're dark blue.

"Very well, come sit."

He pats the stone bench beside him and I sit. As I do, I notice something glimmer from within the fountain. When I look inside, there are countless tiny specks reflecting the pale light of dawn. They shimmer like the scales of a fish.

"What are those?" I ask.

"It's customary to leave trinkets of personal value in the fountain." The boy says, "People believe it will grant them wisdom or luck." He rolls his eyes. "I personally believe it is a waste. Someone spent a lot of time creating those trinkets. They could be traded for goods and services. Something of equal value. Instead, they're thrown away on unfounded beliefs."

He speaks with a musical cadence, as though careful thought is put into every word uttered from his mouth.

It's fascinating.

I tear my eyes away, worried he'll notice me staring at him. I peer up at the goddess statue, and as I do, the sun begins to break over the horizon in the east, shining almost directly through the water that pours from her divine jug. The water beneath reflects brilliant yellow.

"Is this statue for the river goddess?" I ask.

He nods. "Her name is Sionnan."

His hand hovers over the water, and the sunlight that catches it casts a shadow upon the water.

"She was a maiden of no title and no known heritage. She wandered the mainland feeling lost until, one day, she heard whispers of an ancient fish that granted wisdom to those who ate it. Despite being warned against it, she traveled to the well in which it swam and caught the fabled fish. She ate it and became the wisest being on earth. Her heritage was revealed to her, a daughter of the sea."

I smile at the thought of a woman becoming wiser than any man, but his sad eyes tell me there is more to the story.

"Her knowledge came with a price. A massive wave burst forth from the well and swept her away."

Mother always said no one was meant to have everything, but to be punished so harshly feels tragic to me.

The boy reaches into his pocket and pulls out a small red book. The light of the sunrise shimmers off the gilded title and I have to stop myself from snatching the book out of his hands when I read realize what it says.

He opens *Dr. Carnelian's Book of Poetry* to a notched page and reads a portion of a poem to me:

River run with Sionnan's blood;
Tendrils of everlasting wisdom.
All the way to Elding Sea
Sionnan's heart bleeds.

I peer up at the statue again. She stares so lovingly at the water that pours into her fountain shrine.

"In our village, the fountain shrine is referred to as Persephone's Light."

He nods approvingly.

"What is this one called?"

"It is as the poem says. Sionnan's Heart." He replies.

"And what is your name?" I ask.

"Torin."

His smile is charming. He looks like a boy but he acts like something else entirely. Mature, maybe?

I peer out at the cobbled streets that stretch from the square out to the fields of muddied snow. Sionnan's Heart beats steadily, breathing life into the city of Neró.

"Perhaps I could give you a tour of the rest of the city, if you'll allow me."

Yes, mature is definitely the word.

"I would love that."

"Excuse me."

Torin peers around me and I turn to see Bradán, the young guard.

"Ah, errand boy," Torin jokes. "What are you here to fetch?"

Bradán reddens slightly but pulls his shoulders back and stands tall as he replies. "Alira, the elders have agreed to speak with you."

"Pretty name," Torin whispers behind me, and goosebumps race up my neck. I'm thankful my hair is long enough for no one to notice.

"They're very excited to meet someone from the Earth Queen's realm. They gave an estimate of two to three days. I'll find you when it's time."

"Thank you, Bradán." He smiles when I say his name. Then he nods to himself and walks away toward the city gate.

"So, what will it be, *Earth Princess*?" Torin asks.

"Meet me here after breakfast," I reply.

He nods in agreement and I stand to bow.

"It was lovely to make your acquaintance, Torin."

Shockingly, he stands and returns a bow to me as well, causing my cheeks to burn.

"See you soon, *Alira*."

My name on his lips drifts through my mind as I walk back up the road to breakfast.

~

"You just missed him," Quill says.

"Who?" I ask.

I take a seat along the kitchen countertop and she slides a plate of eggs, bacon, and bread in front of me.

"The merchant, Tayn. He hopped right down the stairs and out the door before I could even tell him about you all."

"Oh."

I must seem disappointed, because she quickly adds, "It's only a matter of time before he talks your ear off."

"I hope he does! I don't know much at all about the Sun House."

Kai walks in, yawning.

"Why do people get up so early?" he asks, looking directly at me.

"I'm only up because I was too warm," I explain.

"Is it cold where you're from?" he asks.

"It's not much different, but we don't have fires to warm

our houses. We build our houses underground, close to the hot spring, so the temperature stays the same year-round."

"What's a *hotz pring*?" He climbs into the seat next to me, eager for more. His hunger for knowledge reminds me of my own.

"A *hot* spring." I say it slowly and he perks up.

"Oh! Is that like a spring that's hot? We have springs here but they're super cold," he says.

"Yes. Just like that."

His eyes are such a bright blue, especially when he smiles.

"Kai, have you cleaned your room?" Quill interrupts.

"Can't I eat before that?" he whines.

"We had a deal. No breakfast until you clean your room."

"Okay." He stares at my bacon longingly before turning away and bumping right into Joe.

"Whoa, there, little guy. Almost ran you over." Joe chuckles.

Kai's face is beet red, "Excuse me," he squeezes by and runs away.

"Did I say something?" Joe asks.

Quill sets a plate of food down next to mine. "He doesn't like being reminded he's little," she explains.

"Oh, well, I'll have to work on that." Joe settles into a stool beside me, but it wobbles beneath his weight. He stands up to inspect it.

"You got any tools around here?" he asks.

"Not particularly," Quill admits.

"I'll fix this later," he says and settles back in, only for it to wobble again. His jaw tenses in annoyance.

"How's Jane?" I ask. He blows air out of his cheeks as he thinks of a reply.

"She's nauseous all the time. She didn't want dinner last night, and she doesn't want to eat this morning either. She's worried it'll just come right back up."

"She seemed fine on the ride in yesterday." Though I can't remember her eating lunch.

"Yeah, well, I don't know. We'll just have to wait and see, I guess."

When breakfast is over, I grab my coat and head outside. Torin is already there.

"Hi," I squeak in surprise. He smirks.

His earmuffs sit squarely on his head and his hair hangs over his face, landing just above his dark blue eyes. Nothing much has changed about his appearance since before breakfast and I wonder if he ate at all.

"You have many questions about Neró," he says, "and I have answers, but there are some things that are best left to be seen with your own eyes. Which is why I'm taking you straight to the top."

I gaze uphill, following the river and the road. The city hall juts out of the mountainside where before it was shrouded in cloud cover. I grin with excitement.

"I can't wait to begin."

"Very well, then." He holds out his hand and I freeze for a moment. Is it normal to offer your hand to someone outside of a greeting? I reach out to take it hesitantly, but he pauses, staring at my ring.

I take my hand away, embarrassed.

"Sorry, it's a gift from my mother."

His confusion fades and he smiles. "Shall we?"

He offers his hand again and I take it. Together, we walk up the mountain.

I need to distract myself from it all, so I try to come up with a quick question. When we reach the first familiar bump in the road, I take a large step over it.

"Could you tell me what these mounds are for?" I ask.

"And so the questions begin." He smirks.

The light of the morning sun on his face gives his hair a

depth that I hadn't noticed before. His hair isn't just yellow. It's like a flower bouquet of daisies and daffodils, with strands of flax and delicate honey. A cold and misty breath escapes as he answers.

"The mounds cover pipes that are shallowly buried into the ground so that if there is a pipe burst, we can easily replace it."

"What are the pipes for?" I ask.

"Water from the river flows with great force downstream. The pipes collect water at each level of the city and transport it to the houses for freshwater supply. As the pipes disperse water farther and farther from the river, the pipes become smaller to preserve water pressure."

I think of Quill's bathroom. The shower I took last night was short and frigid, but it was a far cry from having to walk to the hot spring, where I'd have to bathe amongst the other women in awkward silence.

Torin's hand squeezes mine lightly as we cross another mound. He pauses, pointing to it as it disappears behind a house.

"The pipes run past the back of each house, looping around and running past another round of houses before unused water is returned to the river. The design creates pockets in the city matrix."

I hadn't noticed these pockets before. The snow had covered them yesterday, making them seem barren and unused. Today, though, they're cleared of snow and vibrant with life as children play in each one.

Each pocket seems to have a unique use. Some are lined with tables for merchants to market their goods, while others are lined with benches and picnic areas, with stages set up for various events. Most of the pockets, though, are orchards planted so thickly that they could be mistaken for the forests of the wilds to the east. I spot a few children hidden in the dormant trees, swinging from branch to branch with gloved hands.

It doesn't, however, explain the other mounds. The ones that extend down each of the cobbled alleyways.

Torin anticipates the question, answering before I can ask.

"Sanitation pipes run separate from the clean water of the river. They collect used and dirtied water for field irrigation."

"I've never heard of irrigating farms with more than just rain," I say.

"Water refuse has what plants want," Torin explains. "When the city first implemented the practice many years ago, they saw a huge harvest. It allowed the city to grow."

With Neró being so large, it makes sense. I wonder if our house might grow, too, or if the elders would even want it to.

"Back home everyone grows their own food, but here, it seems like you do things differently."

He nods emphatically. "Segregating chores was perhaps the best thing the city did for its growth. It allows people to take on the occupations they want. Currency is unnecessary because everyone has something to offer and everyone has something others might need."

"You sure do know a lot about this."

He hesitates to answer, his hand loosening briefly.

"Well, I live here," he decides to say, though I feel like there's something more he's not telling me.

We walk in silence for a while, with my hand in his. It's warm and comfortable and fits perfectly. We pass other people, couples and children, but no one is holding hands like we are. It makes me wonder if . . .

I blush at the thought.

Torin's hair begins to take on a sweaty sheen and our breaths come quicker now as the top of the mountain gets closer and closer. I feel fine, but I know tomorrow I'll feel sore—the same kind of sore I used to feel after making several trips to the hot spring, lugging water and eggs and bread.

I stop for a moment to give us both a break. When our hands separate, I try to wipe my sweaty palms against my pants as discreetly as possible and spot the steplike structures lining the edge of the river.

"What are those?" I point them out.

"Those are fish ladders. The salmon swim upstream to reproduce as part of their natural cycle, but our pipes and turbines make it difficult for them to navigate to their spawning grounds, so we installed fish ladders to help them migrate."

"Oh, I like that a lot."

"My grandfather devised them," he says. When I turn to ask more about his grandfather, he's already started walking again. I rush forward to keep up.

"We're almost at the top," he explains. He doesn't take my hand, but that's okay. I allow myself to fall behind a little as I take in everything. It's more of the same, really, but I like it. I like seeing the city come alive as the sun rises higher in the sky.

When we reach the top, there's another bridge. The river splits into several ponds, and finally, I see a massive waterfall just next to the doors carved into the mountain that lead into the city hall.

I turn and my breath hitches at the sight of the entire city below us. The river rushes down the city slope, and looking down, I can see each pocket clearly now. The city of Neró is beautiful and grand. I can see almost everything from here.

"So," Torin says, "you can see why the walk was worth it." He stands next to me, pointing out all the important sections: the inner city, the farmlands, and the stables in between.

"I'd love to see the farms."

"We can visit the stables tomorrow," he says.

The thought of seeing Torin again makes me blush. I

barely know him, but he already seems interested in seeing me again, and that's not something I'm used to.

"I'd like that."

He takes my hand again, leading me to a pond beneath the waterfall where a bench sits. Foxes and fish are carved into its wooden frame. For a time, we sit and watch the city breathe to the sound of the water rushing by.

It feels absolutely divine.

17

OBSIDIAN

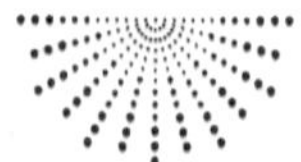

I LIE awake half the night thinking about Torin's hand holding mine. It's silly, really. I'm sixteen years old and I'm crushing on a guy when all he's done is hold my hand. And give me a tour. And offer to show me more.

I can't tell if I'm reading too far into it or not. I've seen people flirt—I've seen Gemma flirt, and Clay, and Gemma with Clay—but I can't tell if that's what this is or not.

Besides, I don't know how long I'll be here. It wouldn't be right to be with someone for such a short time. It wouldn't be fair.

And yet here I am, thinking about how wonderful it would be, going around every day hand in hand with Torin as he tells me about the city and all its intricacies.

So when the second day of touring begins, I resign myself to assuming that he doesn't want anything. I go into the morning determined to not give him any clues at all into how I'm feeling. I don't want to seem dumb, and I definitely don't want to go into this with expectations that will only lead to disappointment, and the only way to do that is to pretend I feel nothing at all.

The knock at the door comes right after breakfast and my hair's still drying. I pull down my sleeves past my hands and anxiously try to pat it dry as Quill opens the door.

Torin is there, holding a fishing pole.

Two fishing poles.

Oh, Hades. I'm screwed.

My stomach rises right up to my throat as his eyes find me, my hands still up in my hair. He smiles.

"Oh, Torin! What brings you here?" Quill asks. My face must be rose red because his smile grows even wider.

"Alira wanted to see some of the farms. I thought I'd take her to the pond. You know, make a day of it."

"When did you become so charitable?" she asks.

Torin shrugs.

"Well." She turns to me. "You found the best tour guide. Torin knows the city inside and out. I would expect nothing less from the son of the city planner."

This time, Torin's face is red, which isn't something I expected.

"What does the city planner do?" I ask.

"Well, I'll let him tell you." She opens the door wide to let me through and closes it behind me, leaving us standing awkwardly outside.

"It's not that big a deal," he says, forcing a laugh. "I just don't like to tell people that my dad runs things around here. Sometimes they treat me differently. But now that the cat is out of the bag, I suppose it doesn't matter."

"What do you mean by 'runs things'?"

He starts walking down an alleyway in the direction of the farmlands.

"The city planner helps to develop the city. It's a super important job, and one that is passed down from family member to family member."

"Oh, so does that mean that you'll be the city planner one day?"

"Yes," he says, "but it comes with some unfortunate downsides."

"Oh?"

Before he can explain further, I sense movement nearby. In a small space between one house and the next, a pair of foxes play.

Torin stops, too. "Do you know about the foxes?" he asks.

They nip and paw at each other. Lunging and leaping and rolling onto their backs. They have no clue how close we are to them.

"All I know is that I've seen far more here in the city than I would expect," I reply.

"They are a sacred animal," Torin explains, leaning perilously close to me.

"Sacred meaning you don't kill them?" I ask, tearing my gaze away from the pups.

His eyes cut into mine. "To do so would have disastrous consequences."

"But surely they would target your chickens!"

He smirks. "If a fox steals a chicken, it was never ours to begin with."

He looks out into the alley as the pups continue to play. His voice is quiet, careful not to scare them away.

"In death, it is said that Sionnan was reincarnated as Sionnach, a fox spirit. He carves rivers into Rhizole and guides salmon to spawn.

"So she became a he?" I ask.

"When one life bleeds into the next, concepts of he and she need not exist."

Finally, the foxes spot us and dart away down the alley.

"I saw one when we arrived." I remember, "It had a fish in its mouth."

"To see a fox with a fish is an omen of a lesson to be learned." He starts walking again. "Knowing your quest, it doesn't surprise me at all."

I wonder if omens are always that simple, telling you what you already know.

He points up ahead. "Those are the stables. We'll go there first. It's on the way to the pond, and I figure you'll want to see your horse."

"I didn't realize Quill had brought him here," I say.

"She has a small stall for late arrivals, but as far as I know, it's meant to be temporary. The stable manager is in charge of long-term care and boarding. Most of the horses here are his own, trained and lent out to residents in need, but some, like yours, are welcome to stay in the extra stalls, especially during times of heavy travel, like the spring."

What does he get in return?" I ask.

"It depends. Everyone has something to offer. There's an animal specialist who lives close by. His horse boards for free because if any of them need medical assistance, he's the one they call."

His words give me pause. "I don't have much to offer other than holy water. Do you think the stable manager will want something more?"

"If it hasn't come up, then it's possible Quill asked for a favor. She's well-liked around here, so it wouldn't surprise me."

We pass the first stable and I peek inside for ours, but all ten stalls are completely empty. It isn't until we pass the third stable that I start to see the pastures, wide-open grasslands with horses grazing in small herds. I walk up to the fence line, searching.

"If I had a lyre, he'd come right out for me. Pretty much any animal in the House of the Earth Queen will come to the sound of it."

"A lyre?" he asks.

"Yeah, you know, the stringed instrument," I say, before realizing they might not have them here.

"Oh, you mean a harp."

I look at him quizzically.

"Here, hold these." He hands me the fishing poles and walks around the side of a house, grabbing a strange looking lyre leaning against a wall.

"Here." He offers to trade.

"You're just taking it?" I ask, peering warily back at the house.

"Don't worry, I know who owns it. They won't mind."

I take it gingerly. It feels as light as a feather in my hands. I worry I might break it.

"Will it do?" he asks. He's adorably uncertain.

"I think so." I straddle the fence, set the lyre carefully on my thigh, and begin to play "Persephone's Descent", the tune that Jade played at the Harvest Festival.

Within seconds, our horse comes bursting out from the herd, galloping at full speed before skidding to a stop in front of me and nuzzling my leg. I laugh, almost falling over, but Torin catches me.

I stand up straight, my cheeks burning, and hand the lyre back to him.

"Thank you. It's been a while since I've been able to play."

"It was a nice tune; is it from your house?"

I nod.

"I'll go put this back." Torin takes the harp, leaving me with the horse.

He nibbles at my shirt and his chin whiskers tickles my stomach. I giggle before squirming away.

"All right, are you ready to go?" Torin asks, taking up the fishing poles again.

"Yes."

I give the horse one last pat goodbye before following Torin away.

~

The pond is about as large as the hot spring. There's a small wooden dock from which, Torin says, people fish, but there's no one here today. Torin walks out to the edge and takes out what he calls a bait box.

"So what about you?" he asks.

"Huh?" I'm busy looking at a bunch of geese gathered in the field. A shepherd's dog runs toward them, but they're pretty adamant about sticking around. It's fun to watch.

"What's the House of the Earth Queen like?" he asks.

"Oh." I refocus on Torin. He's taking his gloves off so that he can have a better grip on the fishing pole.

"It's nice," I say.

"That's it?"

"I love my house," I clarify, "but growing up there was . . . difficult. I looked different and therefore I was treated different."

"Different how?"

I blush. "Well, a lot of the people in my house have dark hair and eyes."

"Why don't you?" He glances at me and bites his lip. "Sorry, that's probably personal." He hands me a pole and I take it from him tentatively.

"So how does this work?" I ask.

"Well, there's a hook on the end of the line that you cast out into the water. If you put bait on it, a fish will bite it. If it does, and you're lucky, then you can hook it and reel it in."

"Do you eat it?" I ask.

He laughs. "Sometimes. Winter is actually the best time to

eat fish from the pond, but we'll be releasing what we catch today."

He takes a stance behind me and reaches around to show me how to hold the pole. It's awkward and I feel like we are way too close.

"Why don't you just start and I'll watch?" I suggest. He moves away and I regret it instantly, but he doesn't seem too bothered.

"Okay. There are two important things when it comes to fishing. One is the bait. You need to know how to lure the particular fish you're looking for. You need to know what bait they'll jump for." He leans down and grabs a fluffy-looking thing from the bait box.

"Live bait is best, but if you can make your bait seem alive, it doesn't really matter." He attaches the piece of fluff to the string of the pole and pauses, glancing at me.

"You're going to want to be on my left." He shifts so that I can move around him, then begins casting the string back and forth before letting it loose and letting it fly out into the open water.

"The second important thing is setting the hook." He pulls the string back bit by bit, trying to emulate the movement of live bait.

"You don't want to pull in the hook before the fish bites. You have to make sure the fish is biting, not just nibbling. In other words, the fish needs to show you it's committed before you can catch it." He's intensely focused, pulling the string little by little until a splash pops up in the water.

"There." He tugs at the line, setting the hook, and pulls the fish in.

It's huge.

"This is a largemouth bass," he says. It wriggles and squirms against the line as he pulls it up and onto the dock.

"How many types of fish are there?" I ask.

"Plenty. And I know them all." He pulls the hook out and plops the bass back into the water.

"Wow."

"Do you want to try?"

"I'm kinda scared to," I admit. He reaches over, takes my hand, and places the pole inside it.

"As the fisher, you must never be afraid of the fish," he says.

I stare at his hand on mine.

"Okay," I say. "I'll try."

Voices rumble beneath the floorboards. I open my eyes and realize it's the first time I've been able to sleep through the night. Sunlight slants across the room and settles on the deer-skin knapsack I left by the door. A fuzzy lure is latched onto its side; a keepsake from yesterday.

The smell of freshly baked bread crusted with rosemary is what draws me out of bed. It smells so good I can practically taste it. I get dressed quickly, worried Joe might eat it all before I get there. As I slip on my boots, I hear a door close in the hall. Quick steps descend the stairs and rush out the door. It isn't until I'm halfway down the stairs myself that I realize it must have been Tayn, the merchant, and that I've missed him again.

I walk into the kitchen and pause at the sight of Torin.

"And after she said she wasn't sure she could, she went and caught not one, not two, but five fish!" Torin exclaims. Joe slaps him on the back.

"That's Alira for ya. Always surprising, she is." Joe spots me and waves me over. "Ay," he greets me, "this one's been telling us all about your fishing expedition."

"It was fun," I say.

"Fun? It sounds like a blast. I gotta get myself a teacher," Joe says.

Quill rolls her eyes. "Anyone could teach you. I could do it myself if I weren't so busy."

When she hands me my plate of food, she leans in close. "How was your day yesterday, hun?" Her voice is tinged with worry.

"It was great!" I assure her. I sit on a stool and notice it doesn't wobble at all. Looking down, I spot a slivered piece of wood stabilizing the shortest leg, affixed with birch bark tar.

"Well, Torin was kind enough to offer some fish in exchange for breakfast," Quill says, "so I'll be cooking those up tonight with a mushroom sauce. I made sure to tell the merchant, so he'll be there."

"I met him yesterday." Joe grumbles, crossing his arms, "I don't like him."

Quill laughs. "He likes to make fun."

"Well, I can't wait to meet him!" I say, breaking off a piece of bread. It's warm and fresh, tearing apart easily.

Rosemary and butter melt on my tongue. I pair it with a bite of egg, soft like pudding. I realize, with wide eyes, these eggs aren't boiled or fried; they're steamed. It slides down my throat with comforting ease.

"So, Alira," Torin says, "I was thinking today we could—"

A knock raps at the front door.

"I'll get it!" Kai's voice calls from the great room and Quill smiles to herself. When he comes in, his face is bright red.

"Alira, Bradán says the elders want to talk to you today!"

"Oh, good!" I get up from my seat, having only eaten half my breakfast, but Quill gives me a withering look.

"Now, hold on, you need to finish. The elders will be there when you're done," Quill says.

I sink back into my seat and inhale my food, realizing belatedly that Torin is probably watching me.

He laughs, "You're cute."

I blush uncontrollably, pushing the plate aside. I gulp the last of my milk and stand up to leave.

"Can I go with her?" Kai asks.

"Did you clean your room?" his mother asks.

". . . No."

I stoop down to his level, eye to eye. "I'll tell you all about it when I come back."

His eyes light up. "Promise?"

I nod. "I'll be back soon."

"I'll be around," Torin says. His words are the last I grab my bag and leave.

Upon entering the city hall, I am reminded again of how small my world has always been. Slate runs along the floor in curved scalelike shapes. The outer edges are covered in panels of glass. The glass channels twist to meet at a miniature well set within the floor. When I tap my foot against the glass, it doesn't budge, but the fish beneath it swim fervently, following me as I cross the floor to the front desk.

"Excuse me," I say.

The woman's hair is white with age, and her eyes are almost silver, with just a hint of pale blue. She smiles up from her book at me.

"Are you Alira?" she asks. I nod. "The elders will be ready in a few minutes. You can wait in the chamber if you would like." She points to the stairs next to her before looking back to her book.

"I have one question," I say.

She smiles. "What is it, dear?"

"It's just, I've never seen anything built quite so beautifully, and with such a mix of different materials. How were they able to get the slate to look like that?" I point to the scales along the floor and she sets her book aside.

"This building was a cooperative effort between the House of the River Goddess, the House of the Illuminator, and the House of the Earth Queen."

"Really?"

She nods. "Dr. Carnelian offered the designs, and the merchants provided the glass, but we mined the other materials ourselves."

"How?" I ask.

"The process is called hushing. Back when the city was being built, it was common practice. Water was used to break down rock and expose the minerals and ore beneath. We don't do it much anymore."

"And the slate?" I ask.

"Oh, that's not slate," she says. "That's obsidian."

"Obsidian?" My mind immediately shifts to the recorder, black and shimmering in even the faintest light.

"Do you have machines here?"

"What kind of machine are you looking for?" she asks.

I pull out a spool from my satchel, which I had been keeping in hopes of finding another recorder, and show it to her. "I had a machine that could record voices onto these, but I lost it."

"Oh!" Her eyes light up and she leaps from her chair with youthful excitement. "Follow me."

She leads me to a room behind her desk. It's massive, divided into numerous aisles of floor-to-ceiling cabinets.

"They are quite rare. We have one for recording important meetings between the elders, but I wonder if your spools would fit in there." She stops at a shelf along the far side of the room and slides open a wooden door to reveal a much larger recorder than the old one.

"Here, let's try it out."

I hand her my spool and she slots it into place.

"Hmm. No, that's not quite right." She turns some knobs before sighing in defeat. "Sorry, hun. It seems this recorder is a bit different from yours. There's a chance it could have been custom made or, if it's old, it could be a prototype."

My heart sinks. "Thank you for trying."

I turn to leave but catch myself.

"Sorry, I almost forgot." I pull out *The Queen's Acuity*. "I wanted to make sure you have a copy."

"No need." She assures me, "We already have one. You should keep yours, though. From what I understand, they're quite the commodity."

I thank her again, stuffing the book back into my bag before walking up the curved stairs to the second floor. I study every inch as I go, unable to drag my eyes away from the sheer effort it must have taken to build this place. The glass railing filled with water ripples all the way down to the well, and the sound of it leaves me relaxed as I rise to the top floor.

From the highest step, the intricate pattern laid about the first floor is easily visible now, and far more breathtaking than I expected. Obsidian scales decorate the body of a massive salmon along its winding channels. The circular panel where the fish tried to nibble through the glass takes on the shape of the salmon's eye. Water ripples and goosebumps spread through me.

Even the door to the elder's chamber is made of glass. A blur of rushing water slips between the two panels and disappears through a crack in the floor. I watch it in awe, wondering how it all works.

A lever sits beside it, and I touch it gingerly before pressing it down.

A hard grating noise of rock on rock grinds above. The water stops flowing and I can access the doorknob. I step into the eerily quiet chamber.

The sound of trickling water is gone, replaced by the jarring sound of my boots against the floor. Rippling channels that follow the path swirl away as I reach the front where a massive glass table sits, filled to the brim with water and teeming with fish.

Hovering over the table are three elders. On the left is an elderly man with balding white hair and stern eyes. On the right is a young woman in a pale blue gown covered in a white mink shawl. Her blond hair is braided intricately around her head, with little wisps falling out to frame her face.

At the center of the glass table is an older woman. Her dress is rich green. Her hair is fine, light blond, and cut short. She stands.

"Welcome, child. Allow me to introduce you. I am Onora, lead elder. To my left is Patience, our youngest, and to my right is Keane, our eldest." Patience sits still and Keane simply nods.

"It was brought to our attention that you hail from the House of the Earth Queen and that you come bearing an important message regarding the water villages. Please introduce yourself and explain the situation so that we might understand."

Onora sits, her movements smooth and calculated. Her eyes are inquisitive, like Demeter's, stripping me to my core.

"Elders." My breath shakes and I bow slowly to hide my face until I can collect myself. "My name is Alira. It is true that I hail from the House of the Earth Queen. I have been sent on a quest, with the approval of my elders and with the company of my companion, Clay, to seek out the knowledge of the other houses to inspire innovation within our own." I try not to make it obvious that I am sucking in air and attempt to continue, but before I do, Patience speaks.

"Have you seen the other houses yet, Alira?"

"No." I blush. "This is my first stop, although I have met the lumberjacks."

Patience closes her lips tight, as though to hide her displeasure.

"And what of this traveling companion? Clay, was it?" Onora asks.

"We ran into some trouble on the road so he's still at the outpost, healing."

"Very well," Keane says, pensive. "We shall teach her and the boy our ways before sending them into the fray." He chuckles, "Have a little patience, Patience."

She scowls, her displeasure shifting to annoyance. Meanwhile, I'm trying not to jump for joy.

Onora brings me back to earth, "It's settled then. We will send Marilla, our head professor, to teach you and Clay. Now, please tell us what you have learned about the southern water villages."

My ring becomes a comfort as I spin it around my finger and relay to them what Clay told me.

"They think it's coming from the river?" Patience asks.

"They do."

Her brows furrow. Onora takes over questioning.

"Was the man at the outpost coughing or sneezing?"

"He was coughing," I reply.

"If it isn't the river," Onora asks, "were you close enough to him to become sick?"

"I don't believe so."

They all let out a breath of relief.

I get it: Letting a disease loose in the city could be catastrophic. But Ripley isn't just sick. He's dying. Others are, too. If it is the river, which Ripley was positive it was, we could evacuate them sooner rather than later.

Before I can say any of this, Keane speaks up.

"Winter is in full swing now, child. No one can go south until we can be sure they can do so safely. Understand?"

I nod weakly.

Onora explains further, "In order to make the most of our resources, we need to take into account only the facts. The facts are that there is a man at the outpost who is ill, and that the source of his illness is undetermined. Also, as the villages are a separate entity and are governed by their own elders, there are many variables to take into account. We will take some time to deliberate the matter, but in the meantime, take advantage of Marilla and her teachings."

I feel nervous leaving without having a solid answer. I want so badly to help Ripley and the many others who are facing the unknown. I keep my mouth shut, worried that I might push my luck. Patience senses my concern.

"The water villages have rainwater storage. If they are in need, they can cease all use of river water and use the storage tanks until spring."

It works. A weight is lifted off my shoulders. I delivered my message, and they are going to do what they feel is best. There is nothing more I can do except wait for their decision.

I bow deeply and thank them for their time, leaving the chamber and the problems at the southern water villages behind.

18

MARILLA

Two weeks have crawled here. I've been doing my best to learn about the city and its culture from Quill and Kai but I've had limited success. Quill has a lot of practical knowledge, but she doesn't know the minutiae of how things work, and Kai's explanations are so choppy and interspersed with distractions that I yearn for the recorder.

The books in the great room are a welcome source of learning material: books on horse care and herbalism and wood sculpting. I read them when I can't sleep, when nightmares dig at me: nightmares about our travels, alternative routes, and different endings. Nightmares about Clay never returning or falling ill like Ripley.

Even when Marilla is here, I can't focus. Between Clay and Torin, I feel like I'm working with half a mind. Each time I look to the south, I search for Clay and see nothing but the cobblestone road leading to the gate. Then I think of Torin, his soft hands guiding mine around the fishing pole, and I blush. Now that I've started my studies, he's stopped visiting as much. Last time I saw him, he told me he's working on something special for me but wouldn't give any hints as to what it is.

The last few days I've resigned myself to enjoying the time inside. Joe likes to challenge me at wooden puzzles, seeing who can get the most pieces in. Kai loves chess but always changes the rules when things aren't going his way.

And Jane. . . She's been very isolated lately. When I ask Joe how she's doing, he doesn't quite know how to answer. In the beginning, he was so adamant that she would pull through this, but lately there is this look of pity on his face every time I ask. I think he believes her hardships are his fault, somehow.

And then there's Tayn.

The merchant has skin like fertile soil after a soft spring rain. He is warm and bright and always so happy to entertain me. He waves his hands around emphatically, bracelets and jewelry dangling. It's a wonder no one has tried stealing from him.

He talks and talks and talks all day long, telling stories of islands in the Sun House, or as he calls it, the House of the Illuminator. From him, I've learned that his house is full of travelers and merchants. They take advantage of whatever they can trade for, claiming that if the sun touches it, then they can use it.

Unfortunately, his knowledge is limited. His job is to know something well enough to sell it. And so I settle for what he can tell me, which still amounts to quite a lot.

"You may think the term ant is an insult, but it is quite the opposite," he says. We sit at the chess table as he procrastinates his next move.

"For a time I actually sold a variety of ants to a client of mine."

"What?" I abandon the chessboard.

"Yes, their saliva has practical uses in medicine. The green weaver, for example, is a beautiful iridescent green. They clear the sinuses right up."

"I've never heard of them," I say. I thought all ants were small and black.

"They are by far my favorite." He says, "They weave nests from leaves and glue them together with their silk."

His distraction works; I'm thoroughly invested in his musings about ants.

"Ghost ants are a close second," he continues. "They have dark brown bodies and legs, with abdomens of milky white. They blend in easily and are hard to see, but I have my ways."

"How did you transport them?" I ask.

"The island of Solaris is warm year-round, but when traveling, I had to build a special cart with a custom greenhouse, split into sections for each unique ant species to keep them warm. Pharaohs, honeypots, pandas, I traded them all. That is, until my client built an enclosure of their own, and now they have no need for my services."

He finally moves a piece and I'm forced to bring my attention back to the chessboard. He watches me closely as I move my knight into place.

"When you come to the island of Solaris, you will see many fantastic things." His gleaming smile shines brighter than all his jewelry combined. His dark brown eyes light up orange as he remembers something, the firelight caught in his irises.

"And Farah, you've got to see Farah! She is the finest of them all, I tell ya. None can compare!"

He speaks of his girlfriend with admiration as he sets a knight down in a new spot on the chessboard.

Joe cuts, in chastising him, "Yesterday it was Freja, the day before it was Fanny, and tomorrow it will be some other 'F' name."

"You know nothing, Jack."

"It's Joe."

My smile turns into a laugh. "I'm sure he knows that." I make my final move, swinging my queen sideways to swipe Tayn's knight off the board.

"This one is smart. You should listen to her, Jim." Tayn chuckles.

I open my mouth, intending to ask more about ants, but someone raps at the front door.

Tap-tap-tap.

Quill sweeps into the room. Her fishtail braid glistens in the firelight. She opens the door and a gust of wind blows through, causing the flames to flicker.

"Marilla! It seems a crime for them to send you over here in a storm like this," Quill exclaims.

"This is important work," Marilla replies.

The house professor enters quickly as Quill shuts the door behind her, removing her hood to reveal bright white hair braided regally atop her head. She hands a lantern filled with fish oil to Quill, who blows it out and sets it aside. Then, she assists Marilla in removing her layers, each one revealing more of her fragile frame.

She's like a watercolor painting. Her powder-blue dress is embroidered in a vibrant hue that matches her eyes. Fish seem to swim across her hem as she approaches me and Tayn. She exudes a confidence that I wonder if I will ever attain, and yet her eyes are calm and patient.

Tayn takes his hint to leave. He sweeps the pieces into a basket below the table and moves the board aside before bowing goodbye.

"Until next time, Antoinette," he winks. I can't help but smile as he leaves.

Marilla takes Tayn's seat, placing the heaviest book I've ever seen between us. It thumps against the table, a faded blue against the dark oak below.

"What is that?"

My hands drift toward it, uncertain, before touching its fabric cover. It is rough on the edges, with dark yellowed pages that hint at generations of knowledge.

"This, my dear, is a very important tome. Every house should have one, for it is an incredible teaching tool. We call this one *The Goddess Binding*. There are only a few in print. It is a reference of different tools and mechanisms used within the house; everything from fish ladders to pipes to wells."

It vaguely resembles *The Queen's Acuity*, the book Ms. Ilesha gave me before we left home. I sit on my hands to avoid rudely snatching it from the table and opening it.

"We have much work to do, as always." Marilla opens the tome and another day of studies begins.

I listen far more eagerly this time as I realize this isn't a lecture on waterwheels or fish ladders but rather the history of the house itself, in such detail that I feel I am a part of it, somehow.

There exists, beyond the sandy shores of the mainland, a sea so vast and deep that no one could travel upon it without finding themselves lost. For millennia, our people resided on its shallow edge, collecting all the fine things the tides would bring in. They charted their patterns and found them linked, in some way, to the moon.

Stories sprouted, lores and legends of an ancient being that pulls the moon across the sky each night. His name is Máni and he became our Lunar Deity. Turning our gaze skyward, we found a map amongst the stars.

Boats were built, sails were made, and off our ancestors went, exploring the vast unknown. But for some it was short-lived. Salt water and barnacles ate away at ship hulls, harsh storms snapped them like twigs. Women returned to the main-

land to raise children, watching them grow into sailors destined to be devoured by the sea.

One day, a young boy watched the salmon return to the river, an annual migration, and asked his father why they loved the river more than the sea. His father decided to find an answer.

He took a band of men upstream and found lands rich with food. Weeks of travel felt far less terrifying than an equal length of time at sea. Before long, they found the source of the river: a mountain surrounded by fertile grasslands. There, the salmon spawned, and the foxes feasted. When the men slept, they dreamt of Sionnan, and when they woke, wisdom flowed through their veins. They returned to the women and relayed their experience to them.

The result was the splitting of the House of the Lunar Deity. Those who believed the stories followed them upstream, and those who refused were left behind. The people of the House of the River Goddess settled where the salmon spawned and developed what is now known as the thriving city of Neró.

Over time, our understanding of the river has strengthened, but our connection to the moon remains. When one of our own comes to the end of this life, we send them down the river under the light of the moon toward the sea, hoping that the people of the House of the Lunar Deity will treat them as long-lost friends and provide them with a proper sea burial, guiding them into a peaceful rest.

19

CHERRY & PINE

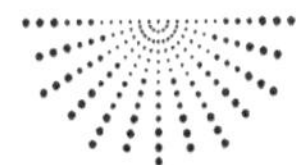

WHEN THE STUDY SESSION ENDS, the sun is far below the horizon. Marilla stands in front of the door, donning all her many layers and taking up her lantern of fish oil.

"We have covered much of the material you need to continue to study on your own. I will be back in a few weeks to quiz you on your knowledge. In the meantime, I encourage you to spend some time interviewing the cityfolk. Some have working knowledge that the book does not provide. These tools will allow you to learn and will, in turn, allow you to get Clay caught up when he arrives."

She sets out into the snow. It falls slow and wet in large clumps of flakes. I clutch *The Goddess Binding* close to my chest as I watch her leave.

It isn't until I close the door softly behind her that I turn to see how utterly empty the place is. I go upstairs to place the tome on my bedside table and all the other rooms seem dark save for Joe and Jane's.

When I return downstairs, the fire is burning incredibly low. I take it upon myself to grab the mitts hanging beside the fireplace so that I can toss two more logs into the flames. They thump heavily, sending ashes swirling around me. The smell of burnt wood permeates my nose and I squint in disgust.

In time, I'll learn to adore this smell, but right now all it does is remind me of the fire and Clay.

My stomach grumbles, and I realize I've not eaten. The candles in the kitchen still seem to be lit, so I go in.

When I enter, everyone is huddled, speaking in hushed tones. Joe waves me over to them.

"Alira, great timing. Today is Jane's birthday," Joe whispers. I look around and realize Jane is the only one not here. Quill quietly hands a glass of water to me from across the counter.

I drink it thankfully, realizing I'm as thirsty as I am hungry. As I do, they fill me in on their plan.

"Jane doesn't leave her room much," Joe explains.

"But," Quill points out, "she always comes down for a late night drink after everyone else has had dinner."

My stomach grumbles on cue. Kai giggles quietly beside me.

"By Ra," Tayn insists, "give the girl some food!"

Quill turns to the wood stove while Joe continues.

"Basically, when she walks in, we're all going to yell 'Surprise!' and wish her a happy birthday."

"Do we have any gifts for her?" I wish they had given me more time; I could have crafted something for her.

"I've got it handled," Joe reassures me.

Kai leans in, pulling at my arm so that I'll bend down to listen to him. He cups his mouth between both hands and whispers in my ear.

"I made a cake!"

I smile. It feels nice to celebrate Jane, even if it is a little bittersweet.

Quill places a bowl of soup in front of me, paired with two hearty slices of bread. I barely manage to say thank you before stuffing a piece in my mouth. I try to hover over the bowl so that the crumbs will fall into the soup.

"You let me know if you need more bread," Quill orders. I simply nod.

Back home, we call birthdays *birthmoons*, but I can only name a few that mattered to me. Flint was born on the first waxing gibbous of the winter season, and Clay on the Strawberry Moon, but I was born on a black moon in summer.

Mother says it's good luck, but the kids at school had different ideas. It earned me the nickname *black sheep*.

After a while, I stopped caring about my birthmoon. I usually spend the day in the fields, playing my lyre for the sheep. Gemma makes me a cake every year and Mother gives me a day off from chores. That's more than enough for me.

Something moves in my peripheral vision. Jane.

"SURPRISE!" everyone yells. I can only manage a mumble with my mouth full, trying hopelessly not to shoot bread bits everywhere.

Jane stands frozen in the doorway. "You planned a birthday party for me?"

"Of course I did." Joe walks over to her, giving her a hefty pat on the back. "I've never missed one!"

She smiles timidly.

Kai stands on his chair, drawing all eyes to him.

"I made this for you!" he announces, pointing to the cake on the counter next to him. The frosting is uneven and the candles are crooked, but I have no doubt it will be delicious.

"Off of the chair, please," Quill chides, bringing a match to meet the candles. Kai complies, lowering himself down from the chair and waving Jane over with boisterous energy. She takes a seat next to me and, after a moment of anticipation, blows the candles out in a single breath.

We all cheer as Quill reaches over to take the cake for cutting and serving.

"And now it's time for the main event," Joe announces. He digs into his pockets and pulls out a ring. My eyes widen. It's the ring I saw in the jewelry box in the cart right after the fire. The one that looked so much like Mother's.

"I had this fixed up nice and pretty for you, with Tayn's help of course." I glance at Tayn, who winks at me subtly.

"Go on," Joe prods as Jane takes it from him tenderly. "Read the inscription."

"Inscription?" She turns the ring over between her fingers and pauses, staring at the words. I strain to read them over her shoulder:

Cherry and Pine, forever mine

"So?" Joe asks. He's having trouble containing his excitement. "Do you like it?"

There is a moment of silence as everyone waits for her answer. The ring is sheltered tightly in the closed palm of her hand as she speaks.

"I thought someone stole it," she says softly.

"What?" Joe booms. "When would someone have done that?"

Jane doesn't look up. She reopens her hand slowly, tilting it so the light shines on it in such a way that the words glimmer. Slowly, Joe's smile fades and his eyes catch mine. We both know what this means.

"I couldn't find it before the fire." She rubs a finger softly over the inscription before pressing the ring softly to her lips. My mind blurs.

If Joe hadn't hidden the ring . . .
If Clay hadn't gone out to the cart . . .
If Jane hadn't assumed it was Clay's fault . . .
Losing Clay, burning my foot, and leaving behind the recorder. None of that would have happened. And most of all, Joe and Jane would still have their childhood home.

Joe makes a decision then to stay silent, and I decide to

respect it. None of us have approached Jane about her actions, and now he is making sure we never do. We share a quiet moment of agreement before he lets it all go.

"I've had it for a while," he explains. "I had been holding on to it with the intention to polish and clean it for your birthday. But we ran out of polish a while back, and the merchants stopped coming . . ."

The sound of bones clacking together is so clear in my mind, sending a brief shiver down my spine.

"Thank you," Jane says.

When Quill begins to cut the cake, I set my soup and bread aside to taste Kai's creation. The frosting is hard, but when I chip some off and stick it on my tongue, it melts right down. It's sugary sweet and utterly divine.

Then I bite into the cake. It's fluffy, though a bit dry. The milk helps it slide down. Kai did a wonderful job for his first try.

Everyone disperses after they've eaten. Kai is sent to bed, Joe and Tayn take up a game of chess, and Jane sits next to me drinking milk as Quill cleans up the mess.

"Alira," Jane says, her voice subdued, "I'm so sorry."

"Sorry? What on earth for?" I play into her confusion because I've made up my mind. Joe and I are not going to make her feel bad about this. Not now, not ever. She made a mistake, a costly one, but she's more than paid the price for it and I won't let it determine the rest of the trip.

"I didn't know, I couldn't be sure. All it did was—"

A knock on the front door is so loud and strong that it makes us both jump. Quill almost cuts herself on the knife she's cleaning.

"Who could possibly . . . ? Excuse me." Quill rushes out of the kitchen and I can't help but follow. There's no good reason for anyone to be knocking on the door this late at night.

"Oh, sir, please come in and out of the cold!" Quill exclaims, pulling the hooded visitor inside.

I try to get a peek at him, but Jane surges in front of me, almost knocking me over.

"I'm so sorry." She rushes past me and turns a sharp corner, escaping up the stairs. When I turn back, Clay is standing there, looking at me.

"Clay!" I lunge forward and hug him, breathing in the wet wool of an unfamiliar winter coat. I remove myself from him briefly, suddenly aware of the scene I'm making, but he pulls me right back in.

"I missed you very much," he says. His voice is deep and husky. He pulls back to look at me, his eyes dripping from snowmelt. He smiles his usual bright, boyish grin that is oh-so contagious.

Joe pops up from his chair. "This is cause to celebrate!"

"Come, there's cake in the kitchen," Quill says. She takes Clay's coat and we all walk back into the kitchen to celebrate.

"Do you think three houses a day is a good pace to keep?" I push hair off my face and glance at Clay, who is sipping tea dangerously close to *The Goddess Binding.*

His bulky autumn figure has become far leaner in the time we've been away from home. Veins protrude from his arms and hands and I feel a pang of worry for him.

For the past week I've been catching him up on what I've learned. I'm not as good a teacher as Marilla, but the book is certainly helping. He's reading a chapter on plumbing, trying to wrap his head around the inner workings of Quill's bathroom.

He looks up from the book after a moment, processing what I've said. I continue, knowing now that I have his full attention.

"Maybe we should aim for more. I want to learn every-thing I can before the elders agree to send us to the southern villages."

He sets his tea down and makes a point to riffle through the book's innumerable pages. Each one flutters beneath his fingertips before gathering at the bottom and closing with a satisfying *snap*.

"There's a reason Carnelian made this his life's work. It's going to take a while. All we can really do is take advantage of the time we have. We can always come back."

I smile at the thought of coming back to all the friends we've made, friends we have still yet to meet.

After breakfast, we begin. Our plan is to follow the pipes from the waterfall out to the fields before returning to the river and moving downstream, one pocket at a time, until we reach the gates where Delta and Bradán stand watch.

Coincidentally, when we knock on the first house, at the very top of the mountain, Bradán is the one who answers the door. His hair is so dark, I almost mistake him for Flint.

"Well, hello." He laughs, "I'm usually the one visiting you. What brings you here?"

"We're trying to conduct interviews to learn more about the people who live here," I reply.

He steps aside, inviting us in.

"Please, sit wherever seems most comfortable. Have you eaten breakfast yet?"

"Yes, Quill is quite adamant that we eat," Clay remarks, sitting on a wooden bench covered in cozy cushions along the windowsill. I sit next to him, allowing our legs to brush against each other. Reaching into my satchel, I pull out my list of questions.

"We have two goals here: to learn and to teach," I explain. Bradán sets down two cups of tea before taking a seat on a leather-bound chair. He nods in understanding.

I study my list of questions, but something tells me to put them aside. I don't want my experience with the residents of this city to be so prescribed.

"I'm surprised you live so far up the mountain," I say.

"It's my mother's house, really. My father would love to

not have to walk up and down the mountain every day, but he also refuses to let this place go. Just part of the grieving process, I suppose."

"I'm sorry," I say, but he shakes his head, undeterred.

"She didn't die. At least, I don't think so." Bradán says, "She left."

"Oh?" Clay leans forward. I do, too.

"Well, to put it simply, she didn't really like the city. She felt claustrophobic here. She wanted to leave and Father couldn't agree to leave his post to join her, so they separated."

"Does that mean she went to the southern water villages?" Clay asks.

"We thought so, but two years ago she stopped visiting during the Spring Festival, and when we asked around last year, the villagers said she left there, too. No one knows where she is now."

"That's so odd," I say. I can't imagine why anyone would leave their family or the security of an entire village. In a way, I'm no different—I left my family and friends to come here, but my intent is to go back. This is different. This is . . . weird.

"We should move on," Bradán says, stirring me out of my thoughts.

"Oh, okay, let me refer to my notes." I skim them quickly and we begin.

Bradán answers each of our questions quickly and concisely. He doesn't stray into storytelling, simply stating facts. He does, however, have many questions for us.

"What do your homes look like?" he asks.

"Do they have running water?"

"How do you wash up?"

"What is a hot spring?"

"How do you irrigate your fields?"

The list goes on.

Clay and I take turns answering his questions methodically. He seems just as intrigued by our answers as we are by his. It makes me feel like what we are doing here is well worth it. So far, everything we've learned has been well beyond what I considered possible. But Neró was built around the river, and our villages were built around the spring. I can't imagine how it would be possible to implement a similar design.

When we leave, the snow has stopped falling. Everything is crisp and clear and white against the sky's bright blue. The sun is almost hot against my back, but the occasional wind gust keeps us huddled in our coats. As we walk to the next house, a child bursts out from a walkway leading to one of the pockets and stops abruptly next to a stone pillar on the other side of the alley. It's connected to one of the mounds, and when he steps on a lever, fresh water comes pouring out. He drinks from the pillar until he's gasping for air. Then, he darts back to the pocket.

It sparks an idea.

"Do you think we could source water from the ground?" I ask.

"I never really thought about it." Clay says, "I suppose it's no different from sourcing heat from the ground. All we need is the mechanism to back it up."

"If so," I point out, "it would be a good safety net for if we have a drought, and we could use it to pipe water into gardens or homes."

The potential of having running water, of taking showers, washing clothes and doing dishes at home, is delightful to think about.

"I think there's some merit to it."

Clay pauses as I continue searching for more stone pillars or anything that I might have missed before. Realizing I should wait for him, I turn around.

A hard ball of snow smacks me in the face.

"Ow!" I yelp, bringing my hands to my cheeks. They're already red from the impact.

"Shoot," Clay says, running up to me, "I meant to hit your back." He pushes my gloved hands away to get a good look at my face. His eyes are searching, his fingers tracing my burning cheeks and settling on my jaw. I tremble.

"I'm fine." I flinch away before my face gets even redder.

"Are you sure?" he asks.

"Just give me a second." I turn away, setting my satchel down to sit on a wooden bench. As I lower into my seat, I reach beneath it and grab a handful of snow, lobbing it at his chest.

"Ow!" he whines.

I grin mischievously as he wipes the shock off his face. Then we both bend down, and the snowball fight begins.

~

After a few days, we reach the farms on the far side of the city. The homes here are secluded from those at the city center, each one with its own custom design and structure. Some are tall and skinny, with three floors above ground all encased in red brick. Others are only one story, half the size of Joe and Jane's cabin.

The first house past the stables is the latter, a small wooden dwelling abutting the stable pastures. A young woman stands facing a small garden with an easel, sketching out a watercolor painting of a frosted gladiolus flower. She hears our boots crunch against the hardened snow and turns to face us.

"Oh, my," she exclaims, "You must be the academics!"

I blush and nod in reply. Most people just call us ants or earth dwellers. She's the first to use such a distinguished term. She leaps into action, quickly setting her tools aside. Before I can react, she's enveloped both of my hands in hers for a firm handshake.

"I'm Isla. It's so nice to meet you both! Everyone's been saying such nice things about you two."

Her eyes are a soft and delicate gray blue, like rising steam from the spring. She takes my breath away.

"Please, come in! I'll make you both some tea."

Isla's dwelling is stuffed with paintings. She rushes around trying to clear off the dining table, swiping small canvases off the chairs and leaning them against the wall. I skirt around the remaining paintings, feeling drawn to the far side of the room. Countless works of art hang upon the walls: Peonies in bloom, tiger lilies, daisies, cherry blossoms, daffodils, and more all adorn the paper canvases on which she paints. Even common plants like chickweed and violet, dandelion and purslane are given center stage in each of their own portraits.

"Do you paint from memory?" Clay asks. His hands are stuffed in his pockets as if he is afraid to touch anything.

"I paint what I see," Isla says. "Though sometimes I'm inspired by old memories. It's fun to mix the two."

She goes on about her process, but I'm distracted by clouds. They cover the opposite wall. Isla notices me and starts naming them: cirrus, cirrocumulus, cirrostratus, noctilucent, all mixed with different landscapes. Some are in the fields, others over the fountain shrine, but most look as though they were painted right from her back garden.

One painting in particular catches my eye. Isla calls them stratocumulus clouds. Soft puffs of magnolia pink and violet purple against the mountain at sunset.

"I never imagined clouds to have names."

"Aren't they wonderful?" She gushes, "The merchant I trade them to tells me all of their names. He's wonderful, really. He's due back in the spring, so things have gotten quite cluttered."

Clay and I sit gingerly on the chairs. I take my notebook from my satchel.

"Are the farmlands different from the inner-city houses?" I ask.

"Not by much," she replies. "The inner city is close enough that everything I could possibly need is a short walk. My garden is more than capable of feeding me and even the flowers provide me with the pigment I need for my paint."

"Really?"

"Yes. Do you make art in the House of the Earth Queen?" she asks.

"The potters are probably the closest thing." Clay says, "Some try chalk, but it washes away with the rain."

"Pottery is quite interesting." She says, "I wonder if my flower pigments would work on a pot."

"Unfortunately, probably not." I say, "The potters use a lot of heat and that heat would likely destroy any floral coloration." She frowns slightly and I feel like I've broken her.

Clay speaks up for me, "There are some things that work, though, as far as I know. Eggshells can offer a white glaze, but ash is the best source of color."

Her eyes perk up. "Ash provides color?"

"Yes. When done correctly, they can produce all kinds of colors: blues, browns, yellows, but also pale greens and grays. There are some rather beautiful pieces in the community center back home, but those are very distinct. They're almost impossible to replicate with our current setup.

Clay knows far more about this than I realized. I suppose it helps that he's the best source of ash in the core villages.

"That's wonderful," Isla says. "Perhaps someday I'll be able to try it myself."

We continue to talk, but as time goes on, my mind latches on to one inconsistency that I fear I shouldn't bring up. It may be rude to ask, but curiosity gets the better of me.

"You live alone?" I ask, sneaking a glance to measure her reaction. I mean nothing by it; Quill is single herself, though she has Kai and her guests to keep her company.

"Oh, yes," She replies, "I could never live with anyone but myself." She smiles when she sees our confusion.

"I once met a man who I thought I loved. I was willing to do anything for him. I even stopped painting for him. He always fussed about how dirty the place was, so I cleaned it up. But the hole I carved out for him in my life became exceedingly large. It seemed like even one or two paintings hanging around was a nuisance to him. Eventually, I stopped painting altogether.

"One day he left for a long trip to the southern villages, and to pass the time, I started painting again. It gave me such joy. For the first time in a long time, I was at peace. When he returned, he was infuriated at the mess I had made. He told me to clean up and I told him to leave."

Though her voice is smooth and undeterred by her rocky past, I can see in her eyes a glimmer of sadness. She did, at one point, love someone enough to abandon herself and her art for them.

"I'm happy for you," Clay says. "It seems he was the one taking up space, not your paintings."

The hint of sadness behind her smile dissipates. Her eyes well up as she smiles.

"Thank you. You are both so kind. Everyone thinks a woman ought to marry, but I will never settle. My work thanks me for it every time."

We stop at several more houses before we head back. Each one is unique. We talk to an elderly woman living with her grandchildren, a newlywed couple expecting a baby while starting a brewing business, and a plumber who fosters kittens. I feel light on my feet, as though walking on air.

"It's so nice to see people pursuing what makes them happy," I say.

Clay smiles. His brown hair curls up against his wool hat.

"Feels pretty good to say we're doing the same thing."

It feels more than good, it feels amazing. I feel so utterly happy.

We reach Quill's, anxious to return to lounging at the hearth, but I pause.

Beyond Quill's, past the bridge, and perched on the edge of Sionnan's Heart, is Torin.

"Is that him?" He asks. I told him about Torin the morning after he came, but it's been a while. Last time I saw him, he said he was working on a gift for me, but I haven't seen him since my studies began. Now he's just here, and I don't want to assume that he's waiting for me. It feels presumptuous, even egotistical.

My cheeks burn. I have to know.

"I should talk to him," I say. "Do you want to come?"

If Torin rejects me, I'll have Clay there as a crutch.

He nods, his eyes hard.

The wind picks up and the air feels crisp; it burns my nose with each inhale. As we approach the fountain, I tap my finger on the thin ice that spreads along its outer edge. It cracks under even the slightest pressure.

Torin's eyes look past me and narrow into a scrutinizing glare. I realize, belatedly, I never bothered to mention Clay. Not once.

His eyes drift over to me and the corners of his mouth curve up before his smile tears me apart.

"Good afternoon, Alira."

Butterflies soar through my stomach. A book wrapped in paper and twine sits on his lap. My gift.

He has been waiting for me.

I smile dumbly for several moments before realizing I'm being rude.

"Torin, this is Clay, my traveling companion. Clay, this is Torin."

Clay offers his hand in greeting, but there is an odd delay. Torin inspects Clay's hand before offering his own. For a moment, I think I see his eyes flit to the ring on my finger before speaking.

"Clay, what a fitting name. Alira never mentioned you."

My face turns rose red.

"Should she have?" Clay asks.

"I just thought you'd trust me with that sort of thing." Torin directs the statement at me, his blue eyes scalding.

I stumble on my words.

"I . . . Well I just wanted to . . . um . . ."

Clay cuts in, "You guys have known each other what, a month? I'm sure there's plenty she hasn't told you yet." He grins.

"Right."

I feel like a ram has shoved its horns into my stomach. I should have told him. I'm utterly stupid for it. I thought it would be safer not to. With the way Torin's eyes dwell on my ring, the knowledge of Clay would have surely turned him away. He's the only one who's shown any interest in me. I had to make sure.

But if I say any of that . . .

"Anyway," Torin says, "I have your gift." He hands me the book that he's been holding. The paper bends against the twine that binds it. I unfurl the careful wrapping and find a leather-bound sketchbook with stained edges. I open it carefully.

The first page is a watercolor painting of the grand city of Neró.

"Torin, this is beautiful." I sit next to him in shock.

"Most of what I know about the house is in there. It could help you visualize things."

Each page depicts different sections of the city in astounding detail. Pocket by pocket, he's managed to give each brushstroke meaning. Every detail is a decision painted in soft blues and grays. Fishermen stand at the pond, children play in the city square, and in each one, there's a shadow of a girl with fallow hair.

Torin leans in, his breath hot against my neck.

"So watercolor is your thing?" Clay interjects, creating a void between us as Torin turns away to answer him.

"It's more of a house thing."

"You're very talented."

Poison seeps deeper and deeper into every word. I don't know how to fix it. I want to apologize, then and there, for not mentioning Clay before, but when I open my mouth I spot Kai running toward us.

He slips on the masonry near the base of the fountain and quickly rebounds, hopping up to greet us.

"Hi!" Kai waves excitedly. "The iceman is here!" Without waiting for a response, he turns about and runs away as quickly as he came.

I jump up in excitement and hand the book back to Torin, but he refuses.

"It's a gift."

I smile, clutching the book close to my chest as we leave. The feeling fades quickly. When I glance back, he quickly averts his gaze. I feel a tug at my heartstrings, wondering what I could have done differently. Apologies spill out of me.

"That was the opposite of how I imagined that going. I'm sorry."

"It's no big deal. He kinda seems like a jerk anyway."

"He's actually really nice," I note, a weak attempt at vindication.

"I'm sure he is."

A chestnut horse with flaxen hair waits patiently at the entrance to Tranquility's B&B. It's harnessed to a cart. I circle around it and find exactly what I'm looking for. Etched in large letters on the cart's broadside is one word.

ICE

Clay chuckles as I rush inside, bursting through the door and into the entryway. I continue into the kitchen, where a hulking man twice the size of Joe sits with a minuscule cup of tea.

"Hi!" I say, a little breathless. "I have questions."

The man sets down his cup and regards me with mild amusement. "They told me you would."

"Hey now," Joe says. He recognizes the look on my face, the same one I had when he was telling me how to make paper. "I'm not done with him myself."

I take the chair next to the iceman and badger him with questions.

"What's your name?" I start.

"Vale."

"Where do you get ice from?"

"She leads with the big punches," he observes, feigning a laugh. I barely notice Clay enter and take a seat by the door. He seems content to listen in.

"In the summer months, my brothers retrieve ice from colder elevations and bring it to me. I, in turn, deliver it to those in need. Next year, I'll swap duties with them."

"Sounds like a hard job," Clay interjects.

"Depends on who you ask. Retrieving the ice isn't easy, but it's seasonal work. My brothers are relaxing at home right now while I deliver ice almost year-round."

"Where do you store it? Won't it melt?"

"I store it in our underground storage room. Not many houses have one, but for us it's essential. We pack it pretty tight down there. We have to. You see, ice has a way of insulating itself, so if you stick enough of it together and add some straw for good measure, it will stay solid for quite some time."

"That must be great in the summer," Clay says, "having ice like that."

"It comes in handy. Whenever I'm in need of certain goods, I'll rent out the room for a period of time in exchange for whatever I need."

After that, the interview becomes less of an interrogation and more of a conversation. Clay and Joe continue to chat with Vale, and I listen intently for any other hints he has to give, but it's short-lived.

Vale rises from his chair and Joe lets out an audible groan in protest. Quill can't help but giggle.

"I should get going," Vale says, handing his empty cup to Quill before turning to Joe, "but you, you are welcome for a drink at my place any day."

"Should I bring something to trade?" Joe asks.

"Bring your own tankard and I'll supply the rest."

Joe beams.

"Thank you, Vale," Quill says. "I will send for you when we need more. We may not need it weekly yet, but the Spring Festival will be here sooner than we think."

"It's a good time," Vale says. "You're not the first to put a request in."

He says one more goodbye before heading outside, but I'm lost in thought. Spring is coming, Quill said, and the elders will need to make a decision soon.

STORYTIME

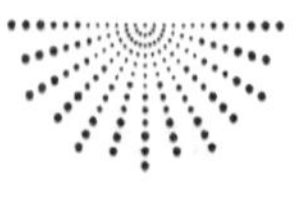

CLAY

ALIRA ALWAYS GOES to bed early. She has for as long as I've known her. It's not hard to imagine why. Her mind bounces from one worry to the next until exhaustion wins. The earlier she sleeps, she claims, the better she feels the next day.

I have no such habits.

As Alira excuses herself for the night, I remain by the fire with *The Goddess Binding*. Despite all the days we've had to study this thing, I've barely even made a dent in it. Each page is so packed with information that I have to sometimes reread paragraphs two or three times before I can even try to grasp the mechanics they are describing.

I'm searching for any information I can find on how to pump water from the ground into homes. Without a river to push the water for us, I'm not sure what mechanisms we can use. Joe isn't helping. He's focused on a puzzle of a waterfall. Every couple of moments he sighs loudly, frustrated, and every now and then he exclaims, "Aha!" and fits a wooden piece decisively into its proper place.

He stands up suddenly. "I need a drink, you?"

I nod in agreement. As he dashes into the kitchen, I

take a seat at a table unburdened by chess boards and puzzle pieces. It's been a while since I had a drink. The last time, I realize, was with my father the night before we left.

I can hear Joe from here.

"Hey, Quill!"

"Hello, Joe. How can I help you?"

"Clay and I were looking to have some cold beer."

"Of course." I hear her move toward the icebox.

"You should join us," Joe adds.

"Oh, no," Quill replies, "I have a lot of cleanup left to do before the night is over. Thanks, though."

"Oh, come on, you deserve a break. I'll even help clean up after."

There's a pause as she considers his offer.

"Perhaps if Jane joins us," she proposes.

"Jane? I spend enough time with Jane. I'd rather spend my time with people who aren't so serious, you know?"

Two tankards thunk against the countertop. Quill's voice is terse.

"Sorry, I don't think I do. Here's your beer."

I'm unsurprised when Joe walks through the threshold looking dejected.

"Did you just try to flirt with Quill?" I ask.

He shrugs. "Maybe."

"Well, you're not very good."

Joe rolls his eyes, "I'm seeing that now."

He sets one tankard down in front of me, tipping his own back for several gulps before taking a seat.

"Got any advice?" he asks.

Joe wants advice from me? As my eyes narrow, his dart away.

"Oh, you *like* her," I realize.

"Sh! Don't let her hear you."

"Oh, that's cute." I glance toward the kitchen, but Quill is still busily cleaning. Faster, even, now that she's angry.

"Rule number one." I say, "Respect all women, even if you don't like them."

He nods solemnly. "I should be more careful how I speak about Jane."

"I get it. I can't imagine sharing a room with my siblings."

"It's just"—he pauses—"with everything that happened, I want to make sure she's okay. I want to keep an eye on her. But lately it's getting really hard to listen to all her ranting and raving about when and how we should rebuild."

"She burned the place down, and now she wants to build it back up. She wants to right her wrongs." I pause, thinking of Flint. "I've been there."

"Yeah, well, I don't know how to tell her I'm not interested in leaving."

He hides behind his tankard, chugging it halfway down. When he finally stops, I let silence draw his eyes back to mine.

"Don't tell me you're down that bad?" I ask.

His smirks. "Love will hit you like an ax to the head."

My thoughts jump to Alira, but that's not quite how it feels. I know her too well, and if I met her today, I'm not sure I'd chase her for more than her looks. I wonder if she'd feel the same.

Joe doesn't seem to notice. "I just feel like I could live here forever and be happy, you know?"

"Are you sure you aren't just getting spoiled?" I jest.

"Can't say for sure. But the opportunity's staring me in the face like never before."

I drink some more, mulling it over. It makes sense, in a way. Back home, there's entire villages' worth of girls to date. Joe, on the other hand, has spent his whole life with his father and Jane.

"So, you got a girl back home?" he asks.

I grin mischievously. "Depends on who you ask."

He laughs. "I thought you'd say that. You and Alira get along quite well, but I don't like to assume."

"I had a debt to pay," I explain, "and I wanted to make sure she was protected."

"She fought tooth and nail to turn back for you," he says.

I lean in, leaving my tankard off to the side.

"And when that wasn't an option, she made sure you wouldn't run into the same problems. That claw trap really did its job." He speaks so lightly of it now, but that woman, with her stubbed foot and her eyes like a starless night—I won't ever forget her.

"Alira needs you," Joe says, bringing me back to reality. "You're her rock."

"I made the trip a reality for her." I realize, "Without me, she must have felt lost. She kept up hope, though. She left those jars out and that made all the difference."

"Oh, no, mate," Joe reveals, "that was me."

"*You* left the jars?"

He laughs at my surprise. "Aye, and by the looks of you when you arrived, you needed them."

"Hey, now, I can handle myself." I argue halfheartedly. "But when I realized what you guys had seen up ahead, I booked it to the outpost. Probably missed a bunch of jars along the way."

"Could have been worse," he says.

I shiver, despite the heat in my belly.

"Well, since it all worked out, I think we can agree not to dwell on it." I take another long swig.

"Certainly." Joe says, "No need to fell a tree twice."

We continue to chat and drink, stumbling up the stairs in the darkest hours of the night and falling into our respective beds.

The next morning, I'm sitting at the table, still hungover, when Joe asks Quill if he can have his own room.

"Is something the matter?" Quill seems overly concerned.

"I love my sister, but I'm tired of living with her." He excuses himself to the bathroom and pauses in the doorway.

"Was that crack always there?" he asks, motioning toward the window next to me. Splintered wood cuts through the sill and branches down the wall.

"I . . . um . . . Yes," Quill stutters. "I've been putting it off."

"I'll fix it later. And I'll fix that leak in your bedroom, too." He leaves.

Quill, dumbfounded, leans over the counter and asks in a hushed tone, "Jane is his sister?"

I nod and my head spins. I hold my head in my hands to hold off the headache that ensues.

"Oh dear, I thought they were . . . Oh, never mind." I drop my hands and catch Quill smile to herself as she turns away.

After Joe's request, the day is uneventful. Rain turns to snow turns to rain and then thunder rolls in. Quill advises us not to set foot out there unless we have a death wish.

Alira seems unhappy, spending time by the window looking out at the fountain shrine, but eventually she accepts that not every day can be productive, and we spend some time studying from *The Goddess Binding* instead. I quiz her on the chapters we've read and we make a sort of game out of it.

"What's a watershed?" I challenge her.

"Oh! Oh! I know this one. Joe told me about it once. It's an area of land through which channels of rainfall and snowmelt drain into creeks, streams and rivers. Just like how our creek back home drains into the Sionnan River." She grins when she gets each question right, her eyes gleaming with confidence.

"Yes, yes, correct. Your turn."

"What is a watershed with no outlet called?" She asks.

"A sink," I reply. "Really, Alira? You can do better than that."

"I just wanna get to the next one."

She bounces up and down in her seat excitedly. She's so cute when she's competitive like this.

Suddenly, Joe sweeps into the room looking like he has a grand announcement to make.

"Everyone, listen up. I have a brilliant idea and you are all about to hear it."

Kai jumps up from his puzzle table, almost knocking the pieces over.

"I wanna know! Tell me, Joe!"

Jane appears from behind Joe, smirking. It's been a long time since I've seen her make any face resembling enjoyment.

"It's about time that we burn the night away telling stories," Joe declares. Alira and I look at each other and smile. Tayn, who has been absent all day, suddenly appears on the staircase.

"Did I hear someone say *stories*? Oh, I do very much enjoy stories."

"We know," Joe jokes. "You seem to make one up every day." Joe pulls up a chair by the fire. Everyone else follows suit. Quill comes in last, setting down a glass of milk and a plate of cookies for us to munch on. She sits awfully close to Joe and he smiles uncontrollably.

"Why don't you go first, Tayn?" I suggest.

"Splendid." The merchant claps his hands together in delight, keeping them clasped as he begins to tell his story.

"In the esteemed House of the Illuminator, there are very

few laws. However, there are some that are non-negotiable, especially those involving thieves and vagabonds."

I notice Alira lean in at the mention of the word. Tayn continues, "There was once a young boy who was the best thief in all the island of Solaris. He was always trading things with people with no indication as to where he got them from. He taught the other kids, too, and for a fair bit of time, the island was teeming with thieves. Women clutched their pearls closer to their necks and men walked with a pep in their step." He clasps at his own set of pearls, feigning offense.

"Well, one day, the little sand shrew got caught. He was found guilty—his finger cut off as punishment." Tayn's voice grips at me, surprisingly, sending me to the island of Solaris, where a little boy stands trial. His storytelling paints a picture so clear I can almost see white sand for the first time.

"That's a good story." Quill nods in approval. The moral is clear.

"But that's not the best part, my dear! He tricked them and got away!"

Kai moves closer to Tayn in earnest, just quick enough to escape his mother's grasp.

"But what about his hand?" Kai asks.

"Well, you see, on the night before the trial, he escaped his containment, but he knew that his escape would not last long. So he stole a fake hand from the props in the theater and stuffed the fingers with red dye so that they would seem to bleed. The man doing the cutting barely looked, and so the boy got away scot-free."

"So he didn't learn his lesson?" Quill asks, exasperated.

"He learned it was time to move on, which is why he stole a ticket on the next ship to the neighboring island."

Jane groans, "Vagabonds."

"One time I stole a trinket from the fountain!" Kai exclaims proudly. Quill shoots him a judgmental glare.

"I put it back." Kai adds, "I just wanted to see if it was real."

"Yes, that's good!" Tayn praises him, "Always make sure that the goods you steal are real."

"Oh yes, Kai is quite the thief," Quill says mischievously. "When I was pregnant, he decided to steal some sunshine and arrived a tad bit early."

"Mom! That's embarrassing!" Kai objects. He bolts away, running up the stairs and out of sight. From the corner of my eye, I can still see his hand grasping the banister, a bit of red hair peeking from behind it. He's simply too adorable not to notice.

"He was so tiny," Quill remembers, "his little hands could barely grasp my pinky finger. His skin was the softest I had ever touched. Sometimes I miss that first year of motherhood. Well,"—she pauses—"most of it, anyway."

Her face darkens and she stares into the fire as if remembering something sour. I decide to take the spotlight off her.

"I have a story."

All eyes turn to me.

"I got into a bet with Flint once, Alira's brother." They all nod in understanding.

"He told me there was a pest getting into the berry bushes and I told him I could catch it for him, but he got all offended about it, since he thinks he should do everything himself. So we made a bet on who could trap it first. We had no clue what we were dealing with, but I was pretty confident I would win." I lean forward and everyone seems to huddle together for a moment, excited to see where this goes. My leg brushes against Alira's and she decides not to flinch away this time. My heart beats a little faster.

"We made our own traps, set them, and checked on them separately, until one day, I came over to check on my trap and ran into Flint, and this overwhelming smell was just *wafting* off him. So I asked him, 'What on Earth did you get into?'"

I smirk. "Of all the things that could have gotten into the berry patch, he found himself a skunk."

The room erupts into laughter. Even Kai giggles from atop his perch. Alira perks up.

"I remember now, Mother was furious. She ordered him to go wash up in the spring before even thinking of stepping foot in the house."

"From then on, every time I saw Flint, I called him Stinker." I pause. "Until, of course, we had our fight. Then we kind of stopped talking altogether."

It feels weird talking about it now. Almost a year has gone by and I'm still trying to make up for my mistake. Joe can sense that I'm done with this topic and shifts everyone's attention to Jane, but Alira leans in and whispers low enough so only I can hear.

"I don't understand. You guys fought all the time. What made this fight any different?"

I can't tell her the details, but if I don't give her something, she will find them herself.

"The difference is that it was about you."

She stares at me a moment too long before refocusing on Jane, but as for me, I'm caught thinking about that crisp spring day where it all went wrong.

I had been dating Gemma quietly for some time. I'm honestly surprised Flint didn't catch on sooner; secrets don't last long where we're from. But Gemma was on her way home from visiting Alira and I was on my way in to see Flint, so we shared a kiss and Flint just happened to find catch us.

I had never seen Gemma walk away so fast in all her life.

Flint just stood there, waiting for me to explain myself. When I didn't, it only served to feed his frustration.

"She's too young for you," He groaned.

"Not really," I argued. "She's only two years younger than me."

"Two years is too young and I don't think it's appropriate for you to date her."

I looked at him for a good long moment, wondering why he cares. "Are we talking about the same person right now?"

Flint laughed. "Alira would never fall for your nonsense."

That much was true, but at this point I was having fun messing with him. "Maybe you overestimate her."

It was then that Flint punched me square in the nose. It was so unexpected that I found myself knocked onto the ground.

I tried to back-step. "I'm just messing with you." I said.

But it was too late.

"Get out," he said. "*Get out!*" He erupted into an anger so rare that it was scary to see. I left without a word and every time I tried to talk to him afterward, he simply turned and walked away. And Alira—if I'd made any move toward her that he might see or hear about later, it would have only made things worse. So I stayed away. That was the last fight we had.

"Do you have a story, Alira?" Quill's voice shakes me out of my memory.

"Not really," Alira admits. "I've always been pretty plain that way."

Not true. But I'm not going to offer up any stories without her feeling comfortable.

"Well, this trip is bound to change that for you," Joe says, leaning in to pat her on the back before launching into his own story.

"I nearly broke my ankle once." He boasts. "I was climbing one of those big hulking trees in the forest behind the cabin. A traveling medic had to come by and treat it. She was the prettiest girl I'd ever seen." He smiles. "Not as pretty as Quill, though."

Quill blushes. Jane's eyes narrow and I wonder what she'll do if he decides to stay.

When the stories have finished, Tayn claps his hands as he did at the very beginning, jolting everyone out of their thoughts.

"Splendid, absolutely splendid." He says, "You are all true storytellers at heart. I am happy to have shared this moment with you all." He excuses himself to his room for the night, followed closely by Jane.

The rain slows to a soft and steady patter outside the window. While Alira and I start a puzzle, Joe and Quill sit close together by the fire, reading a book. Joe seems incapable of wiping his smile off his face and Quill is quite the same.

Then a knock comes at the door. Quill's face drops. She doesn't want to get up. I do them both a favor and offer to answer it for her.

Alira follows me, and when the door opens, we both are surprised to see Bradán. His jacket is wet, though not yet soaked through. His face is a mix of relief and disdain.

"Good, you're here," he says. He seems out of breath.

"What's wrong?" Alira asks.

"The elders made a decision regarding the villages downstream."

"They did?" Alira perks up.

"Don't tell anyone I told you this. They want to keep it under wraps to avoid anyone getting upset."

"What do you mean?" I ask.

"The elders have decided to leave the villages to govern themselves. There are no plans to assist them. In fact, they are limiting travel to the villages and asking us to keep an eye out for anyone who seems sick to avoid the spread of possible disease. They're only having me tell you out of courtesy."

Bradán's disdain makes sense now. He disagrees, and so do I.

Alira shakes her head in disbelief. "I told them it was coming from the river. Why don't they believe me?"

Bradán shrugs. "The Spring Festival is the biggest event of the year. If there's any chance you're wrong, it could cause some massive problems. They don't want to cancel it, but they will if they have to."

Ripley saw firsthand what the water was doing, and even the village elders were taking precautions against the river water. The city elders refuse to act, and so they leave us no choice. It may be too late for Ripley, but I know there are plenty of people left to save.

"Bradán, I'm going to ask you something," I say, lowering my voice.

"Certainly." His eyes bore into mine.

"If we wanted to leave to go evacuate them and investigate the cause of all this, would you let us through?"

"Happily."

"Give us a week."

He nods. I hold my hand out and we shake before I back away and close the door.

"Clay," Alira whispers, concerned and uncertain.

Joe and Quill sneak confused glances our way, but the conversation was so hushed that they must not have a clue.

"Everything's fine," I assure them. "We got news from the elders. Quill, I'll have to talk to you about it tomorrow, but I think it's time we go to bed, right, Alira?"

Quill accepts this and sinks deeper into Joe's side, but Alira looks at me worriedly. I lay a hand softly on her shoulder.

"Let's get some sleep and talk tomorrow."

I lead the way upstairs. She follows slowly. It's for the best. I know she won't sleep well tonight, so the earlier she goes to bed, the better.

CHAMOMILE

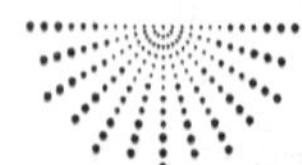

"Do you really think they would consider canceling the festival?" Quill asks. She hands us our food with deep worry creased into her forehead.

"We're hoping to sort this out before then," Clay replies.

"How exactly?" Quill asks. "If you evacuate the villages, they'll come here, and if the elders don't want them, it will cause problems."

"Part of my plan is to send someone from the outpost in with them." Clay says, "They've watched this sickness from the start, and they know it's not contagious. They are trained medical professionals. The elders will have to listen to them."

I know he's talking about Misty, but it still feels tricky. Ignoring the elders is one thing, but evacuating the villages and sending them straight here is going to cause a stir.

"Regardless, you'll need supplies," Quill says. "By cart, you can expect a round trip of over a fortnight. How much time do you have to prepare?"

"I told Bradán to give us a week."

"I'll see what I can find, but it will be difficult without drawing attention to myself."

"I'm sorry, Quill," I interject. "You've done so much for us."

"I'm not one for ignoring elder orders, but a lot of people have family in the villages. What you're doing is important, and I want to help."

"We don't want to draw any attention to this," Clay adds. "We need to give the impression that we agree with their decision. Therefore, we will continue to interview as normal."

Focusing on the interviews is hard knowing that we'll be gone soon. My brain is already mapping out all the obstacles that could be in our way. Clay keeps watching me with burning eyes, making sure I'm all right. He stays close, grounding me and allowing me to give all my attention to the people we are visiting.

Yesterday we ended in the far reaches of the farmlands, so today we work our way back in. Creek and Serenity are the first couple we meet. They breed dogs for various purposes: hunting, shepherding, and interestingly, guiding.

"Guide dogs are like guard dogs," Creek explains. "They protect their owner and allow them to live their life without fear. They're great for people who have weaker eyes, but I train them for a mix of other things as well. Dogs have a knack for reading us. They know when we're stressed, weak; heck, Dribble here knew Serenity was pregnant before we did."

I look at Dribble. His eyes are vacant, his jowls thick with saliva. He takes my attention as an invitation and rests his head on my pants until they're almost completely soaked in his drool.

"Are you stressed, hun?" Serenity asks.

"Just a little bit." I pet Dribble and he huffs hot air onto my lap.

"Stay as long as you like," she says, handing me a cup of tea. "It's chamomile, great for relaxing."

It's enough to settle my thoughts, for now.

Next to Creek and Serenity's house is a curiously small home with a roof not of slate or thatch, but of sod. Evergreen plants climb the windows and line the yard in organized chaos. It reminds me of the community center.

"Come on," Clay says, pulling me toward the door.

It opens before we even get to the knocker.

"Muriel!" a tall woman calls behind her. "They're here!"

Her hair is pulled into a tight ponytail; her eyes are sage green. The wisp of hair that falls away from her head is a shocking purple hue.

"We've been dying to meet you guys," the woman says. "Pun unintended, of course." She opens the door wide to let us in.

"I'm Morgan," she adds, "And this is my wife, Muriel."

Behind her is another woman, shorter and slighter than her, wearing denim pants and a white shirt of very smooth material.

"Nice to meet you," Muriel says, her voice melodic and pure. "Isla told us all about you."

"Isn't she adorable?" Morgan asks, placing a plate full of fresh bread on a table.

"She's great!" I reply.

As we sit around the table, Muriel sets our a wide variety of teas to choose from. Clay pours for me. He chooses chamomile.

"Morgan is a pocket-scaper. She helps the city planner design the pockets for each season." Muriel explains.

"It's mostly just weeding," Morgan groans, "but I make it fun by hybridizing the flowers in my free time. I like to see how bright I can make them flower." She points to her head. "This color came from indigo flower."

"Really?"

"Really, really." She grins. "But Muriel does the really cool stuff."

"Oh yeah?" Clay asks.

"It's nothing," Muriel squeaks. "I just make fishing line, is all."

"Not just any fishing line," Morgan corrects. "The strongest in the city. The smoothest, too. You see that shirt she's wearing? It's the same material."

"Silk." Muriel says.

"I've heard the word before," I say, though I don't know where it comes from. It reminds me of the steamed eggs Quill made. Soft like pudding.

"It comes from silkworms," Muriel explains. "I raise them myself. They wrap themselves in silk cocoons, and when they mature, they turn into silk moths and leave their cocoons behind. I take them and process them into silk, which can be braided into fishing line."

"What does everyone else use?" Clay asks.

"Depends on what they can get their hands on." She says, "Horsehair, cotton, linen, even kitstring will do, but none are as good as silk string."

When Torin took me fishing, he used a linen string. It can be quite soft, but this is far softer, slipping between my fingers like water.

We continue to chat until most of the tea is gone.

"If y'all are here for the fishing tourney in the spring, I'll have plenty available." Muriel giggles, but the mere mention of the Spring Festival is enough to pull me back into spiraling thoughts.

"We'll be sure to look for you," Clay says, pushing me out the door. The second it closes, he turns me around to face him.

"Look, I can tell you're stressed, but everything's going to be fine."

"Is it?" I ask.

"Yes. I have a plan," he says.

"You keep saying that, but I haven't heard it yet."

"We're going to collect our supplies, head to the outpost, and follow the river downstream. We'll bring extra water along, and dole it out to them before evacuating. After that, we will guide them back to the outpost in time for the Spring Festival. The city will already be preparing for an influx of travelers, so there will be plenty of room for them, After that we can go home."

"You're not worried about the dangers we might face?" I ask.

"Our portion of the Travelers' Road only ever saw merchants, and the cannibals were a problem, but this stretch of river is well traveled, and the only real danger is going to be the water."

I'll admit; it sounds like a decent plan, but it almost sounds too simple.

"We will not stop at any cabins." He assures me, "We will remain by the cart at all times. We will be safe. I promise."

A few months ago, I wouldn't have believed him. His arrogance would have driven us to ruin, like it almost did at Joe and Jane's. It would have been the same with the cannibals, if we had made it that far together, and I cringe to think of it every time the thought rises in my head.

But he's changed, somehow. When Bradán knocked on the door last night, Clay didn't miss a beat before making a decision. In one week, we'll be sneaking out of Neró and onto the Travelers' Road. It's something that would have taken me a lot of time to decide, worrying about all the different issues that could arise if we took such a chance, but Clay didn't waste any time. His ability to think through his decisions is quickening.

"Okay," I relent. "I trust you."

"Good. For now, just enjoy the time we have left here. Are you ready for more interviews?"

"Yes."

～

Around noon, we walk up to a house nestled up against a pocket. It's a little shoddy-looking, with a weathered roof and a cracked window. The kids in the pocket behind it are eerily quiet as they pass. They whisper amongst themselves as though it's haunted.

When we knock on the door, a man opens it and frowns.

"Ugh, ants." The door slams shut in our faces.

"Wow, that's a first" is all I can manage to say.

"That's okay," Clay says, "I don't think I want to interview him anyway."

I step down from the front stoop and freeze up.

"What?" Clay asks, but I can't answer. My eyes are glued to Torin, who is walking into a house across the way.

I gravitate toward the door, and Clay follows.

All this time, I had been hoping Torin would appear at the shrine, or show up at Quill's, or even invite me over to his house himself. But ever since meeting Clay, he's been completely out of sight.

There is a chance, I realize, that I may have missed him at the shrine. I stopped looking after a while. I feel guilty just thinking about it.

And now here we are, standing at his front door, knocking three times and waiting to be let in. He opens it and, upon seeing me, smiles broadly.

"Hello, Alira."

Butterflies flutter through my stomach in a whirlwind of emotions that I try to tamp down.

"Please come in, take a seat; my mother is in the back." He opens the door wide and we step inside. Then; he closes it firmly behind us and disappears into a dark hallway.

The home is much bigger than most of the ones we've seen. Quill's is the most comparable in size, though the layout is mirrored. The front door opens up opposite a staircase, along which lies the hall that Torin took to find his mother, but the great room sprawls out on our left, rather than our right.

Two plush couches sit in the middle of the great room with a table between, atop which are various blueprints for city projects. Beyond it is the fireplace, where a reddish-brown sphere spins over a cauldron, attached by two tubes.

"My mother will be right out," Torin says, returning from the hall. "Allow me to take your coat."

His hands graze my shoulders as I take off my jacket and I shiver. He turns to the wall on our right, where two fishing poles lean against the wall, and hangs it on the coatrack beside them. I open my mouth to ask about the strange sphere over the fireplace, but a voice interrupts us.

"You didn't tell me there were two of them!"

I turn to see Torin's mother, a beautiful woman in a sweater dress of periwinkle blue. She sweeps through the house, picking up the plans off the table and rolling them up before offering us a handshake.

"Hi, I'm Cordelia, so nice to meet you. Please excuse me while I find something to serve you." She prattles on anxiously, "Should I warm some bread? Oh, it's delicious, one of my best. You really must try it. And Torin, you really must get better at warning me about these things."

"Sorry, Mother."

Before she can find her way to the kitchen, Cordelia spots herself in the mirror.

"Oh," she groans, "my hair! This is unacceptable."

Her hair, of course, is pristine. It's a rich blond, like daisies and honey, clipped up into a messy bun. She storms back into the hall, and just before being swallowed by darkness, she removes her clip, letting loose a cascading mass of hair.

"I apologize." Torin says, "She can be a bit much, but she really cares, you know?"

I nod dumbly, unable to formulate words. He leads me to the table and sits across from me. When I sit, the plush cushions feel different from most.

"What are these made of?" I ask.

"They're stuffed with horsehair." Torin explains, "Most are stuffed with cotton or straw."

"Figures," Clay says, sitting next to me.

"So, I hear you two have been all over," Torin says.

"Yes, we've met many wonderful people," I reply. "We won't be able to talk to everyone before we leave, but we are learning a lot regardless."

"When are you leaving?" Torin asks.

"Soon," Clay says. The word is sharp like a blade. I pray Persephone will forgive his rudeness.

"Why not wait until the summer? That's when the city is the most beautiful. Ripe for a proper tour." Torin winks at me and I almost crumble. If I don't hold my tongue, all of what we've learned about the southern villages and the elders' decisions will spill outward.

"Torin, dear, you really ought not badger our guests with questions." Cordelia rushes in from the kitchen and shoves a slice of bread into his hand, placing several more on the table before us. He rolls his eyes and takes a bite.

"We're just going to visit the villages." I try to say it lightly, searching for a segue into another topic.

"Traveling to the villages this time of year?" Cordelia asks. "Why, I can't think of any reason to do that."

My eyes drift to the fire and the sphere that rotates within it.

"Is that sphere rotating on its own?" I ask.

"Yes, well, kind of," she answers, pulled away from her thoughts. "The steam pushes it so it turns. It's called an aeolipile."

"Now, hold on," Torin interjects. His eyes slice into mine. "Why are you going to the villages this time of year?"

I glance at Clay. He looks unsurprised at the hole I've dug us into, smirking at me as though he expected it.

"We are looking into a problem we heard about at the outpost," Clay replies.

Cordelia's eyes widen and her voice trembles. "What kind of problem?"

"Well," I start, but I don't know how much I should say. Telling more people will complicate things.

"My sister is there," Torin explains.

Cordelia grabs a piece of bread for herself and begins to tear it apart anxiously.

Clay nods, and so I tell them the truth.

"There are reports of sickness downstream. They think the water is compromised."

"They think?" Cordelia's hand shoots to her mouth, a poor attempt to avoid shooting crumbs at us.

"They haven't checked?" Torin asks.

"That is what we are setting out to do," Clay explains.

"I should go with you," Torin volunteers, but Cordelia explodes, tossing her bread aside completely.

"Oh, no, young man, I will not have you gallivanting toward a plague. We have no clue what this is!" She waits for us to agree, but we could use the help. Besides, I really want Torin to come.

Clay, though, is happy to pipe up. "More people means more supplies. You'd need a way home, as we won't be returning with the evacuees."

"Then I will go purely to fetch my sister and the kids."

He seems adamant, and I hope that he's fighting not just for his sister or her kids but for me. It feels selfish, but my entire body is tense waiting for the answer to form.

"Your father will not agree to this, and neither will I," Cordelia argues.

Torin's face darkens. He stands to face her and I shrink into my seat as I watch.

"You really think Father won't agree to bring the family home? Or is it just you?"

Heavy steps thunder from beneath the floor. I watch Torin's face shift from anger to fear.

A man with ice-blue eyes storms through the door in the hall. His anger is writhing beneath calm waves.

"What is so important that you must raise your voices and disturb my work?" he asks. His voice is smooth as silk.

Cordelia sniffles, wiping away tears.

"I'm waiting," he says.

"Alira, Clay, this is my father, the city planner." Torin's voice begins to shake. "Father, we have received word that Brook is in danger. The village's water supply is compromised."

There is a long bout of silence as Torin's father thinks.

"I suppose it can't wait until spring?"

"Spring is close; we're just making sure no more time is wasted," Clay says. He turns to Torin. "You really don't need to come."

"He does." His father says, "He must retrieve his sister and her children. We must preserve our family."

He turns to Cordelia. "He has traveled this path many

times; you must trust that he is capable. If you continue to coddle him, he will never be ready to lead."

She buries her head into his chest, unable to hold back sobs.

"Cordelia, sweetheart, I don't have time for this. Please collect yourself and assist Torin with packing."

He breaks away from his wife and leaves without a good-bye. All the tension in the room leaves with him. Cordelia, having lost her battle, crumbles.

"Excuse me," she whispers, her voice rasping, before running away.

Clay stands up from his seat, his tone resigned. "I suppose there is no need to interview you since we'll be traveling together."

"Yes, I agree," Torin replies.

"We should be leaving." Clay walks over to grab his coat, but as I rise to follow, Torin blocks my path. He sets his warm hand on my shoulder, and when he speaks, I barely register what he says.

"It should comfort you to know I have traveled this road many times. I know all the little secrets it holds."

I grin uncontrollably. "I look forward to it!"

Clay hands me my coat and Torin steps away, watching us leave. It takes me a moment to realize that this is real. That I'm leaving and that Torin is coming with us.

SIONNACH

There's a fox on the mountain,
Ears tipped in frosted snow,
Descending from the clouded mist
Unto the land below.

He carries in his jowled grip
A silver salmon limp,
The vestiges of life and all perceived.

He trots on thirsted soil,
Each splash a beating heart,
Carving out a path toward the sea.

We call him Sionnach.
A river god is he.

—Dr. Carnelian

23

MOONLIGHT

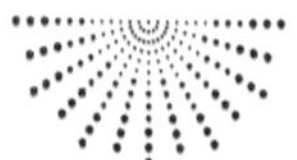

WHEN I WAKE, it's still dark out. I know, deep down, it's time to get up, but I detest the bitter cold that waits for me outside. Instead, I clutch the blankets closer, clinging to a waking dream.

A knock raps on the door to my room.

"Alira, breakfast is ready!" Kai's whisper is urgent and just loud enough to cut through my half dream, causing it to dissipate like the mist of Sionnan's Heart. He sounds excited that we're leaving, but I know that's not the case. He's simply excited for the adventure we are about to embark on. But I'm not.

The road is terrifying. So much so that I find myself praying to Persephone that our experiences have left us wiser and less likely to fall to ruin. Sionnan gets a prayer, too, on behalf of Torin and Ripley and the villagers who await us.

When I gaze out the window toward the gate, I find nothing to abate my concerns. No more than a sliver of the moon is visible tonight. We will be riding by lanternlight until sunrise.

Begrudgingly, I pull on my boots, grab the last of my

226

things, and walk downstairs, setting them down by the door. I feel numb and unwilling to move, but the smell of warmed bread pulls me into the kitchen.

Joe and Jane are already at the counter, drinking tea and munching on toast.

"She's off on another adventure," Joe says. When I sit, he pats my back so roughly that I jerk forward, almost tipping over my tea.

"Sorry," he says, patting a little lighter. "I almost envy you."

"Lies." Jane says, "No one envies you."

"I wish I could stay longer," I say, cupping the warm tea in my hands.

"You are both coming back, right?" Quill asks. Kai looks at me intently, hoping for me to say yes.

But it's Clay who answers him.

"Not until we've seen a few other houses," he says. He steps past Kai, roughing up his hair as he goes, and settles into the far chair next to Jane. He's wearing his leather jacket, the one that smells like woodsmoke.

"Clay . . ." Jane stumbles over her words. "I just wanted to say that I . . . Well, I thought you should know that . . ."

"All is forgiven," Clay says, biting into his toast as soon as Quill hands it to him.

"Really? You're not just saying that?"

Clay shrugs. "You lost more than I did."

Jane falls back into silence and we all eat without another word. The crunch of teeth on toast and the occasional sip of tea is all that stands between us and imminent goodbyes.

Tayn bursts in, abrupt and half-dressed. He grins at the sight of us.

"Ah! Barely awake but just in time. I hear my favorite insects are leaving already? No matter, I bring gifts for the wise wanderers."

He walks up to Clay first. He pulls a packet out of his pocket and hands it to him.

"Mixed spices from a faraway land. Use it on your next batch of jerky. It will change your life."

Clay stares at it with stoked curiosity, shaking it a little before stashing it in his pocket.

Tayn steps over to me next.

"Your house values pomegranates, correct?"

"Yes," I say. My eyes shift toward his robe, wondering if he's hiding one inside.

"And you have heard my stories of greenhouses that allow my ants to survive even the coldest temperatures."

"Of course."

"Well, I have a habit of making my services obsolete. First ants, and now this." He takes my hand and turns it wrist-side up, placing a small packet much like Clay's in my hand. I shake it and it rattles quietly. Curious, I open it and gasp.

"Pomegranate seeds!"

"That's not all." He says, "I managed to find my greenhouse blueprints. I'm sure someone handy enough could make do." He takes a finely folded piece of paper and hands it to me. I stare at it in awe.

"This is everything." I tell him, "If we can grow our own, then we won't have to worry about running low."

He grins wide. "I have one final gift for my favorite ant."

"All I got was spice," Clay complains.

"You have no idea the value of that spice." Tayn's grin turns into a scowl and his eyes slice into Clay, whose eyes grow wide at the merchant's sharp tone, but then Tayn laughs and the mood lightens, as though a dark cloud just skimmed over the sun.

"As I was saying. Your ring, dear, it's very pretty."

He motions to Mother's gift. The ring used to bother me.

Its cold surface rubbed up on my finger and snagged on every little thing. But now it feels like a piece of me.

"It saved my life," I remember.

"I have something even more beautiful for you, my dear." Out of his bag, Tayn pulls out a gemstone. It's the exact same shade of clouded yellow that clings to my ring. At its center is a dramatic black eye, with a line crossing the two bottom lashes, which makes it look like the letter "A."

He places it in my hand. It fits snugly in my palm, the perfect size for me to rub my thumb along the engraving. I trace it from one end of the eyelash to the other and back again.

"Oh my." Quill leans in.

"Are you proposing?" Joe jokes.

Tayn ignores him.

"That worry stone has been in my bag for some time now." Tayn explains, "Couldn't quite decide what it was meant for. It's the Eye of Horus, you know, except that cross in the middle isn't supposed to be there. Not sure why anyone would put it there except to give to someone, and by Ra, it's perfect for you."

"Oh, Tayn." I drag my eyes away from the gem to meet his gaze. "I never thought anything could look so beautiful."

"Do not forget to visit the island of Solaris."

While everyone finishes breakfast, I excuse myself to put

the gemstone in my bag by the door. I set it in the outside pocket with the pomegranate seeds. The satchel is far fuller than it used to be. It's got *The Queen's Acuity*, Carnelian's map, and Torin's book neatly tucked inside. I spot *The Binding* in Clay's bag and reach for it.

A soft knock on the door startles me. The knob turns and the door cracks open. Torin's deep blue eyes peek in.

"Am I too early?" he asks quietly. His jacket hangs from him unbuttoned, and the white, cotton shirt beneath is open slightly at the collar, revealing the curve of his collarbone. I lean in as if I am a fish on a hook. He smells of citrus and peppermint.

"Hi." I squeak.

He smiles that slight smile and my stomach flips. I stand up quickly as Clay walks in. Everyone follows him.

"Time to go." He says.

Torin holds the door open and I walk outside. The air is crisp and cool, but not as bad as I expected. The winter winds seem to have spared us, this morning.

The horse awaits us, already hitched to his cart. He seems anxious, shifting his weight from one leg to another. After emptying the cart of Joe and Jane's remaining treasures, all that's left is what Clay and I brought and several water jugs. Only two of them are filled in an effort to avoid tiring out the horse too soon.

I look to my right and see Kai looking at me expectantly. Everyone is, really. I kneel down to look him right in the eye.

"We'll be back, I promise."

He hugs me tightly for a long time. When he finally lets go, his eyes are rimmed in red. "I know why you're going," he says. A tear burns a path along his cheek. I wipe it away delicately with my sleeve.

"Then you know that this is a good thing."

He nods, his hands trembling. After a moment, his face

shifts into something stern and unbreakable. He wipes his eyes, turns to Clay, and bows.

Clay smiles quietly, bowing back, before climbing into the front of the cart. I sit between him and Torin, undeniably warm as they both press against me.

"Keep an eye out for evacuees," Clay instructs. "If all goes according to plan, they will be coming in droves."

Everyone nods in understanding, and so Clay takes up the reins, directing the horse across the footbridge, past the fountain shrine, and down to the gate where Bradán sits. Without uttering a word, he rises from his seat and calls upon the mule to pull the gate up for us to leave. The weight of his decision feels heavy, and may fall harshly on him later, but I tell myself he knows what he's doing. We all do.

The gate closes behind us, and we're on the road again.

There's a crowd forming outside the outpost. They walk across the path in front of us, coagulating at the riverbank. When we reach the stables, I notice makeshift beds. The horses have been released to the paddock, blankets fastened to each of their backs.

I can't imagine all these people are here for the Spring Festival. It's far too early for that.

"Hey!" Clara runs up to us from the front of the outpost. She wears a black cotton dress and is wrapped in a thick, gray wool shawl. Her hair falls in long and cascading waves, with two braids pulling hair away from the sides of her face. She waves us over to the paddock gate, where several carts are parked. Clay pulls past the end of the line and we all climb down.

Clara doesn't hesitate. She unhitches the horse fastidiously in four quick movements.

"You came at just the right time," she says, leading the horse to the paddock.

"The right time for what?" I ask.

"Ripley's funeral."

Clay looks like his heart's been ripped out of his chest. We're too late. Ripley is dead.

"Come with me." She leads us to the arch of the bridge before joining Lynn, who sits on a boulder near the riverbank with a lyre leaning against her shoulder. Next to her is a boat.

Ripley lies in it, wrapped loosely in linen cloth. He is peaceful and unmoving, as though in an endless slumber. Countless trinkets are laid about him: fox totems, fish totems, and a fishing pole. Hazelnuts are carved into the boat's side, and judging by their number, I gather they're meant to symbolize the number of years of life lived before death took him.

He was sixty-three.

Clara joins Lynn at the bank of the river, and a solemn hymn begins. Its melody is light and delicate, Lynn's hands float effortlessly up and down the instrument. The men begin to push the boat as Clara begins to sing. The notes are low and light, rising up and down like water lapping at the boat's edge. The hymn builds into a delicate trill at the climax before descending into a hopeful conclusion.

> *Watch the boat as it drifts by,*
> *Undeterred and featherlight.*
> *No more pain and no more cries.*
>
> *Bathed in your divine moonlight.*
>
> *Treat them like a long-lost friend*
> *Sent to you by Sionnan.*

I grip my worry stone tightly as tears stream down my face. Lynn's fingers continue to run over the lyre, playing the melody over and over. I commit her notes to memory. When her hands fall away, the hymn continues to echo through my head. Its cadence is burned into my worry stone one stroke at a time.

Together, we stand in crowded silence, watching Ripley's boat disappear beyond the horizon.

Clara returns to us after the ceremony.

"I'm happy you guys made it. I tried to send someone for you yesterday, but the guards have been turning everyone away."

"That's because they don't want the disease spreading to the city," Clay scoffs.

"What do you mean? I thought Alira told them it wasn't a disease?"

"They didn't believe me," I answer.

"But how can they not! Ripley was sure of it, and all the travelers since have confirmed it. The water south of here is running black as death now, tainted by water flowing in from the west. They say you can't find clean water past the tributary."

"I'm sorry." My chest tightens and I turn away, unable to meet Clara's eyes. If I had been able to convince the elders, then we could have seen Ripley one more time. The villages would have been evacuated already. Instead, the infirmary has become a revolving door of death.

"It's fine." Clara says, "We don't need the elders' permission."

"We?" Clay asks.

"I'm coming with you," she says.

"Can the horse handle that?" Torin asks.

"We have so many in the paddock," Clara says. "We can hitch on one of the orphaned ones."

"Orphaned?" I almost crumble right there, but Clay's hand grips my arm and squeezes it lightly. It feels like he's trying to absorb my pain. It's silly, and yet it works. I take a deep breath.

"Misty and Lynn might object. Marshall definitely will." Clara notes, "But I'm practically an adult now and this is important. Besides"—she looks out at the river, where Ripley's boat was—"the villages are going to need a medic."

"I see no problem with it," Clay says. "We're going to need all the help we can get."

2 4

RIVERBORN

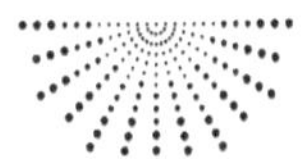

THERE ARE four chores split amongst us: horse care, water maintenance, food gathering, and fire duty. For the first night, fire is my chore.

Gathering wood is mindless work. I follow the deer paths carved into the forest, winding in and out of berry thickets. Hoofprints in soft loam mark where they've been. The space between strides indicates whether they were walking or running. Their scat burns through the stubborn snow that has yet to melt, and I find myself wandering deeper than needed in my search for deadfall and kindling.

A rustle of leaves pulls my eyes up from the ground. There's red in the brown brambles. At first, I mistake it for a fox, but looking closer, I almost drop my wood in surprise.

A little girl with red hair is nestled in the bushes. She stares at me with fallow eyes.

"Are you lost?" I ask, my words cracked in confusion.

She doesn't answer but remains frozen, like a deer. Her skin is pale, her feet are bare, and her baggy brown dress is two sizes too big.

"Do you need help?" I ask again, but there's no reply. A

breeze blows, sending chills up my spine. If the weather turns, she won't make it through the night.

I step forward and she bolts away, disappearing into the forest. I try to follow, but something grips me.

"Don't follow her," Torin says, his voice dripping midnight.

I turn and his eyes pierce through me like pins in moth wings. His irises are flecked with subtle fear. I look down at his hand tightly circling my wrist.

"What if she needs help?" I ask, looking for red hair in a forest of brown.

"Doesn't matter. Never follow children into the wilds."

His grip loosens and he leans down, taking up the wood I dropped.

"Let's go," he says, leading me back to the campground.

"Why was she there?" I ask, but he doesn't answer. His pace quickens until we break away from the tree line and into the light of the roadside meadows. There, he takes a moment to pause. His breathing is jagged. I've never seen him so rattled.

"Torin I—"

"Don't worry about it," he says. He starts walking again.

"Why was she there?"

No answer.

The campgrounds that lie between the outpost and the villages have all the basic necessities. When we return, Clara is tying up the horses to a post and Clay is sitting at the ashen firepit, waiting.

"What took so long?" he asks, eying me specifically.

"There's a problem," Torin says, dropping the wood into the pit. "You may not know this, but there have been more than a few disappearances in the last few years involving strange children."

"Oh, is this about the Flower Tribes?" Clara asks, "I heard

stories from some of the travelers. I thought they were just seeing ghosts."

"Me too," Torin says. "But Alira found a girl just now and almost fell for the trap."

"Trap?" Clay asks.

"Rumor has it that when you follow a child into the wilds, you give yourself to the Flower Tribes," Clara explains. "We don't know a lot about them except that they live in the wilds and, for some reason, they use children to lure people in." She pauses, glancing at me. "Especially women."

"Why would they do that?"

Torin shrugs. "I don't want to know. But let this be a warning to you and Clay. Do not follow children into the wilds. Ever."

Clay and I share a glance. Without Torin or Clara, would I have fallen victim to the Flower Tribes in the same way we almost fell victim to the cannibals? Would it really have been that easy?

"Let's get dinner started." Clay begins to sort the firewood and I kneel down to help.

"Are you okay?" he asks, taking wood from the pile as I sort it by size and thickness.

"Yeah. It's just . . ." I glance at Torin, sifting through the cart for food. "I had no clue I was in danger until Torin showed up. I would have followed her. I was worried she was lost."

Clay leans each stick against another, creating a tent of wood.

"I don't like him, but"—he grimaces—"it's not something I would have caught on to."

"Don't go blaming yourself again," I chide. "This one's on me."

"It's on no one." Clay says, "But that doesn't make me feel any better about it."

He sparks the fire with skill and precision that only a hunter could possess. It's annoying; fire is my chore, but he claims it saves time and everyone's hungry.

Not me.

The girl emptied me of all craving. I feel numb and moronic. When I left home, the only worry on my mind was vagabonds. Now the terrors are multiplying. I don't know what to expect anymore.

The fire grows quickly, licking up through holes between the logs and reaching for the pot above. The smell of fish stew is a mild comfort. We eat silently. As we do, both Torin and Clay keep a watchful eye on me. They don't trust me to keep myself safe.

It's a grievous pain.

I thank the Earth Queen when they retire early, leaving me and Clara to ourselves. I feed the fire as she watches the horses graze, and when she pulls out her lyre, I watch her play. And as she plucks each string, I find my eyes drawn to the river. I notice something bobbing downstream.

A boat, dark and dreary.

Every day we spend on the road is another boat out to sea. They always float by when the moon is high, long after the sun is swallowed by the horizon.

Tonight, we wait for boat number four.

Clara is the most solemn, sitting by the fire with her eyes fixed on the river. Every boat that passes has a name. She knows them by the number of hazelnuts carved into their wooden hulls.

I ache to make her happier. The bright sun that shone within her gets darker each night, fading behind blackened storm clouds. I move to sit next to her just as Torin swoops into the empty seat beside me.

"I'm sorry about the other day," he says. His face is painted in dusk and firelight. He smells of peppermint, reeling me in.

"No, I should have known better," I admit.

"That's not true." His eyes take on a warm glow, matching the flames that crackle like crumpled paper. "I think it shows how much of a good person you are." He says, "You want to help people."

"Yeah, well, clearly that's not always a good thing."

"I think it's a strength, not a weakness." His hand brushes against my back, settling on my hip.

It feels like a lightning strike.

"Um . . ." I try to find something, anything, to take my mind off his hands burning through the cloth of my shirt. "Can I ask you something?"

He smiles. "Of course."

"Why does your sister live in the villages?" I ask.

His brow furrows and his hand twitches slightly. When he speaks, his words are steeped in poison. "My sister revoked her birthright."

"Her birthright?"

"My father was grooming her to be the next city planner, but then she went and married a lumberjack."

"What does that matter?"

"It means that her children aren't riverborn."

"Oh."

"Not yet, at least. I suspect my parents allowed me to fetch her to convince her to remarry."

"What?"

"Her husband died two years ago. She's a widow. If they can convince her to remarry, convince her to have more kids, then they won't have to rely on me."

"Is that something you want?" I ask.

"It doesn't matter what I want," He admits, his eyes staring deep into the blazing fire. "My path is already charted. I'm swimming blind, but that doesn't remove expectations."

I shrink away uncomfortably. He doesn't seem to notice. In fact, he moves in closer until I'm left sitting on the edge of my seat.

"Torin!" a voice calls, rescuing me.

I break away from Torin's loose grip on my waist and see Clay.

"Can you help me with this?" he asks, holding a pole in his hands. "I don't think I'm doing it right."

Clay winks at me and I relax.

Torin glances at Clara, whose eyes are still fixed on the river, and sighs. "I suppose so."

He walks away, leaving the entire log for me to sit on. He took up so much space. I breathe deep, but it catches in my throat.

I can't be with Torin, I realize.

I can't fall for someone who can never be with me. I can't build a foundation on *nothing*.

Somehow, this feels worse than grieving.

I glance at Clara and sit up straight. I'm being selfish. There are more important things.

I walk around the fire and take a seat next to her. Her entire body is rigid, as though carved from ice. I can't even see her breathe.

"Clara?"

"Hmm?"

"I was wondering if you could teach me the funeral hymn."

Her eyes spark, latching on to mine. "You play?"

I nod and she grins.

"Wait here, I'll get the lyre." She walks away.

Her steps are lighter than they've been in days. I can't say I feel the same.

When I look at Torin, I feel like deadweight.

~

"We are at the midpoint of the journey," Torin announces at breakfast. "We've made good time."

Maybe in his mind, but six whole days have felt like an eternity to me.

"The weather has been favorable, but the clouds indicate that it will start snowing again sometime today. We should aim to reach this tributary before dinner." He points to a section of the map where the stream forks.

I only take a glance, avoiding his gaze before returning to my meal.

Every time he speaks, it burns. Every time he looks at me, it hurts. The feeling of longing I get is stifling and we're only halfway there.

"Drink all the water you can before we get there. Once we refill, we will want to restrict our use of it to conserve."

"And where exactly will we be refilling?" Clay asks.

"Don't worry, there will be a clean source right before the tributary."

Torin rolls his sleeves up and turns back to the horses, giving them a quick rubdown before we continue on. I stayed up all night looking after the horses. Now it's his chore. With his eyes on them, I allow myself to watch.

His hand glides over their hindquarters, double-checking each of their fastenings. Every movement is calculated and certain.

Then his eyes catch mine and he smirks.

Heat rises to my cheeks. I get up abruptly, grab the jug from the back of the cart, and drink as much as I can. I hand it to Clay, who gives it to Clara, followed by Torin. It circles us like a fish trapped in a well, swimming restlessly.

I climb into the back. Torin will be at the head of the cart today, and I just can't let myself be near him.

Clara climbs in behind me, settling between two jugs. She grabs a blanket and takes up *The Queen's Acuity*, thumbing through the section on botanicals. I take a blanket for myself, feeling tired after watching the horses all night, but sleep is elusive. My heart is bursting with each beat. I want to tell Clara what I'm feeling, but I shouldn't. It's far too selfish.

Here we are, racing against the clock to get to the villages, and I'm torturing myself over a *boy*.

As the cart lurches along, I take out Clara's lyre, practicing the funeral hymn over and over. Clara hums along to the tune.

It's muscle memory now. I don't have to think about it. It takes the place of my worry stone, pulling my hands over the strings and giving my head the space it needs to think.

I wonder, what would Gemma do?

I draw her heart-shaped face in my mind. Her dress is a soft peach pink. Her eyes are locked on me, waiting for me to speak.

There's a boy, I tell her. Her eyes light up with excitement.

A boy! Tell me more.

He gave me a tour of the city. He showed me how to fish. He likes me . . . I think.

That's adorable! Are you dating?

Well, that's just it. His family is purist. Pursuing him would be fruitless.

You want my opinion?

Yes. Obviously.

I think you need to relax and have some fun.

Have fun? People are dying, Gemma!

You're moving as fast as you can, right? The horses can't

walk through the night. You'll have plenty of time to mope when you get there. Until then, you might as well enjoy the ride.

I don't even know what that means. Enjoy the ride?

My hands scrape along the kitstring as the cart lurches to a stop, pulling me away from my reverie. I'm lying on my side, the lyre pressed against my cheek. I've fallen asleep. Clara sits up, rubbing her eyes.

"I don't think we stopped for lunch," she says, her voice drowsy.

It's possible the boys ate what little food they had up front, figuring we would sift through the jars back here for ourselves. But that begs the question:

"Then where are we now?"

I pull the fabric to the side and see white snow drifting down. To the west, the sun skims over the tops of the trees. It's late. We definitely missed lunch. It's a good thing, because when I look down, my stomach drops.

BLACK WATER

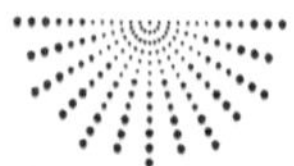

Crisp mountain water roars beneath a wooden bridge just ahead, only to crash into a wave of dark, opaque liquid. The air around us is steeped with the stench of rotten fish. It stings my sinuses. I pull the sleeve of my shirt up to my nose in a weak attempt to block it.

"Turns out *black water* wasn't an exaggeration," Clay says. His eyes follow the source of it. It courses down to the river from a hill to our right, just beyond the bridge, and disappears behind a snarling thicket of trees.

"I really hoped it was." Clara plugs her nose.

"We should set up camp here for the night," Torin instructs. I spot Clay rolling his eyes. He doesn't like Torin taking the lead. He doesn't seem to like him at all. But we all agreed that he was the best equipped to guide us.

"Here, everyone should take a drink. Afterward, we can settle in. Clay, you go find wood. Clara, don't set any traps. No animal has a poor enough sense to wander around these parts. Look for chickweed and wild onion, instead."

As we each take a drink, Clara starts to search along the roadside for fresh greens.

"Don't bother." Torin redirects her. "Nothing that grows this close is going to be healthy." He points out past the fields on the other side of the road. "You should try there instead. It's farther, but we'll be guaranteed to find something. Good for wood, too. The thicket over here is a bit too knotted with thorns."

Clara doesn't question it, walking off toward in the direction of the fields. Clay follows her lead, handing me the emptied water jug before walking away.

I turn to Torin, "So where do we fill this?"

He smiles. "Follow me."

He leads me across the bridge, ignoring the overgrown path that parallels the Travelers' Road. Instead, he treks up the hill and into the thicket.

"Torin, where are we going?"

Black water rushes past, circumventing large rocks in the riverbed. Tall pines tower over us, darkening what little sunlight we have left.

"Trust me," he says. His voice is calm and determined.

Up past the rocks, crooked trees and brambles grow wildly. We duck and sidle to avoid thorns. They become so thick that I want to turn back, but the villagers need this water. Every jug matters.

Torin sees my struggle and makes a path for me through the last of it. When I pass through the gate of thorns, my eyes widen at the sight before me.

"Oh, wow."

"I've been wanting to show you this. It's a well-kept secret."

The river forks again. This time, the water that crashes into the river is bright and clear. I stoop down, letting the clean water of a babbling brook rush over my hands, and gaze up at the waterfall off to our right.

I never would have considered looking up the polluted

river for clean water, but it seems the force of the waterfall prevents the pollution from backing up into the glistening pool below. I can only imagine how long this waterfall has been working to dilute the black waters.

"This water is as close to the source as it gets. I was sure it would be untainted. I'm happy I was right." Torin reaches out, taking my hand.

We stumble across the mass of rocks that line the edge of the waterfall. I slip on the moss more than once, almost falling into frigid waters, but Torin quickly scoops me up. The movement is so fast I find myself breathless. Each moment alone with him makes me more and more feverish. I realize this is the first time we've been truly alone since we went fishing in Neró.

So much has happened since then, and even though I've learned that a relationship with him is impossible, I still find myself drawn to him. I've never felt this strongly about anyone before.

We reach the waterfall quickly, climbing carefully up the rocks and into the darkness that lies behind it. The last light of dusk streaks in through a dim and shallow cave.

"This is amazing." The waterfall is so loud it drowns me out as Torin pulls me deeper into darkness. He stops abruptly. Before I can react, his hands are on my waist.

"Alira." Torin's voice is low and deep, a mere vibration against the sound of falling water. He leans into me, whispering in my ear.

"Do you want this?"

He pulls back, cupping my chin so that I cannot avert my eyes. The blue that glimmers in his irises keeps me tongue-tied.

Do you want this?

I don't know.

Is that bad? Shouldn't I know? Why don't I know?

Suddenly, the decision is being made for me.

Torin nudges me backward, pinning me up against the rock wall. Jagged stone digs into my back.

Everything in me screams to move, but I don't. I can't. I'm caught between want and fear and nothing makes sense. This is what Gemma was talking about. This is what I want. I want him and he wants me, and that's something I can't let go of easily.

He leans in, pressing his lips softly against my neck. A rush of satisfaction flows over me, something I've never felt before. It's so alien, so undeniably strong and sudden that I can't help but whimper. In return, his grip tightens. His lips drift up to the sensitive skin below my jaw, breathing softly as his lips trail up near my ear.

"I've waited so long."

"Torin," I whisper breathlessly.

"Shhh." He quiets me with his lips.

But all I can focus on are his hands. Even as my lips are pressed against his, his hands feel hotter and hotter as they wander down to my hips.

Panic bursts through me.

What am I doing?

I don't want this. I want him, sure, but I don't want things to go this quickly. I don't want to do this only for him to leave when everything is said and done.

But I can't move. He has a steady hold on me, his hands drifting ever farther.

My anxieties begin to flutter through my head. The sun is getting lower, the jug is not yet full, and Clay will be wondering about me.

"Clay," I gasp.

Torin freezes against me and I panic.

"I'm worried about him," I clarify, "I mean, I'm worried he's—"

"I should have known." He backs away. "I *did* know. But I convinced myself otherwise. Now, I feel a fool."

I try to reach for him, "Let me explain."

He grabs my hand, pulling it toward him with such force that I feel confused. When I gaze into his eyes, they are blackwater.

He pulls at my ring, ripping it off my finger and flinging it behind him.

"I hate that ring." His voice roars louder than the waterfall. "I hate all the time I wasted trying to catch you. It was all a waste. You're a *waste*." He walks away, taking up the empty jug from the ground and leaving me in the darkness of the cave.

I feel like I'm waking from a dream, trying to pull the memory of what happened out of nothingness.

A sliver of clarity pulls me back into action. I fall to my knees, feeling around in the darkness of the cave for my ring. Water pounds through my ears. My chest tightens and I can't breathe. I feel like I'm scrambling beneath the cart next to the cannibal cabin again.

I want to run and apologize for hurting him, beg him to help me find the ring. When I peer out from the cave, he's gone.

Light has faded into darkness. I'm running out of time. This isn't what I wanted. I feel broken.

My knees buckle and my arms give out. I lie down on the cave floor curled into a ball. Sobs escape in broken gasps and my whole body shakes. The feeling of satisfaction that coursed through me moments ago has drained out in a pool around me. I wish I could drown in it.

How could I be so stupid?

The seconds that pass feel like hours, until time itself breaks into shards of obsidian shadow.

I hurt Torin, but that ring is everything. I can't go on without it.

I get on my hands and knees and focus, forcing my eyes to adapt to darkness. A shallow pool at the entrance of the cave reflects the rising moon. At its edge is a faint shimmer. I crawl toward it.

It's ice cold, but it's there. It's not lost. I slip it on and exit the cave, rushing over the snow-dusted rocks. Each time I fall, it's a stark reminder that Torin's not there to catch me.

My chest tightens and my teeth grind as guilt, fear, and anguish pull at me. Every thorn that catches me is a piece of my heart torn, but when I feel my ring on my finger, I push on.

There are voices up ahead. A quiet argument. I come out of the thicket and find our cart surrounded by men on horseback.

"You say you need to evacuate the villagers, but you have no elders' decree." A man on a chestnut-colored horse towers over Clay and Torin.

"The elders wanted to leave the villages to govern themselves." Clay explains. The calm in his voice doesn't fool me. He's scared.

"And who are you to defy them?" another man chides. He sits upon a gray horse dappled with white spots. A third man, dark and brooding, sits away from them, watching carefully. His horse is black and utterly intimidating.

I stumble closer, crossing the bridge, where Clara sits anxiously with a basket of chickweed and mushrooms on her lap.

"What's happening?" I ask. My voice is gritty.

"Clay saw them approach the cart on our way back. They didn't have time to steal anything, so now they're trying to intimidate us." Clay catches my eye, nudging his head toward a space next to Clara. It's a silent order to sit still.

I don't comply.

"What's in it for us if we let you go?" the man on the gray horse asks.

"You'll be considered a decent human being," Torin chides.

"Shut up, boy." The man pulls his horse close and Torin turns white as snow. Him, Clay, Clara, they're all frozen in fear. But me? I'm just tired.

I'm tired of obstacles. I'm tired of being scared. I'm tired of feeling helpless and at the mercy of strangers. People are dying and I'm standing here, waiting to be allowed to go and help them.

"Oh, looky here." The man on the chestnut horse has been rifling through our cart. He pulls out a box.

Spools.

"Haven't seen one of these in a while. Could be worth something."

"We need those," Clay says. It sounds desperate, not something I ever expected from him. If he's scared, I should be, too. But I'm not. If anything, I'm angry.

"The only people who need these are the dangerous kind. If you have them, you're dangerous," the man figures. He walks over to his horse, aiming to dump the spools into a saddle bag.

"Hey!" I call out from the bridge, taking a step toward them. I sidestep Clara's hands as she tries to pull me back down.

"Alira!" she cries.

But I don't care. These men are nothing to me. They act all tough, but they're nothing.

They're tamer than they look, Mother had said.

"I don't care who you are, or what you want. People are dying, unable to leave their homes. They're sick and they need our help. If your justification for stealing our shit is that we're lying, then I highly suggest you realign your thinking and fuck off."

Clay looks at me like I'm insane. It's only after I run my mouth that I notice the long curving blades sitting at the vagabonds' sides. I take a deep breath, realizing the hole I've dug.

It's just one mistake after another for me. First the little girl, then Torin, now this. I glance at Clara, wondering if sitting back down is an option, but when I turn back around, the man on the gray horse is in front of me. He hops down and waves his lantern perilously close to my face.

"You look familiar. Alira, was it?"

I have no energy to flinch as the heat flickers closer to my skin.

"Blue eyes and hair like honey. Quite the pup, wouldn't you agree, Peri?" He turns to the man on the black horse, swinging the lantern around with him. It offers a brief reprieve from the heat.

The voice that responds is smooth as river stone.

"Would explain the spools."

The light of the lantern matches his hair, and his figure is far slighter than I realized. The man on the black horse, Peri, is a woman, and their leader.

I try not to let the shock of it change anything. Instead, I hold her stare as she studies me.

Time stands still.

Finally, I sense a subtle shift, and she speaks.

"Put the spools back, Cal."

Cal begrudgingly complies, and the man who questions me hops back onto his horse.

Peri turns to Clay.

"Don't be leaving your things unattended again."

With that, she spurs her dark horse forward. It surges like

the river into the night. The other vagabonds follow closely behind.

"What is wrong with you?" Torin yells, but I walk to the cart, ignoring him. I check the spools to make sure they're not scratched.

"Are you okay?" Clara comes up beside me, lays a hand on my shoulder, but I flinch away. Her hand falls, her eyes heavy with concern.

"I'm going to bed." I climb into the cart before they can see the tears return, wrapping myself tightly in blankets and curling up into a ball in the corner. The soft crackling of the fire and the warm glow that seeps through the cloth of the cart let me know that, for now, we're safe.

But it doesn't make me feel good. Nothing does. I feel like a shell.

Four more days.

26

PROFIT

CLAY

Something happened between Torin and Alira. I'm sure of it.

Ever since that night with the vagabonds, Alira's been a ghost of a person and Torin acts like she doesn't exist. He used to offer to help her up onto the cart, or talk endlessly about his childhood trips to and from the villages. Now he barely utters a word.

I watch Alira warily as I help Clara forage. She's supposed to be on wood duty, but she's meandering, pausing every once in a while to gaze up through the canopy of trees rather than toward the sticks at her feet.

"The vagabonds got really up in her space," Clara points out, noticing me watching her.

"I guess."

They said something about her hair and her eyes, how she looked like a puppy, and how somehow that explained the spools. It made no sense.

Clara tries to ease my mind.

"We still don't know what to expect once we get to the

village. That tributary was a sobering sight. I think she's just overwhelmed."

I've seen Alira overwhelmed, tugging at her shirtsleeves, biting her lip, her eyes glazing over as she worries over problems she can't solve. Now she has her worry stone, but she hasn't touched it.

This isn't Alira overwhelmed. I've never seen this before.

Torin did something to her, and I'll never forgive him for it.

I leave Clara to her work and walk over to Alira. She's looking at the ground now, though still ignoring the sticks. She stoops over a rock, examining the small bugs hiding beneath its wet underside.

"Hey." I almost put my hand on her shoulder but think better of it.

"Hmm?" She begins walking again, spinning a single stick between her thumb and forefinger.

"What's on your mind?" I pick up a stick that she walks past. Then another, and another.

"Just thinking." Her words are crystalline shards, a pause between each one, and her voice is distant, as if lost in space or time.

"Alira, did something happen that I should know about?"

She turns to me in a brief moment of lucidity. A slight smile curves her lips, and she looks at me softly as if *I'm* the fragile one.

"I'm fine, Clay."

After that, she heads for the meadows and I follow at a distance. Torin is sitting at the edge of the cart, his eyes fixed on the horses. He won't let them out of his sight after last time.

She approaches him.

"Torin?" She says the name as a question.

"I'm busy," he says.

I stay off to the side and break down sticks for the fire, convincing myself it's none of my business, but it is. I promised Flint I would protect her and so far I've failed miserably.

"I just wanted to—"

"Waste my time?" he asks.

I drop the remaining sticks and start walking over, but I'm too late to intervene.

"Never mind." Alira brushes past me looking somber and defeated and—it's clear to me now—heartbroken.

We all eat breakfast in silence and continue on the journey without a word. Torin and Clara sit in the front and I take the back, trying my hardest not to interrogate Alira. Instead, I flip through *The Goddess Binding* as she plays the funeral hymn over and over again.

I knew Torin would hurt her somehow. I could see how she looked at him. She had never looked at anyone like that before. Not that I could tell.

I know I can't protect her from everything, but guilt still digs at me. I keep wavering between minding my own business and giving Torin the punch in the nose he deserves.

"Is that a merchant?"

Clara's voice breaks me out of my spiraling thoughts. I swipe at the cloth that separates me and Alira from the front of the cart.

Sure enough, a merchant stands on the side of the road beside a cart pulled by two palomino horses. His hair, glinting in the sunlight, is blindingly white, though he looks no older than Tayn. He smiles broadly at the sight of us. Behind him, a casket floats downstream. It feels like an omen.

"Greetings, young travelers. Allow me to introduce myself. I am Profit, the only merchant on this side of the river."

"Clearly." Torin snickers. The merchant continues, undeterred.

"The path you are on is dark and dreary, riddled with disease. Allow me to illuminate your day with these fine curatives." He pulls open one side of his wool coat and reveals a soft underlying fabric pocketed with several fine glass bottles, then takes one out and swirls it in his hand for us to see.

"This water replacement is sure to keep you healthy on your journey!"

Our cart inches forward, the horses restless.

"Alas, if that does not interest you, I also have these enhanced water filters!" He sinks his arm into his cart and pulls out a bulky contraption. Alira's side brushes against me as she tries to take a look, but Clara isn't interested.

"You can't go selling things claiming they're cures without being more specific. Where are you from, anyway?"

Alira hops out of the cart and stretches, yawning.

"You know where I'm from. Why, you can see it on my skin," he replies.

"What's in it for you, then? Travelers like us have nothing to offer you that is worth the price of that."

Profit smiles wryly. "No payment is required. If I do the work I have been given, I will receive all the payment I require in the form of coins."

"Coins?" I erupt into laughter. "You can't be serious."

"Who is giving you coins for this and why?" Clara asks, digging deeper. Alira moves closer, curious, peeking into the cart behind him and perusing his wares.

"To assist those affected by the product of their comforts, the House of the Soul Keeper has purchased my help."

We all freeze. Even Alira falters as she rummages through the merchant's wares.

We all knew that the sickness plaguing the southern villages was waterborne and that the source is upstream of the tributary, but this proves that another house is causing it. And now it's clear that they aren't just causing it. They're aware of it.

"You mean to tell me you work for a house that is willing to pollute these waters and then sell a 'cure'?" Clara holds up her fingers in the form of quotation marks, mocking him.

"Try it out and let me know what you think!" he goads us.

"No way," Clara scoffs. "That's how people die—trusting terrible people like you with their lives."

Alira returns to the cart, seemingly unsatisfied with the merchant's inventory. Torin picks up the reins as soon as she's settled in.

"Move aside, merchant; your goods are worthless to us," he says.

"Very well, travelers. Till we meet again."

The cart lurches forward and I feel sick. I sincerely hope I never see that man again.

Clara whips open the divider cloth, addressing me and Alira.

"What a terrible salesman!" she fumes.

"Yeah." Alira smiles, her eyes devious. "He didn't even see me take this."

Clara's eyes widen as Alira hands her an elixir.

"How did you manage it?" Clara asks, awe clear on her face.

"In my blood, I guess." A frown tugs at her soft pink lips. "I wish I could have grabbed that water filter, too."

"Vagabond blood." Torin sneers. "Figures."

It takes every muscle in my body not to lurch through Alira and Clara and toss him into the black waters.

"Okay, let's see what kind of scam they're trying to sell us." Clara opens the bottle and sniffs it gently. "Weird. It doesn't smell like anything specific." Then she drops a small amount onto her fingertip and sets it on her tongue. "You've got to be kidding me." She groans, "This is just plain water!"

She inspects the faded green glass closely and I feel my stomach drop. If this house is working closely with the House of the Illuminator, then we have bigger problems than we thought.

~

As we continue on, the energy in the cart shifts. Torin and Clara take their turn riding in the back, but the closer we get to the villages, the more restless they seem to be. Alira sits quietly beside me, scanning the horizon. She's stoic and determined. She knows what's coming, and she's ready to face it.

The time we spent in Neró was necessary, but seeing the river as black as it is worries me. So much time has slipped out from under us. Daffodil clumps line the road, crocuses and hyacinths sprout between them. and snowdrops are already in full bloom. We're moving as fast as we can, but will it be fast enough?

A dog barks in the distance, then two. Torin opens the fabric of the cart.

"It's just around this bend," he says.

Sure enough, the tree line recedes, revealing a wooden fence carved with foxes and fish. Beyond it, thatched roofs stretch out as far as I can see.

A man stands at the gate. His eyes are narrowed and his frown draws a deep crease into his brow. I pull the cart up to him, but he doesn't seem happy to see us at all.

"I don't know how you all got here," he says, "but we don't have any resources to spare. The river only gets worse from here. I advise you to turn back immediately."

"Yeah, well, I advise you to evacuate." Alira hops down from the cart and takes two jugs of water with her, ignoring the man completely as she begins to walk into the village. I can't help but smile at her snarky behavior. It's a welcome change from the past few days.

"Is she serious?" he asks. When I nod, he smiles, but it's brief.

"Wouldn't happen to be healers, too, would you?"

Clara hops out of the cart and his eyebrow hitches in surprise. She holds out her hand in greeting and he shakes it firmly.

"Clara. Healer. I'm ready to help those in need."

His eyes harden. "We don't need you to heal. We need you to help prepare the dead."

Silence washes over us. Torin, who was busy unloading two jugs from the cart, becomes completely rigid.

How bad has it gotten?

The guard's stern eyes are sunken and shadowed, with sharp cheekbones that remind me of Ripley.

"Are you sick?" I ask.

"No." He replies, "We switched to water stores weeks ago, but we're dangerously low, and . . ." He spares a glance behind him. "Food is scarce."

"Where's Brook?" Torin asks.

The man studies him as if trying to recognize him.

"You're her . . . brother, right?"

"Yes, where is she?" His voice rises, sharp with anguish.

"She's fine. She's at her house with the boys."

Torin rushes past him, making a beeline into the village.

"We've brought supplies to be split amongst the villagers." I explain, "If we can get people organized into a caravan, they should be able to make it to the tributary. The water is clean past that point. For now, I need you to inform the elders that it's time to leave."

"Also," Clara adds, holding up the glass vial, "a merchant is trying to sell these to travelers, claiming it's a cure. He is not a medic and should be ignored. Please inform evacuees as they leave."

The guard nods. I hand him a jug of water and he takes several long gulps before handing it back to me and walking away. People begin to peek out of their homes, wondering why their guard is leaving his post.

Clara and I split up. She goes to find boats and I go to park the cart at the stables on the side of the road opposite the river's edge. They're terrifyingly empty, with only a few horses healthy enough to peer out at me. The rest lie in dirty straw, too weak to get up. It's only when I pour a jug of clean water into all their buckets that they conjure up the strength to stand, sniff, and drink.

Once the cart is secured, I search for Alira.

27

SOUTHERN VILLAGES

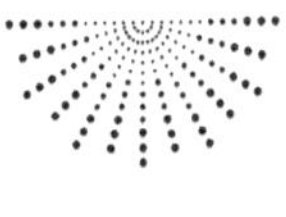

CLAY

I WALK along the road of the village, watching the evacuation unfold. It's clear that Alira has already torn through here. The doors are wide open as villagers rush in and out, gathering their belongings on the side of the road. Blankets and books and fishing poles pile up against the fences that line each garden. One man even takes the fence down, folding up the netting that stretches between wooden posts and setting it aside. Chickens wander out from within. Their feathers are dirtied, their beaks void of color. The man makes no effort to catch them.

The houses begin to spread out as I continue on. I finally spot Alira near a waterwheel that no longer spins. Her two jugs have dwindled to one. She walks down a straw path to the next house and knocks on the wooden door.

"Please pack your belongings; a caravan is forming at the gate and will leave at sundown," she offers them water, allowing each a small sip before moving on. Picking up my pace, I finally catch up to her.

"Let me hold your jug for you," I offer.

"No, I need to do this myself," she says.

We should branch out, divide and conquer, but just as I consider moving on, she pauses and I almost smash into her.

There's a house with a door that's already wide open. Torin stands inside, towering over a woman who holds her head in her hands. His sister, I presume.

I try to tug Alira along, but she won't budge. Instead, she inches closer.

"I was worried sick thinking no one would come for us," Brook sniffles. "The boys are fine, but the horse died early on and traveling with the kids in winter was out of the question." A small boy with dark brown hair stands near her, wrapping his arms around her in a hug. His shirt hangs loosely from his shoulders.

Torin is still rigid. "We must go now. I will take what I can from the cart for us. A few jugs, some food, whatever you want."

A few jugs?

Alira spins around, hands me her jug, and rushes away. I run to follow her.

"I cannot *believe* he is using the water for them alone. It needs to be shared," She fumes. She stops at the cart and jumps in for two more jugs. She takes hers back from me and hands over two more. They're heavy. I can't imagine how she was able to march around with these before.

"Go and deliver this water to anyone but Torin," Alira orders. Her eyes are shards of ice. She hops off the cart and begins to walk away, but I need answers.

"What happened between you two?"

"Later. This needs to be delivered now."

"Hey!" Torin calls. He walks with haste.

Alira veers left and Torin has to decide. Me, or her.

He scowls. "Never mind. Just get out of my way."

He passes me, digging into the cart for more jugs. "Where did all the water go?"

I saunter up to him, doing my best not to show the jugs' weight. "Alira and I have been doling it out. What remains will be split amongst the caravan."

"Was this Alira's idea?"

"What?" I play dumb.

He hisses in reply, "Brook needs water."

"Didn't you already give her some?"

"Give me the water." Torin holds his hand out. I smile, filling the space between us. He's tall, but spindly. More so than Flint. While he was sitting by the fountain drawing, I was carrying game through the woods, splitting logs, and helping in the fields. He's weak next to me.

"Oh, you want this jug?" I ask, shoving it into his ribs. He staggers back into the cart, wheezing out air. "Or maybe this one? It feels like it has a bit more water in it." I pull the jug out and replace it with the other. He gasps at the weight of it.

I lean in. My voice is a primal growl. "I don't know what happened between you and Alira. I don't want to. If you don't get your head out of your arse and help, you'll have something worse than bruised ribs."

I jam the jug in a bit more and he curls into himself, falling to the ground.

"Okay," he croaks.

"Good."

I walk away.

As the sun lowers toward the horizon, a line of evacuees begins to form. Each family has a cart and one horse. It's all they can afford.

The elders, huddled in a trio at the back of the line, have no horse at all. They've refused every offer of a ride in favor of traveling together.

The youngest elder carries a deerskin tent and a blanket. The middle elder, an older woman, carries a small tin of dried meats and a fishing pole. The eldest, a grizzled man with a square jaw and gray eyes, reminds me of Ripley.

There's no way they'll make it on foot.

"Alira."

She turns to me, her eyes bright.

"I saw an extra cart behind the stable. Hitch the orphan to it. "

She nods and gets to work, unhitching the outpost horse and leading him away. I approach the elders, offering my hand in greeting. They take it eagerly. Each one shakes it three times.

"We can't thank you enough." The youngest says, "We tried our best with what we had, but the odds were stacked against us. If it weren't for you. . ."

Alira guides the horse and cart to them and their eyes grow wide.

"That's old Ripley's horse," the gray haired man says. "Has he passed on, then?"

My heart drops like a rock. My eyes begin to blur and when I try to answer, my throat feels sewn shut.

Alira answers for us. "Yes. If it weren't for Ripley, we wouldn't have known to come."

The woman nods. "We will take good care of this one."

We return to our cart and it seems like all our hard work is done. Relieved, I take one last look at our supplies.

"Wait. This isn't right." I dig around in confusion. Our belongings are covered by the deerskin tents and a few blankets remain, but the last jug and the food I had saved for our trip home is gone.

I look out at the caravan line, which steadily shrinks as villagers take their rations and head outside the village walls. Torin is up next. He managed to find a haggard-looking mare and a cart with fabric torn in three different places. In the back, Brook's sons eat venison jerky and pickled eggs. What's more: Two jugs sit beside them.

My steps are slow and deliberate. Anger vibrates up through my legs, emanating out from my chest and reaching all the way to my hands, which curl into tight balls of tendon and bone.

"Yes, there are four of us," Torin says to the guard.

"So four shares of rations." The guard takes jars out of the box we gave him, handing Torin *more* food.

"Hold on," I shout. My voice thunders over the crowded line, causing the villagers to whip their heads around in confusion.

Torin hops into the cart, and takes up the reins but I run around to the front of the horse and block the way.

"He stole our food." I explain, "We don't have enough to get to the tributary, much less get back home."

The guard grabs the reins where they attach to the horse harness and unlatches them in one swift movement, taking full control of the horse.

"This is absurd." Torin says, "We have just enough to get by ourselves."

"Torin, I warned you," I say.

"Warned me?" He gives up trying to escape. He hops out of the cart to face me, wincing when he hits the ground. "You act like you're all tough, but I don't care. My family is more important than any of this." He gestures around him.

"Wait." Brook stares at her brother in disbelief. "You stole their food? They're your friends!"

"Hardly."

"I can't believe you!" She gets out of the cart and walks to the back.

"Elbio, could you be a dear and hand me that box of food there? And the jug, too. Thank you, sweetheart." She whispers some more instructions before returning from the back.

She hands the food to me, her eyes shadowed with exhaustion.

"I'm so sorry," she says.

"What are you doing?" Torin yells, his face beet red.

"You told us this food was for us," she hisses, "but you aren't just stealing from the people saving us, you're stealing from my village, too. These people are my family. They have done everything to help me. But you . . . you're no better than father. In fact, you might be worse. I don't want to be anywhere near you. I'll walk if I have to."

The villagers lined up behind them begin to catch wind of what's happening.

"Brook, come in our cart," a woman calls. "We have plenty of room."

"No, that's ridiculous,"a man shouts. "She should take the cart for herself!"

"Yeah," another villager calls, "he's a selfish thorn in our side. We don't need him!"

More villagers join in on the frenzied chaos. The guard has to yell to calm them down.

"Now, now, let's handle this appropriately," he says. "Are there any villagers willing to take Torin into a cart with them?"

I grin at the silence.

"Very well," the guard replies. "You'll ride in with me."

"You? Why?" Torin asks.

"Someone needs to report your misdeeds to the elders in Neró." He smirks.

Villagers surround the cart, ordering Torin to climb down. He does, slowly, unwillingly, and every second is bliss. I look back toward Alira to see her reaction. Her brows are tightly knit. She grips the side of our cart so hard that her knuckles are white. But when her gaze shifts to me, she relaxes, though only slightly.

For the rest of the evacuation, Torin sits off to the side, his back up against the stables, watching the sun lower over the horizon with glazed eyes.

When the last cart has left the village, Alira and I join Clara by the river. There are a few boats here, what few she could find. Some hold two or even three deceased, with nothing but a thin linen cloth between them. It feels so wrong, and yet it's the best she can do.

Alira takes Clara's lyre from the cart and sets it down near a stump by the bank of the river. She leans the lyre against her shoulder and begins to play the funeral hymn.

Alira has spent almost every night practicing this song. I thought it was merely out of curiosity. Alira enjoyed playing the lyre, and a new song was always a challenge for her, but I feel a surge of emotion when I realize her intentions. She knew Clara would need a lyrist. She knew she would be the one to play the hymn, and she made damn sure she knew how to play it just right.

I'm an emotional mess.

Clara's voice is grittier than at the outpost, her lips parched from travel. But her voice still rises to meet the climax in perfect timing as I push the boats out for her. Her voice only falters at the end, when Alira's final note rings low and steady before fading into silence.

And just like that, it's time to leave. Clara hops into the back of the cart and Alira pauses before joining her.

"Do you think Torin will learn his lesson?" Alira asks.

"No, but he deserves every second of it," I reply.

"I don't know," she says. "A part of me feels like I caused all this." Her voice is a weakened whisper.

"Whatever he did to you was wrong and you know it."

She takes a moment to choose her words. "It was a misunderstanding."

"Alira." I step closer to her, but she shifts away. "Alira, he took advantage of you, and you deserve better."

We stand still for a moment. There's an awkward space between us, one I ache to close. I want so badly to comfort her, and words are not enough.

Then she leans into me, hugging me tightly. I don't want to move. I want to stay here forever. But it's time to go.

"Are you ready to go home?" I ask.

"Yes."

Tears dampen my shirt across my chest as her words become muffled against me.

"Okay."

I wait patiently for her to step away before getting into the cart and picking up the reins. The road stretches out before us, and then comes the rain.

2 8

OFFERINGS

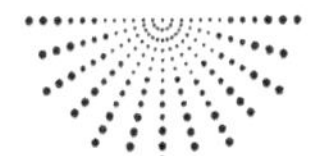

A CARAVAN of villagers travels back-to-back, shifting supplies and fixing broken carts as needed as they make their way to the outpost. Our horse, no longer weighed down with supplies and still in good health, outpaces most of them. We're the first to see the merchant cart, upturned and surrounded by shards of glimmering glass. As we get closer, I notice something etched into its exposed underside: a curved blade.

Vagabonds.

They didn't just take care of the merchant; they left his horses behind, too. They graze in a nearby field, where Clara, Clay, and I spend a bit of time luring them back. When the caravan catches up to us, we distribute the horses to those with the heaviest carts before moving on.

It takes a few days to get to the tributary, but when the smell of rotting fish is far behind us, everyone relaxes. Even the sickest villagers find their spirits have risen once they are able to hold a fishing rod in their hands again.

After that, travel is easy. Each day ends at a campground with a caravan feast. Spring greens sprout readily at our feet and there's plenty of fish to go around.

Torin doesn't partake. He fishes alone. He eats alone. I wouldn't have it any other way.

It's almost bittersweet, reaching the outpost again. But Lynn and Misty, Marshall and Wade—they're all well prepared for the caravan. After we left for the villages, Marshall and Misty went to Neró and spoke with the elders to explain that the water in the villages is tainted, not diseased, and that if it were contagious, everyone at the outpost would be dying. As a result, the elders' reversed their orders and opened the gates ahead of the Spring Festival. By the time we return to the outpost, enough space has been prepared to house the villagers in the dining hall, a temporary measure that allows Misty and Clara to assess each one before they head toward the city.

We stay only one night, but by the time we leave, the sun is warm on my face and the breeze no longer bites; it soothes. For the first time since the start of our journey, Clay and I travel completely alone. It's not as scary or uncomfortable as I thought it would be. In fact, I feel safer than ever out on the open road.

Only the cannibal cabin, quiet and abandoned, serves to remind me of the terrors we evaded. We pass it quickly, but it's not enough. A strong wind blows and the clinking of bones leaves me sleepless for two whole days.

When we reach Joe and Jane's cabin, it's no more than a crumbling mess of wood and stone. A forceful change of wind flips the leaves of the trees upward, revealing their silvery undersides. Dark cumulus clouds roll in, blanketing the sky in pale slate. The sun retreats behind them.

Clay hops down to unhitch the horse and it trots off, taking shelter under what's left of Joe and Jane's shed. The roof is caved in, a dead tree sloping across it, but it's probably the safest place for it.

I wait for Clay at the back of the cart, and just as he enters, thunder rumbles and a steady rain quickly devolves into a sweeping downpour.

The sound of a raging storm is oddly soothing to me. It drowns out my swirling thoughts.

"I looked for the recorder," Clay says, sitting across from me. "I almost missed it. It's out there, in the ruins." he pauses, gazing outside. "But it's useless now. The fire was so hot that the spool melted and hardened over the top."

My heart sinks. If we had the recorder, we could listen to the rest of Carnelian's spools and record some of our own. All we have are the notebooks we've collected along the way, full of scribbled reminders of what we've learned. I open one and begin to write down a list of things we should tell the elders. Wells, plumbing, greenhouses: It's all far more than I ever expected. Even Tayn's pomegranate seeds are tucked safely away in their pouch.

But will the elders agree to let us continue on despite the black waters that stand in our way?

"Clay?"

"Hmm?"

"What do we do next?"

He takes a moment to think, "The merchant said he was being paid by the House of the Soul Keeper to provide a cure."

"A laughable one." I add.

"It might be dangerous," he says, his voice low. "I don't know if we should even try."

"I want to," I say. He looks up at me, studying me, as if he's trying to believe me.

"I know you'll keep me safe this time." I smile halfheartedly and he chuckles.

"If we do this, we need to do it quickly," he notes. "That means we won't be able to stay home for long."

I nod in agreement. Mother will be upset, but it is our

mission, after all, to restore balance to our house, a mission assigned to us by the elders themselves.

When the rain stops, it leaves behind the smell of wet wood and fertile soil. Clay opens the fabric up wide and we watch the world relax.

Our horse walks out from beneath the shed and begins to graze amongst the silvery lupine, pink mountain mallow, and fireweed that bloom in the ashes of destruction. Bumblebees bob from flower to flower, and in the branches of the cherry tree, birds resume their frenzied singing.

"Do you think it will survive?" I ask.

Chalky black burns carve up the tree's side but it's not all bad. Sparse green foliage buds from untouched red-gray bark on the left side of the tree. It's shiny where the flames neglected to scar it, with finely marked lenticels slicing across it.

"Maybe for a while," he replies, "but its growth is uneven. The branches are liable to snap from the weight of it."

My eyes drift down in defeat, settling on the paper-thin petals littering its base.

"It flowered," I say, almost surprised.

"That's good." Clay says, "A sapling will grow in its place."

Even the pine tree, reduced to a spindly stick in the dirt, is accompanied by a tiny sapling. Renewed hope floods through me. By the time Joe and Jane return, the land will be completely healed. They can tear down what's left and build earthen.

Grief, anger, guilt, and sadness dissipate completely as my excitement begins to build. Each hoof strike brings us closer to home. As Clay guides the bumbling cart along the Travelers' Road, the trees become sparse, making way for prairies, fields, barns, and familiar underground dwellings. Lemon balm is scattered across the road, an offering for Persephone. It fills my nose with a sweet, minty aroma.

They prayed for us.

It's not something I expected, though I wonder how far we would have gotten without it.

The first house we pass is Clay's. His two younger brothers emerge from the fields to clamber up and bombard him with hugs. They don't seem hungry or wanting or needing. Clay's absence didn't seem to affect them in the way that I feared it would.

Jasper is the older of the two. His eyes are bright with excitement. "Father's been teaching us how to use the small game traps, and I caught a rabbit yesterday! Are you coming inside?"

"I'll be home later," Clay assures them, tousling the hair on each of their heads. "There's still much to do today."

"Storytime?" The younger, Alan, asks.

"Yes," Clay laughs. It's contagious, sending a joyful warmth through me. "I will have many stories to tell at dinner tonight."

The young boys climb down hesitantly, unwilling to watch their brother leave again. Instead, they decide to run up ahead, alerting the villagers to our return. His mother stands in the open doorway, waving at us from a distance.

As we approach the village center, more and more villagers gather to welcome us home.

Lemon balm isn't the only offering they've left us. The doors of each building we pass as we enter the core of the villages are decorated with spring wreaths of rose, poppy, and lily.

A crowd begins to form as we reach the base of Persephone's Light. Its edges are covered in clay sculptures of bats and rams, symbols of Persephone.

Chatter builds amongst the villagers as we climb out slowly, muscles stiff from the long journey. Gemma is the first to erupt from the crowd, launching in to hug me without any hesitation at all.

"Oh, girl, I have missed you!" We huddle closely together and I watch as Clay hands Jade the reins, discussing the contents of the cart. I should help him, but Gemma's eyes lock on mine, demanding all my attention.

"So," Gemma notices, "are you two . . . ?" It sounds light-hearted, but I know deep down she fears the answer she might get.

"No," I assure her.

Her eyebrows hitch up in question.

"His overconfidence almost got us into quite a bit of trouble," I explain.

I know that Clay has changed. I can see it clearly. He speaks to Jade in a patient and respectful tone. The boy I knew in school would have tried to lure Jade in with a flirtatious joke, spreading his charm like wildfire through the village. He is confident, as always, but not in an arrogant way. My eyes drift past him and I see the girls in the crowd. They all ogle at him like he's a piece of meat. Funny, considering half of them already had a piece.

"Well, I'd be happy to take him back for you," Gemma chides. I push at her lightly before pulling her in for one more hug.

"Alira," Clay calls for me as Jade beckons us inside. Gemma recedes back into the crowd.

Jade leads us through the gathering of villagers and into the community center, where the elders await. Incense sits on every possible surface, smelling of lavender and rose, another offering.

Before she opens the door to the hearing room, she turns to us.

"They will ask you themselves, but I'm dying to know. Will we be seeing merchants soon?"

"Yes," Clay answers quickly. "Though I don't know when. Many of them were . . . compromised."

Jade exhales in relief and nods. "Very well. Let's begin." She pushes the doors open and disappears inside.

The hearing room, normally dark and clammy, is bright with life today. Garlands of spring flowers are hung across the walls. The warm glow of beeswax candles flickers quietly and their drippings are sparse, as though lit mere minutes ago.

Pottery lines the aisles of sculpted benches, each one more detailed than the last. Red and black intermixed with delicate white lines show all the stages of Persephone's descent and, as we get farther down the aisle, her ascent. Flowers billow out of each vase, still fresh with pollen dusting the ground beneath them. The end of the aisle is capped with a beautifully massive black vase. A red silhouetted Persephone walks, her gown of delicate white flowers trailing behind her. She drops red seeds of pomegranate into the soil beneath her, their roots etched deep into the bowl.

The amount of effort they must have gone through to do all this is astonishing.

At the head of the room, the elders sit at the Elder Slate, a long black table stretching from one end of the room to the other.

The last time I was in the community center, I was asking Jade for a chance to see this room. I was shy and nervous and unsure. After all we had endured and after having seen my world expand by so much, the elders no longer seem so threatening to me. Demeter seems more approachable than ever, and Berilo looks like he had a sour apple for breakfast.

"Welcome, Alira and Clayton, back into the realm of our benevolent Earth Queen." Demeter speaks proudly. Her eyes sparkle mischievously, as if she's won some sort of bet. I had almost forgotten how regal she is. Her red dresses always drape so elegantly.

Arani's melodious voice brings me to attention.

"Today's meeting will be brief. We don't want to keep you from your families any longer. However, we must know of the merchants."

Telling them the truth would risk everything, so I have to be careful. Clay nods reassuringly, his eyes kind. The danger is gone; we're home. All that's left to do is assure them that everything is well. I speak decisively, pocketing any unnecessary details.

"We found the reason for the absence of merchants and the problem was resolved. They will return, though they will not be the usual merchants that we see regularly."

To my utter relief, the elders do not press me for more information. They all seem relaxed knowing that the merchants will inevitably return.

"Very well." Demeter stands. "We will debrief you properly tomorrow. Your families are waiting for you."

The elders walk out of the room one by one. It all feels so surreal to me and, honestly, a little anticlimactic. I want to spill everything I've learned in the last several months out onto the floor here and now, but I'll have to wait.

I realize that Clay and I are alone now. I can feel my cheeks burning when I see him watching me. I need to stop getting so lost in thought.

"I can visit tomorrow," Clay speaks as if he's worried I'll shatter without him.

I might.

I hug him, wrapping my arms around his neck. It feels natural now. Ever since we evacuated the villages, I feel myself leaning into him subconsciously, comforted by his calm reassurance.

"Thank you, Clay."

His chest rises and falls once, then twice. On the rise of the third, I remove myself delicately and turn away to hide the red-hot heat emanating from my cheeks.

∿

"I'm home!" I call out. I hang my coat up by the door, but only Pebble comes to greet me. I didn't expect the house to feel so empty.

I call out once more.

When no one answers, I wander from room to room, eventually finding my mother sitting quietly in her bedroom. She reads a book in the light that sneaks through the window, a light so dim I wonder how long she's been sitting here.

"I can't do it," she says.

"Do what?" I ask.

"Pretend I'm not falling apart." She sets her book aside and stands. "Come here." She takes me in her arms.

"I wanted you to think I was okay without you, but you're my baby, and I worried the whole time."

I pull away. "You worried about me? Impossible."

We both laugh, a sound edging on the verge of tears.

"Where's Flint?" I ask.

She sighs. "He's out in the orchard somewhere. I'd rather not talk about it. Tell me, how long will you be home?"

"Not long."

She frowns. "Well, I suppose I should get used to being alone, then."

"Did I miss something?" I ask. I try to understand why she would say that about Flint. "Oh!" Realization hits me like a wave.

I bolt out the door and Pebble sprints ahead of me, as if she means to show me the way.

Flint's birthday was in midwinter. I missed it and his ceremony. Judging from Mother's mood, he must have picked a career that disappointed her. I wonder if he took my advice, after all.

Flint is laid out on the boulder that sits at the gate of the orchard. He doesn't react when I stop to stand in front of him. I cross my arms, but he continues to gaze up at the sky.

"Did Clay try anything stupid?" he asks. It feels underwhelming.

"No," I reply, "but for the record, I don't think this is any way to welcome your sister home." I plop down into the soft green grass and Pebble joins me, licking my face before rolling onto her back. I rub her belly just where she likes it and her tail thumps wildly.

"Sorry, I was too busy sulking about my fate." He smirks to himself. "It's funny, really; that whole pomegranate juice thing doesn't mean all that much."

"What are you talking about? Isn't drinking the juice during the ceremony supposed to seal your fate?"

"For everyone but me, it seems." He sits up on the boulder and faces me, his eyes shadowed by sleepless nights. He used to be happy here, content in an honest day's work. Now it's as if he doesn't know why he gets up in the morning. He waits for me to understand as though I can read his mind, but how am I to know what he wants? He didn't want to come with me, but he also didn't seem to want to stay here.

Whatever you decide to do should be for you. That was the advice I gave him. Had he taken it?

He sighs deeply.

"I told them I want to be an elder."

"Oh, Flint."

Now I know why he felt so trapped in the days before I left home. Elders need to prove they have earthen lineage from both sides of their family. Without Father around, there's no way to prove that Flint is earthen. It's why we've always been outcasts.

But to think I'll be able to carry out my dream while Flint remains here is heartbreaking. I can't think of anything to say that doesn't feel hopeless.

We sit quietly. Pebble lies still as I pet her belly, jerking her leg every so often when I hit a spot she finds satisfying.

The spring breeze pulls at my hair and nostalgia crashes over me as memories resurface; memories of childhood joys and fears, of fights and discoveries.

I miss it here, but things are changing. Soon, I'll be leaving again and, after that, all of Rhizole will be within my reach.

Something about that seems full of hope.

"Flint?"

"Hmm?"

"I'm going to find him."

EPILOGUE

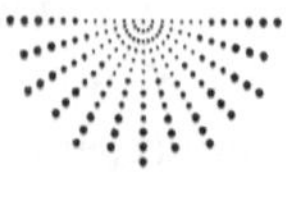

JANE

THE HOUSE I'm looking for is halfway down the mountain, set behind a pocket of trees. It's a bit more run-down than I was expecting. The windows are cracked, the roof frayed, and the flowers out front are wilting from a lack of water.

My hand trembles as I raise my hand to knock on the wooden door. What I'm about to do will set Joe and I back on course. I'm sure of it. We have no other choice, really. With Alira and Clay gone and the southern water villages on their way, there will soon be a question of where Joe and I will stay.

I already know what Joe wants to do, but what about me?

A surge of anger rushes through me as I knock on the door. Joe is selfish if he thinks I would be happy here. I may have misjudged Clay, but I'm certain about Quill. Joe is just too enamored to question her. He's blind to the truth.

Only I know that she's already accounted for.

A voice grumbles through the door. "If it's those ants again, I swear. . ."

The door opens and a man with a thick beard and fire-red hair glares at me.

"What do you want? I'm busy." He looks me up and

down, and for a moment, I'm frozen, sucked into a flashback of terror and trauma. A man with red hair serves me stew.

Then I snap out of it, setting my hand against the closing door.

"It's about Quill."

His grip on the door lightens and he strokes his beard as he considers his options. After a moment, he opens the door wide and walks inside, prompting me to follow him.

I do, with an inkling of doubt.

"Well. . . What do you know?" He asks, making his way to the only chair in the room.

"I know that you two are married."

"Barely." The man scoffs, pulling his chair up and taking a seat.

"Well it's enough to convince me that it is wrong of her to be pursuing my brother."

"*WHAT?*"

Before the man has finished sitting in his chair, he's exploded out of it, knocking it backwards. He stands, his fists closed tightly into large balls of fury. His face looks as red as his beard.

"She's seeing someone else?"

I nod weakly, unable to speak as fear grips me.

"I didn't mind leaving when I was sure no one would mess around with an estranged woman, but if that's not the case then I'll have to do something about it." He pushes me aside and plows through the door. barreling in the direction of Quill's.

Shit.

"Wait!" I yell after him.

I try to follow him, but he's a force of nature, whipping down the mountain like a gust of wind.

This was a mistake.

A huge mistake.

I cut around to the back of the inn. I don't know what else to do. If I follow too close behind, they'll know I was behind this.

I duck under a window and look into the great room just before he manages to break down the door.

"Where is she?" The man yells.

I can see Quill hidden from his view behind the open door, just by the bathroom. He looks ahead toward the kitchen and begins to move. She is frozen in place. The look on her face shows only one emotion, pure terror. Slowly, she backs away into the bathroom, closing the door in hiding.

"Are you the guy who's messing with my wife?" His voice vibrates through the building and he speaks to someone blocking the kitchen door. I feel a stab of fear strike through me at the sound of his voice.

Is this how Quill feels?

"Woah, buddy, no need to get all fired up. What's your name?" Joe enters the great room. He moves slowly toward the man but stops in his tracks.

"My name is none of your concern. Where is my wife?" The man's face becomes even more red. Suddenly, Kai appears behind Joe.

"What's going on?" His voice squeaks.

"Where's your mom?" The man booms. Kai shrinks back, suddenly aware of the situation.

"I don't...know."

The man steps forward, like a wave of water, inevitably crashing down on everything in front of him.

Then Joe swings his first punch.

Oh no.

I can no longer watch the scene that is taking place. I remove myself from the window and run down the hill, past the fountain shrine and toward the front gate, yelling all the way.

"Help! Help! There is a brawl at Quill's!"

Delta hears my desperate call and bursts into action, passing me quickly.

I can barely keep up, now. I feel lightheaded. All this running around is catching up to me.

Delta turns to me at the door.

"Come with me, I want these men to be ashamed."

"But Joe was just–"

Delta is already in the door, grabbing the back of the red man's head and forcing him to his feet. I look past him at Joe. He is on the floor, holding his head in his hands.

"Joe." I swoop between the three men and pull my brother up off the floor as Delta addresses them.

"That's enough, you two, I don't know what the problem is and I don't quite care."

The red man is standing, fuming, yet unmoving. "If that whore doesn't come out here and face me then I'm not leaving until she does."

"Your actions have been reported and you are at risk of deportation. Do not test me." Delta barks.

"Fine. Tell her I want a divorce." The red man pushes his way out the door.

Was this man truly Kai's father?

Kai appears in the doorway, warily looking around. When he spots Joe, he bursts forward and envelops him in a tiny hug.

Quill emerges from the bathroom, a shell of her former self. She does not look at Joe, only Delta.

"Thank you, Delta, I owe you. Whatever you need, let me know."

"Well, I don't need much, Quill, but you need a divorce. I'll see to it that the forms are made up and I'll have eyes on the place until the deed is done."

As soon as Delta is gone, Quill rushes into the kitchen for

ice. Kai helps Joe, and I stand in the middle of the great room, scared to speak.

I walk upstairs and into my room. The model I built for our new home sits in the middle of it, next to the blueprints Clay and Alira drew up. I take the blueprints, folding them and stuffing them into my pocket. Then, I slip off my ring, leaving it on the bedside table.

Joe, Kai, and Quill are in the kitchen when I walk out the door. I make sure to close it quietly behind me before walking down to where Delta's son sits guarding the gate. He jumps up to greet me.

"So, did anyone black out?" He asks.

"No."

"What's wrong?" He asks.

"I think it's time for me to leave."

He looks at me quizzically, "Are you sure? You're not even packed!"

"I didn't have much to begin with." I shirk past him and disappear into the night.

READY FOR MORE?

The Keeper's Machine

Book Two in the Underworld Rising Series

Coming in 2025

Pre-order now at
https://books2read.com/u/thekeepersmachine

Visit www.lydiaruanna.com/links for more

ACKNOWLEDGMENTS

I often say everything happens for a reason, and likewise, my life has been a wonderful combination of things going terribly wrong so that they can later go terribly right.

I call this process Shoveling Sand, after Author Shannon Hale's notable quote:

"I'm simply shoveling sand into a box so that later I can build castles."

Simply put, I would not have published this book without help.

And so I thank the following:

My parents, for always encouraging me to try new things.

My friends, for showering me in excitement over the smallest wins, and prodding me along whenever I paused to question myself. They may not know that they've been instrumental in helping me through countless bouts of imposter syndrome, but I am so thankful for it.

My cat, Church, for waking me up early in the morning to remind me that, yes, there is time to write before work, and for reminding me late at night that, yes, it is time to sleep.

My boyfriend, Alex, for inspiring me to take my writing and share it with the world, something I had been avoiding for a decade. He has been my beta-reader, my marketing counsellor, my map-maker, and most of all, the best boyfriend.

It is because of these people that I am shoveling sand into a box rather than a sieve. Thank you.

ABOUT THE AUTHOR

Lydia Ruanna is a young adult fantasy author from northern New Jersey. As a lifelong writer, Lydia draws inspiration from her appreciation of nature, classic myths, and personal experiences.

Lydia has lived in several states along the East Coast. She attended college in Maine, working in Bar Harbor for a time before moving south to Cape Cod and, finally, settling in eastern Pennsylvania, close to home. She currently lives with her boyfriend, Alex, and their two cats, Church and Mozzie.

If you would like to learn more about Lydia or get in touch, visit her website at www.lydiaruanna.com

Newsletter Sign-up